THE TALKING CURE

KATHY L. BROWN

MONTAG

First Montag Press E-Book and Paperback Original Edition October 2025

Copyright © 2025 by Kathy L. Brown

As the writer and creator of this story, Kathy L. Brown asserts the right to be identified as the author of this book.

Montag Press ISBN: 978-1-957010-63-2
Design © 2025 Amit Dey

Montag Press Team:

Cover: Rick Febre
Author Photo: Jon Aikin
Editor: Charlie Franco
Managing Director: Charlie Franco

A Montag Press Book
www.montagpress.com
Montag Press
777 Morton Street, Unit B
San Francisco CA 94129 USA

Montag Press, the burning book with the hatchet cover, the skewed word mark and the portrayal of the long-suffering fireman mascot are trademarks of Montag Press.

Printed & Digitally Originated in the United States of America
10 9 8 7 6 5 4 3 2 1

This book is a work of fiction. Names, characters, places, and incidents are either products of the author's vivid and sometimes disturbing imagination or are used fictitiously without any regards with possible parallel realities. Any resemblance to actual persons, living or dead, events, or locales is entirely coincidental.

CONTENT ADVISORY

This story's subject matter is murder. It also refers to harm to a child in the past and expresses a character's suicidal ideations. If you or someone you know is contemplating suicide, help is there for you. In the United States, dial 988, text HOME to 741741, or visit 988lifeline.org for deaf, Deaf, and hard-of-hearing support for suicide prevention. Find a suicide prevention hotline internationally at findahelpline.com.

DEDICATION

To Kelly, Allie, Katie, and Thelys. You are my heroes.

PRAISE FOR *THE TALKING CURE*

"*The Talking Cure* is a marvelous story—an Agatha Christie-style murder mystery infused with a strong sense of the Weird... and a hearty dose of magic on the side. It's ideal for all fans of the sinister, the surprising, and the strange."

—Cherie Priest,
award-winning author of *Boneshaker*

"Ms Brown evokes the time and place with terse, vivid prose, and creates characters who stride confidently across the pages to places we never expected."

—Daniel Boyd,
Spur Award Winner for *AESOP'S TRAVELS*

"In *The Talking Cure*, Kathy L. Brown blurs the lines of magic and madness. Is there more to this world than can be known by our five senses?"

—Fedora Amis,
Mayhaven Fiction Prize Winner for
Jack the Ripper in St. Louis.

"A spellbinding tale, *The Talking Cure* unfolds through the unreliable eyes of a woman with missing memories and the man who's been trapped in her forgotten magic. Brown's whimsical imagination and grounded storytelling have plotted a truly mysterious whodunit!"

—Mira Gibson, author of *Who Killed Leeanne?*

"Kathy Brown delivers some insanely spellbinding pulp with *The Talking Cure*, filling her roiling cauldron with all the magick, noir grit, and historic drag to create a modern alchemical tincture worthy of the finest enchanted hip flask."

—Paul d Miller, author of *Albrecht Drue, ghostpuncher.*; *Albrecht Drue: Paranormal Dick*; and the forthcoming *Albrecht Drue in… Aldaemonium!*

"*The Talking Cure* is an exceptional blend, an absorbing historical whodunnit built on a rich foundation of magical lore. The mystery, where 'every witness is a suspect,' unfolds as precisely as clockwork, while grimoires, cantrips, and fae add enormously to its eerie power. The intrigue is deepened by the unusual setting, an asylum in the uncertain early days of psychiatry, as not one but two detectives probe its secrets and unearth the fraught links between madness and magic. In the end, the disparate threads come together into a heady, satisfying whole that leaves the reader enchanted—in every sense."

—Damian Tarnopolsky, author of *Every Night I Dream I'm a Monk, Every Night I Dream I'm a Monster*

Dramatis Personae

Sean Joye: Young Irish immigrant employed in the past by Violet for investigative work.

Violet Arwald Humphrey: St. Louis high-society matron with a tragic and troubled history.

Dr. Henry (Heinrich) Elsass: Deeply-in-debt Institute founder.

Carrie Bartowski, RN: Institute's loyal head nurse.

Percy Emerson: Business executive and volatile president of the Institute's board of directors.

Blanche Emerson: Artist apparently institutionalized by her husband for independent thinking.

Teddy Maderia: Helpful teenaged orderly.

Dr. Ibrahim Cole: Physician from Sierra Leone via Paris, recruited by Dr. Elsass under false pretenses.

Finley (Finn) Osteen: Institute caretaker and son of the mansion's previous owner.

Supporting Cast

Berta: An elderly dementia patient.

Drs. Abel, Bertinelli, and Lieberman: Members of the Institute's board of directors.

Grace Martin, RN; Lottie; Robert; Gretel; and Martha: Institute staff members.

Comfrey Rouse: Mysterious volunteer groundskeeper.

Tomás Maderia: Partner to Finn Osteen and father to Teddy Maderia.

Evelyn (Evie) Elsass: Dr. Elsass's abandoned wife.

People from the Past

Noble Osteen: Finn's dead father and the mansion's previous owner.

Jürgen Osteen: Finn's pioneering ancestor.

Taylor Humphrey: Violet's dead husband.

Kyffin Bernard: Sean's brain-injured lover.

Sean

PROLOGUE

With this sigil inscribed, I do bind you: aid and protect me from this moment forward until the setting of the Yuletide sun.

~From grimoire of "Eunid"
(Violet Arwald Humphrey), October 1, 1924.

My right palm started to itch around three o'clock. Since I just washed a sink full of dishes at my brother Padraig's pub, I didn't pay it no mind. He bought the cheapest of lye soap; t'would take the paint off the floor.

"Youse about to come into money, Sean," said my landlady, Mrs. Charity MacSweeney, a tiny Scottish woman who claimed to be 80. I had my doubts. More likely pushing 90. She had toddled into Padraig's place in St. Louis's Dogtown neighborhood for a cup of tea—with a bit of tipple she added after a sly scan of the room.

It was four o'clock on a gray Friday afternoon, the week before Christmas, 1924. We sat together at an oak table in the warmest corner of the public room. The place was quiet except for the swoosh of my sister-in-law's broom across the plank flooring and the voices of Padraig's two oldest children, Maud and Patrick.

The kids hung fresh evergreen boughs bedecked with red ribbons over the windows, and the clean scent filled the room. *Business must be good for himself to spring for such a frippery.*

Mrs. Mac leaned across the table and patted my hand. "You'll be able to pay your rent."

"I know it's late—" I shrugged as I rolled down my sleeves, fished cufflinks out of my pocket, and inserted them. "Investigations been a mite slow. But I've just cleaned Padraig's entire kitchen and washed every dirty dish in the place." I pointed to the greenery. "He's clearly rolling in it. And it's almost Christmas. Surely, he'll spot me a fiver."

Eliza left off her sweeping to glare at me. "If you're thinking he'll be a soft touch, think again."

I'd started my own job-of-work in October—business of minding other folks' business, if you asked Eliza's opinion. Even if you didn't ask, she'd volunteer her thoughts on my snooping habits, my traffic with the Devil, and my degenerate lifestyle. She didn't even know the half of it.

A child started crying from the family apartment upstairs. Sounded like the littlest one, Francis. "Time you settled down, Sean. You're 24 years old. Get yerself an honest job," Eliza said. "Make a good confession, forget that pilot fellow, and find a nice girl." She tucked the broom behind the bar and headed for the steps. "Hannah O'Grady has set her cap for you and she's not the only one."

"Thank you. For your concern." I scratched my hand. The itch was intolerable. Eliza's dig about "that pilot" reminded me of Kyffin, not that he was ever far from my mind. I hadn't seen my aviator-turned-attorney lover in months. Thinking on him made me think on the person responsible for us ever meeting in the first place, Violet Arwald Humphrey. She'd been whispering at me from the back of my mind for the better part of an hour—since the itching started.

Violet was a witch of my acquaintance. Although it took a while for me to catch on to that fact; I can be a mite dim. For a while I just thought she was a loony, you know, a crazy person. And maybe she *was* a crazy person; she was parked at a fancy insane asylum out in Middle-Of-Nowhere, Illinois. But I knew a lot more about witches now that I was studying magic myself, and she was a witch.

I can tell you the moment she first witched me. Maybe not exactly—she always affected me—but the most important time. She traced a thing in my palm—a pattern. And from then on I'd been unusually protective of her. It didn't feel so unusual to me, but looking at myself, I knew. People who teach themselves magic out of books spend a good amount of time looking at themselves.

Mrs. Mac replenished the whiskey in her cup and smirked at me. "I'd say that bampot society lady's the one what's caught *your* eye. You speak of her often enough." With whatever bridle she kept on her tongue loosened, she continued. "I never did believe that gossip about you being a nancy boy."

Good to know, but we weren't going to discuss my love life at this moment. "Still seeing ghosts?" I asked.

When I first met Mrs. Mac, this lifelong teetotaler was on her way to becoming a lush, finding a drop of the craetur her only escape from a gang of ghosts she'd encountered everywhere she went.

"Just here, here," she said, giving Padraig's pub an airy wave. "No one's going to hire you as a faerie man with your own place full of haunts." She slapped my hand. "Stop that scratching. Do I have to give you mittens, like a wee thumb-sucking bairn?"

"Padraig has ghosts, does he? I'll get on that." I stared at the rough table, struck by the wood grain pattern's resemblance to Violet's profile—her smooth brow, pert nose, and full lips, a curl escaping her chignon to soften her face. An unbearable worry building up in my heart as I pictured her at the asylum.

She'd been whisked away to the "rest home" after the death of her husband—the one I'd shot and killed, but he had it coming. She didn't appear to hold it against me, but we hadn't had the opportunity to talk about it. At her sister's request, I'd been Violet's keeper for his funeral, guiding the trance-fixed woman to walk, stand, and sit at the proper times. She never uttered a word. I've visited her a few times since, and while she was talking to me again, her main nurse, an interesting woman named Carrie Bartowski, didn't think she was up to handling any unpleasant news.

Mrs. Mac stood to go and glanced about for her cane. "I'll be off to the market."

I stared at Violet's image on the table, rubbing my palm. I had sense enough to know my worries over her weren't natural. She was the one making me feel this way. Somehow. But I'd had quite enough of this shite. It had to stop.

The old lady waved her hand in front of my face. "I expect you'll be taking Christmas dinner with your people."

I looked up. *Had she said something about Christmas?*

She raised her eyebrows and glanced up the stairs that Eliza had climbed to the family's apartment. "Unless you truly are on the outs with herself."

"What?" She had me thinking of Violet in that place, at Christmas time. Her there, so lonely. I hated the thought. I hated the fact that I cared enough to hate the thought in the first place.

She shrugged. "'Tis a day for Christian duty, if ever there was one. I'd be happy to feed you."

Christian duty? *Yes, I had a duty to Violet. To protect her.* The itching was a little less intense. *No, no, I wasn't obliged. She wasn't my problem.* More likely the source of my problems. The itching got worse.

"Thanks." I helped her into her coat as I thought about where I could borrow a car. "Talking to you helped," I said, inclined to gnaw off my hand. I had to make Violet leave me alone—today.

"Should I order a roast of beef for Christmas?"

"A roast?" *Would Violet like a roast?* I supposed so. *A goose or turkey might be better.* She liked her fancy meals. Although I doubted the asylum was feeding her anything like she deserved. *Feck it, what did I care how she ate?*

"You should eat here," I said, "with Padraig's crew." I was sure Padraig and Eliza would welcome Violet too. They'd gotten wrong ideas about her, but once they spent some time with her—*No*, I reminded myself. My brother had warned me time and again that Violet and her whole family had used me and would continue to do so.

"Most kind," said Mrs. Mac, "but ask your brother first."

"I will." I slipped on my coat and grabbed my hat, then held open the front door for her. I knew just the man to see next: he both owed me money and had a car to loan out. Violet Arwald Humphrey, loony or not, was due a piece of my mind.

Violet

CHAPTER 1

PAYMENT PAST DUE. THIRD NOTICE.

Dear Mrs. Humphrey,

Please immediately remit payment of $780 for charges detailed below:

~From statement of charges,
The Elsass Institute, December 1, 1924.

"Now see here, Violet," said Dr. Elsass, the asylum's director, displaying a piece of paper on the desk. "This is a serious matter, but—we're all friends here. And I'd appreciate your help."

What fresh hell is this, I wondered. The paper was clean and new, while his scrawl was illegible. But that's not what offend me: it was the rotten smell.

Not now. Just let me get through one normal day. Be reasonable. It's only a piece of paper. It can't possibly smell like a dead rat.

But it did. I shuddered to even touch it, afraid of contamination, and couldn't help turning away as I pushed it back at him with one finger. "You can contact my family attorney," I spit out.

He made a strangled sort of sound as if choking on his own impatience, and then jabbed his forefinger at the long rows of figures. "Room, board, supplies, staff wages—even Dr. Cole's professional fees are in arrears."

I had to laugh at that. "I should pay a man to insult me?"

From outside the office, a squeaking sound approached. The tea trolley. The sound sent a shiver up my spine, and silver splinters spiked my brain. Panic rising, I thought of my friend, Carrie, the head nurse. I'll talk to her again about all the sounds, I promised myself. And the smells. These latest symptoms of my troubles were beginning to abate, we had thought. Obviously, we had been wrong.

I'd been in a fog for months—my only companion the cajoling voice in my head—but the mist lifted on some days. As I had connected with the nurses and staff, I could attend to my surroundings and heard the voice's demands less often.

But today, the sounds, even the sights, of the place were too much. And my perceptions were all wrong. I knew they were wrong. I shouldn't be able to smell things I see or have sounds assault my nervous system—to see, hear, smell, touch, and taste feelings about events and people. At least I hadn't heard *him* all day; the voice had been blessedly silent, or perhaps drowned out in the cacophony of life in this madhouse. *That's not fair. It is a lovely place. Just not my place.*

The doctor hadn't laughed at my feeble joke about his colleague, not that I expected him to. "Violet," he said, "Stay on topic. I have important guests arriving—"

"And bills to pay," I said. "I understand, I suppose." I gripped the chair arms and watched the odors rise off my medical charges statement, wafting at me on a draft from a window that rattled in its frame from the gusts of wind. "It's not that I don't want to pay your staff. Although I do find it unseemly to discuss money so openly. I hope you're not so gauche with your board of directors."

I lit a cigarette to cover the stench of the bill and to kill time. My family founded this city, I reminded myself. Well, St. Louis. Lord knows what town claimed this mansion-on-the-prairie. I glared at the loathsome little man, his cheap suit, and ridiculous goatee. "What will they think of you, complaining about every little penny of expenditure?" I exhaled a cloud of ginger-and-pear scented smoke at him. How remarkable. I glanced down at the pack. Had I picked up someone else's smokes? But, no, it was my usual brand.

The doctor made a face and coughed. "Perhaps you don't appreciate your precarious situation here. Your family influence kept you out of the police investigation, but that could change."

The room spun, and fog closed back in as I clung to reality the best I could. I took a deep breath and pictured myself grounded and tethered to Mother Earth; a bit of my past spiritual practice I was reclaiming. I will NOT go back into the dark. "Are you threatening me?"

My family had brought me to the Elsass Institute in October—two months ago. I didn't remember any of it. My sister Lillian claimed I threatened to murder her baby. I didn't remember that, either. And my sister is a habitual liar. Carrie says I never would have gone through with such a plan—that it had been an obvious cry for help—but I believe that Lillian had made the whole story up.

The last thing I remember from that time...to tell the truth, and I'm ashamed to say it, I worked a spell on a young man, Sean Joye, without his consent. But I needed—no—was desperate for an ally. Things are fuzzy after that. Bits and pieces had started to float to the surface a few weeks ago. Some were horrible, but I could never hurt anyone. I didn't think so, anyway.

The pain of my own child's death makes me acutely aware of other people's pain. I know one thing; the staff and other patients were more helpful than either doctor—Henry Elsass or Ibrahim Cole.

Dr. Elsass smoothed his thinning gray-blond hair, then pushed the invoice back to me. "You're damned right this is a threat," he thundered, pounding his fist on the desk, his face flushing then just as quickly turning pale while beads of putrid sweat appeared on his forehead.

The warm buzz of voices in the parlor beyond his office stopped—perhaps his guests could hear him, just as I'd warned—but he was too incensed to care. "Every day, I see the newspaper headlines about your sister. The money she must have spent on those fancy Chicago defense attorneys—"

I was just beginning to read the news again and had seen the same articles. "Just the one lawyer," I corrected, "although I suppose Jimmy Peel has a staff."

I felt more composed and went to the window. There were a few patients, bundled against the wind, which I could see whirling a weathervane on a distant barn round and round, taking in the fresh air and the expansive view of the Illinois prairie from the wrap-around porch. Blanche, a young woman about my age, had set up her easel; it must not be all that cold.

Before Carrie had given me the newspapers, she had told me, slowly and with great care, that Lillian was awaiting trial for the murder of our father. Most days, I didn't believe it and fully expected Father to show up and rescue me from the Elsass Institute. How Lillian had engineered my abduction, I had no idea; Father was probably out of the country. But I did trust Carrie. Most likely, Lillian had lied to the poor woman.

"One lawyer, a dozen, does it matter?" the doctor shouted.

I faced him as he shook the stinking bill at me. "Would you like Jimmy Peel's phone number? Perhaps you'll need it," I said, not sure why, but I liked the reaction. He staggered and dropped the paper. It floated down to the desk, covering a small, folded note tucked into the desk blotter's corner.

"What do you mean by that?"

I didn't know what I meant and shrugged. "Nothing at all. One hears things, you know. Just nasty rumors, I'm sure." People say all sorts of things in front of catatonic patients. Who knows what was stored deep in my memories?

He turned very red, spluttered, then grabbed the phone off the desk and clicked the switch hook—"Operator, connect me with the sheriff—Hello, Operator?" Faint static noises sounded through the earpiece.

Turning to me, he barked, "You're out of here. Today. You can sit at the McClean County sheriff's office until the St. Louis Police fetch you. I'm sure they'd be very interested in your account of the events last October—"

His words clanked together, steel upon steel, and flew at me, sharp and deadly. The fog swirled around to protect me, catching the threats in a sticky web.

"What are you talking about?" I managed to say.

Amid the phone's static, a tinny voice said, "Num… Plea…"

"Operator, I need the sheriff in Bloomington."

"Sir…" Static drowned out the rest of her response.

"Can you hear me? Sheriff's office."

More static. I found myself pressed against the windowsill, gripping its edge.

Dr. Elsass gave up his phone call for the moment and said, "I'm talking about the step-by-step account of your plan to kidnap and drown your niece."

"Dr Cole said—" I will not cry in front of him, I thought, and ran to the exit. *What had that horrible man said about me? Why couldn't I remember more of our sessions?*

"'That what you say in therapy is confidential?' Of course it is, but you think he didn't keep notes?"

Suddenly calm, I turned back. I'd neglected my magical practice for some time—particularly since my baby died—but maybe it was time to start turning people into newts, not that I'd ever tried it before. I'd practice on him. "You're not my doctor. You had no right—"

"What is worse, do you think? In the law's opinion, I mean. Your attempted murder or me harboring a would-be murderess? Doctor-patient confidentiality only goes so far."

I reached out for support, my fingers finding their way to a basket of junk on a small table behind the door: etched stones, small bottles full of twigs and leaves, and a tiny mirror. I picked up a rock and let its cool, strong curves calm me.

A memory, no, more like an impression, sparked. I was outdoors, standing in the mist and examining my hands. They were covered in dirt and dead leaves, nails broken and caked with mud. "Miss Violet, what have you got there?" a voice said. I held a small star-shaped stone. This stone.

Elsass's sharp words stabbed through the fog. "Oh, no, you don't. Don't even start up with that junk."

I gripped the stone tighter, my fingers tracing its edges. "I never…" It nicked my finger, a tiny jolt of pain on which to focus. "I wouldn't…" The simple stone lent me quiet comfort, somehow, and power. I was tired of people lying about me.

The familiar voice in my head whispered, "This foolish man will pay…"

"Oh no, don't start with me now," I said.

"What? Young woman, you need to hear a few things. I've been more than kind and patient." Elsass was working himself up into a lather. "Oh, you tell yourself you'd never hurt anyone. But, forced to the limit—"

I could see the two of us as if from a great height, the cold stars observing us. We were locked in struggle, one I'd win easily. His weakness, his vulnerability, his softness, his life, inconsequential. My blood dripped on the floor in tiny bursts of power, shielding me from his words.

Elsass returned to the phone. "Operator…" he said, clicking the switch hook. "Damn." He slammed the receiver onto the cradle. "Put that rock down. And consider yourself warned. Do what you need to do to get some money from your sister, your lawyer, that Irish friend of yours who comes around—anyone."

I cradled the stone in one hand and then the other. Suddenly, it leaped away, sinking into the thick Persian rug. I stomped out, slamming the door behind me.

Back in my room, I paced the floor—not *my* room, but the room that I was assigned to in the farmhouse thinly disguised as a Victorian mansion. In no way did I own it. I was alone in the aggressively pink three-bed dormer: a rare occurrence. I would guess that my roommate, Berta, a sweet elderly woman said to have "melancholia," was being forced to decorate the Christmas tree. The other resident,

Blanche, I'd seen out on the porch painting another in an endless series of gray and brown prairie scenes.

Coincidentally, we'd been to boarding school and debuted together, though we weren't friendly. In truth, I wasn't friendly with many people at school, and midwinter of our final year—right after the grand ball when we were presented to society, she got sick and went home. She stayed home.

I looked up at a brisk tap-tap at my door. My caller was likely the head nurse, Carrie Bartowski. Anyone else would just barge in. Yet I took childish pleasure in waiting in silence, just to find out what she would do: go away, knock again, or come in anyway? I could hear her breath, heavy from climbing the stairs. At last, I said, "Come in, nurse."

The knob turned, and the hinges creaked open. Sure enough, Carrie stepped in, her heels clattering across the linoleum, their sound a brittle and violent yellow.

"Since you're here, unlock this drawer," I said, sounding hateful and wondering why. Carrie had done nothing to me. I tried again. "I'd like my journal. Please."

Carrie nodded as she crossed the room to my nightstand. She exuded warmth from her strawberry-blonde curls, her freckled face, and her strong, athletic build. Her appearance and demeanor said, "I'm here to take care of you."

My bedroom, at the top of the stairs on the second floor of the mansion, was a showplace for potential patients' family members. At first glance, it was like any other farmhouse bedroom, a bit sparse and dim, perhaps.

Colorful quilts covered each narrow bed, and cheery, summertime landscapes were bolted, discreetly, to the walls.

A close inspection showed that apart from a small east-facing window, a stolid, institutional fixture in the ceiling provided the only light. No one noticed or cared that the furniture was affixed to the floor, and that the nightstand drawers, each patient's only bastion of privacy, were locked with a key held by the nurse on duty.

Carrie unlocked the drawer. "May I sit with you?"

I shrugged. "You'll do what you like, I imagine." I was taking out my pique with Dr. Elsass on Carrie. I sat on the edge of my bed.

She sat on Berta's bed to face me. "If you want, I can leave, although the door must be open for observation." Shrugging, she said, "I thought you might want to talk. I overheard...some of that."

I sighed, pulled off my shoes, and flopped on the bed. "What I want is to run. Far and fast. I feel like...something, someone...just out of the corner of my eye...will destroy me."

I had been hearing a new, troubling voice since my arrival at the Elsass Institute. A fact that wasn't helping my state of mind. It wanted something of me, although at that moment I couldn't recall what. Innocent things, I was sure. Innocuous, I thought, anyway. And dreams haunted my nights, dreams I'd share with no one. I'd told Carrie some, but not about the dreams. Nor the voice.

Carrie crossed the room and pointed at my wrist. "May I?"

I nodded and offered myself up to her ministrations. She checked my pulse, then held my hand for a long minute. *Gods, my hands are a mess, covered with cuts and scratches, nails broken.* I watched her, watching me, counting the rise and fall of my chest.

"Your hands are ice." She made a few notes on an index card from her pocket. "And what do we know about your nervousness?"

"My thoughts fuel the nerve attacks. They will go away sooner or later."

Carrie sat on my bed and took my hand again. "Want to talk about it?"

"He is so…beastly."

"Dr. Elsass?" Carried smiled. "His bark is much worse than his bite, I assure you. He can be hasty. Says things he doesn't mean."

I wrinkled my nose at the stench filling the room—like a fish had died behind the plaster lathe walls. *What is causing that?* "I'm crazy. I smell and hear the most inexplicable things since I came here. Things I know can't be real."

"Perhaps it's a type of synesthesia, although your pattern is atypical. But, regardless, that trait isn't a symptom of a mental disorder. Many well-adjusted, functioning people take in sensory information differently."

My expression must have been skeptical, as she hastened to add, "You've had terrible trauma—many traumas; with what happened to your baby being the worst—and lifelong anxiety. Whatever we call it or don't call it, your altered perceptions are a protective mechanism for you. Unconsciously, of course."

I assumed a cross-legged position in the middle of the bed and minded my breaths, hoping to overcome the stench coming clearly from behind the wall. And put my little Tony's kidnapping and murder out of my mind. I found the physical culture here, which included a new method from India called yoga, a surprisingly useful therapy. It reminded me of the spirituality I'd abandoned.

The other helpful treatment being my talks with Carrie and other staff members. Certainly not the doctors. "You're the best listener here. The 'Talking Cure' has done me no good."

"That's flattering. But perhaps the good Dr. Cole just doesn't know the right questions to ask. He's quite modern; all about somatic treatment. You know, treatment of the physical body, believing that is all there is to health."

If only there were some sort of pill for mental derangements. I nodded, relieved Dr. Cole wouldn't be allowed to put me in an ice-water bath until I froze or a rotating chair until I vomited. Not with Dr. Elsass's determination to prove the efficacy of the Talking Cure.

"I'm sure Cole does his best to adhere to the treatment plan. If Dr. Elsass were your primary doctor, you'd have a better opinion of psychotherapy."

"Dr. Elsass is pressuring me for payment, knowing full well how tied up my resources are."

Carrie shivered and stood up. "It's cold in here." She touched the radiator under the window and frowned. "I'll get Finn to check the boiler."

I wondered how much she knew about the Elsass Institute's financial situation. "This place isn't in danger of closing, is it? You have backers—"

Carrie returned to my bedside. "Please understand, the director gets...passionate about these things. He's a good man. And a good doctor."

"He threatened to put me out. To turn me over to the police." Angry tears welled up—*I will not cry.* I bit my lip. "I thought that was behind me."

Carrie draped her arm around my shoulders. I fought the impulse to shrug her off. "It is. You've faced your actions and forgiven yourself. And started to write letters to those your actions affected, taking responsibility." She gave my shoulder a squeeze. "The director didn't mean it, but even if he did, I won't let him involve the police. That helps no one."

"Thank you."

"As to money, don't worry about that. We must watch our expenses, of course. It's all rather boring."

"The thing is, I didn't know the bills hadn't been paid. I should make some calls..." I wasn't sure who to call.

Apparently, our family fortune was an illusion that came crashing down when my sister murdered our father. Dr. Elsass claimed my accountant wasn't returning his calls.

I thought of Sean Joye. He *was* an employee, for want of a better word. I'd been told he was the one visiting me.

No one could be paying him to do that, so maybe he cared about me as a person. A pang of guilt hit me; I had put a tiny spell on him. Surely that influence was long gone.

"That would be lovely, and good for you," Carrie said. "Taking responsibility for our lives...it's healing. Your next therapeutic steps will be to ask forgiveness and make amends. This plan feeds nicely into that."

I untangled myself from the yoga pose and blew my nose on a hanky from the night table. Standing, I straightened my skirt. "I'm going to call a friend to find out what's going on with my family. And our money."

Carrie opened my drawer and handed me a hairbrush. "Use the phone in the nurses' office. Then come join me for tea. We have the board members here this weekend."

I unfastened my hair clips, then pulled the brush through my thick, tangled hair. "How exciting," I said.

Carrie laughed. "It's a lot of work. But you've made such good progress and are getting to be so..."

"Presentable?"

Carrie's crooked smile and wrinkled forehead betrayed a little worry. "We need to prove ourselves to the board and our investors—and the work we're doing here." She held up her hand, ticking off her talking points on her fingers. "One: Justify the Talking Cure. Two: Prove that medical science can treat illnesses of the mind as well as the body. Three: Show them that patients can recover." She pointed at me. "*You* can help convince people."

Violet

CHAPTER 2

We found the phone in the nurses' station out of order—the one in the kitchen, too.

"The wind must have blown down the line," Carrie said, clasping me firmly by the elbow and starting down the hall toward the public rooms of the Institute. "It feels like a storm's brewing." I complied, all the while dreading the people in the parlor. I hated the parlor, full of heavy furniture and disquieting curios. And that bedraggled green parrot in a gilded cage, who watched us with evil intent.

"I've got an idea." Carrie paused our trek. "You can write your friend Sean after supper. He seems eager." Carrie lifted my chin, scanning my face. "OK?" Lipstick appeared in her hand, and she applied it to my mouth.

Not my shade, but—did it matter? "Shall we greet those guests?" She kept up a steady stream of distracting chatter as we approached the gathering.

The parlor design was a double one, the room running the depth of the house. I had hope of sneaking in through the servant's entrance so I could disappear among the congregation of tea drinkers, but Carrie steered me to the main entry, all the while keeping up a continuous stream of small talk. I wasn't fooled. We'd make a grand arrival, of course.

A low murmur seeped out from under the parlor's sliding doors, closed against the cold hallway. The sound buzzed about like mosquitoes. We paused on the threshold just as Dr. Elsass entered from the opposite side of the room. Carrie beamed at him, but he glanced away quickly. What's that all about, I wondered.

The doorbell rang. "I'd better get that. Probably more board members." Carrie gave me a nudge into the room, her voice dropping. "Go introduce yourself to Dr. Bertinelli. He's nice." I followed her gaze to a tall, stooped man with snow white muttonchops.

"Welcome, welcome all," Dr. Elsass boomed to his guests. That welcome didn't extend to me, I presumed. "Glad you could come." He walked over to a middle-aged, red-faced Rotary-club-type, his right hand extended.

I searched the faces peopling the room; a bunch of stuffed shirts, as Sean Joye would say. Old White men hogging the hearth. The radio played a Christmas carol concert, making the room at least appear cheery, evergreen and holly boughs hiding the curio cabinets and disturbing oil paintings, though the greenery couldn't mask the faint hint of rot off the artwork.

"I'll be taking Blanche home for the holidays," said the man, as he turned away from a figure seated near the hearth—my roommate, Blanche. Presumably, he was her husband; she'd never mentioned him to me. He smelled of decay.

Cold air invaded the room, and the flames crackled in greeting. Out in the foyer, I could hear Carrie as she passed off the arriving board members' coats and bags to an orderly dragooned into footman duty—"Good evening, Doctor. Ah, Doctor, you remember Doctor? And here's Doctor, right on time."

I scooted as far away from Dr. Elsass as I could, making for the Christmas tree in front of the parlor windows. Its sharp green scent tried its best to counter the guests' stench. As much as I avoided the director, I could still hear him chirping in the background. "We'll talk about that, of course." His voice dropped to a whisper, but the words flew across the room to me like bright budgies. "Do you think that wise, Emerson? She is in a most fragile state."

I found Nurse Martin leading my other roommate, Berta, and two additional patients in tree decoration. "Ah, Violet, thanks for joining us." She held out a sturdy cedar ornament. "Care to help?"

I took it and clung to its warm scent for protection, but despite knowing better—the men would just upset me—I couldn't help watching their dispute. Dr. Elsass was a chess master, and we were all merely pieces in play. Even this Emerson fellow.

"Don't you believe in your Talking Cure? She seems much better to me." Emerson glanced down at his wife and grinned, showing lots of teeth.

The rumor among the maids and kitchen staff was that Blanche was besotted with our therapist, Dr. Ibrahim Cole. Although she was here for "female hysteria"— whatever that was—I had never met a less hysterical female.

Blanche diligently ignored her husband and Dr. Elsass, engrossed as she was in the sketchbook that was never far from her side.

"Aren't you, darling?" Emerson said, paying no attention to her activity. "Wouldn't you like a break from chewing off Cole's ear? You can talk to me if you feel down in the mouth."

Blanche looked up. "I *would* like to see my dog."

Ah, I thought. She *was* paying attention. I bet she notices more than she lets on.

"See? She's fine." Emerson exclaimed to Dr. Elsass, as if he'd cured her female hysteria himself.

"Perhaps a weekend pass," the director mused, pretending to consider the matter. "We'll discuss it at the staff meeting. Mrs. Emerson has made remarkable progress, it is true." He glanced around the room, caught my eye, and beamed. *Damn.* "And speaking of remarkable progress, you know Mrs. Humphrey, I'm sure."

Emerson strode across the room and held out his hand. "Percy Emerson. We've met, but you may not remember. I knew your father from the Piasa Club."

I made myself take his hand, briefly, despite his rotten odor. And the maggots I could see writhing about on his palm. Not real, I told myself. Not real. "Please call me Violet."

"And you should call me Percy. I'm...Sorry for your loss."

I nodded and made for the tea cart, aiming for a napkin to wipe his stench off my skin. My losses were many. To which did he refer?

Percy drifted back to Dr. Elsass and winked. "Nice try. As I was saying, Blanche is much more...tractable...than before." He patted his wife on the head. "But your cure takes an awful lot of time and buckets of cash—who's to say she wouldn't have snapped out of it on her own?"

For her part, Blanche seemed oblivious to the conversation that was transpiring, intent as she was on sketching the Christmas tree. Percy at last noticed the sketchbook on his wife's lap. "That's nice, honey. Gonna puts some colors on there? Lots of green and red?"

She looked up at him, her face blank. Eventually, she said, "Do you think I should? I was interested in the pattern, you see, the way the light—"

"Oh, yes, definitely. Christmas trees are green. With red balls. That might be good enough for a holiday card, if you color it up right." To Dr. Elsass, he said, "Nice little scam you got going here, doc." His voice boomed over the chittering noise of the room. "Well played."

The guests ceased their conversations and turned to the two men. Dr. Elsass and Percy stared at each other for a long minute. At last, the director laughed out loud. "Ah, Mr. Emerson. Always a kidder, as the young people say."

The room grew darker as the afternoon faded, with just the glow of the hearth and the lights on the Christmas tree. When a fresh contingent of board members lumbered into the parlor, the parrot squawked, and the elderly tree trimmers equally took fright. Dr. Elsass approached the new arrivals, arms outstretched. "Come in, gentlemen. Have a hot drink. There will be 'something stronger,' and a fine meal presently."

Suddenly, a passing shadow blocked the glow from the fireplace, a darkness that smelled of decaying fish, sulfur, and algae bloom. Then Berta, who'd been so calm, sank to her knees, her eyes darting about, and croaked in a wavering voice, "Dagon lives. Mighty Dagon. Dagon. Dagon. Dagon."

The bird joined in as a chorus, "Dagon, Dagon, Dagon."

Having no idea to whom or what they referenced, I was struck for a moment with total conviction that Berta, and perhaps the parrot, knew some secret of infinite portent. I utterly believed them, the words a carillon to my ears. I took a deep breath. *This wouldn't do at all.* I'm sure it was just what Carrie had been worried about, one of us crazy people acting crazy at the normal-people party.

"Let's find a quieter place, shall we?" I said in Berta's ear as I took her arm and hoisted her to her feet. "And brighter. It's turned quite gloomy." At least helping Berta would get me away from these men.

"Thank you," said Nurse Martin, glancing at the other two patients warily. They were becoming a little glassy-eyed.

"What should I do with her?" I whispered.

"Can you take her upstairs?" She looked Berta in the face, trying to make eye contact. "Go now with Violet, dear. You've worked so hard, and the tree is lovely. Stop by the kitchen for a cookie, then maybe a nice lie down before your supper. Understand?"

Percy clapped Dr. Elsass on the back, hanging on his shoulder. "That doesn't say much for your so-called Talking Cure, does it?" He waggled his coffee cup, then drained it. "Say, don't you have anything stronger?"

The director shrugged out of the man's embrace. "Alas, melancholic dementia hasn't proven amenable to the method yet. However, the strides we've made are notable. If you'd seen Mrs. Humphrey a few months ago—"

I was trying my best to escape when Carrie appeared in the doorway. "Everyone is here," she announced. "I'll show you to your rooms. You'll find your luggage there."

Dr. Elsass nodded, all smiles again. "Gentlemen, take a moment to freshen up and meet me here at five o'clock for cocktails."

I distracted Berta with food, then walked her up the stairs to our bedroom. Guiding her to bed, the room's unusual chill rang in my ears like tiny bells. When I touched the radiator, I found it was stone cold. Wind rattled the window frame, and cold seeped in under the sash; outside, it was almost dark.

I tried not to think about Berta's disturbing words. The poor woman was demented, talking gibberish. "Rest now," I said to her, aiming to catch the particularly soothing tone Nurse Martin had used.

Berta gave no indication that she'd heard me, but did sit down on the bed. Might as well use what I know, I thought. "Berta, I'd like to help you feel more at peace. Would that be alright?" I took her hand.

I didn't expect her to answer me with words, but I waited for her to accept my touch—a subtle signal, yet always there, always real. When the muscles of her hand relaxed into mine, I slowly traced a loop across the palm, over and over. "Calm and relaxed," I said. "You're calm and relaxed. Nothing disturbs you—any sound you hear is just a sound of everyday living."

The spell worked; Berta's eyes fluttered, and her shoulders slumped.

I had but a moment to feel pleased with myself when my intrusive thoughts reappeared to spoil the moment I'd conjured. *How could they take him? My baby. Why? Whywhywhy?*

Cautious not to pass on my own anxiety, I dropped Berta's hand and helped her to lie down on the bed, then covered her with a thick quilt. I stared out the window at the trees—they claimed to be my friends—shifting in the wind. I breathed deliberately and aimed to fill my head with calming thoughts, to will myself to a place of peace and safety. But the voice intruded. I was coming to think of him as a voice of this place.

"I offer you all the peace you could ever desire."

I glanced over at Berta; she slept quietly, having not uttered a sound. I slid down the wall to sit on the cracked linoleum floor, hugging myself. *Not now.*

For a distraction, I turned my mind to the real, concrete problem of paying my bill. Other people had to deal with such irritations all the time, but it had never been an issue for me. I started a mental list of possible solutions: Call our family man of business in St. Louis to find out what was going on. Or write him a letter. Yes, a letter is more official. I could do both, and have a backup letter as well, maybe even a telegram.

I had no idea if Mr. Orthwort was working for our family; apparently, Father's brokerage company was in arrears at the time he was killed, at least according to one newspaper article I'd read.

It might be better to contact Sean Joye, as Carrie had suggested. If anyone could make our lawyer pay attention to me, it would be him. I continued to fill my thoughts with the details of a plan. Solving a mundane financial issue was so much preferable to the deep loneliness, the empty arms, the separations by death and deceit. And the voice.

"Join me. You'll forget them if you join me."

Anger burst through my mental lists, and self-pity swirled around the room in a gray haze of putrid sewage. I grabbed the quilts and pillows off the beds and flung them to the floor, followed by my shoes and a metal water mug. It rattled and rolled across the floor as I wept into the pile of quilts.

Berta cried out in her sleep and began to bleat a deep, thrumming sound, not her voice at all, but rather the voice in my head. "Come. Come. Come."

"Leave her alone," I shouted. "Or I'll…I'll—"

The door opened and Teddy, the teenage orderly, wagged his finger at me, smiling.

Childhood measles had damaged his hearing; I wasn't sure how much, but I had learned to always turn so that he could see my face. The nurses wrote him notes quite often; his habit was to carry a small notebook for that purpose. "I know," I said. "Sorry. I know the rule: Doors open always."

Teddy glanced at the quilts heaped on the floor, then crossed the room and crouched close to me. "Miss Violet. Really?" He always sounded like fresh blueberry muffins, a kind of muffled sweetness with bursts of clear tanginess.

"I was angry. Sorry. I'll straighten up the beds."

He pointed to Berta, snuggled under the quilt. "Should I get a nurse?"

"Nurse Martin knows she's here," I said. "And I think she's just about asleep." I remembered the voice I'd often heard in my head now coming out of Berta's mouth. What good would a nurse be against that? "She had a fit downstairs, but seems alright now."

Teddy nodded, then tapped my forehead. "And you?"

"I'm fine. I know what I need to do."

It wasn't particularly cold when I put on my coat and scarf. I paid no attention to the wind whipping the birds into a frenzy, and frankly, I didn't care that it was dark out or if it snowed. I had to get away.

The property held a beautiful woodland of elms, maples, and sassafras trees, and I loved to ramble among them. Sometimes, I explored the ruins of a log cabin and a nearby artesian well, which tapped an aquifer to bring water to the surface, in this case flowing into a large, stone-lined basin. The water was heavy in minerals, which encrusted the stones and path with crystals. It was also warm, nourishing moss, cattails, and other plant life. Its warmth misted in the cold surface air.

I was drawn to the artesian well from the start, yet it always felt a bit sinister. Maybe I liked that. It felt like home. I wondered if someone else felt at home there, also. I had found a shifting collection of fossils, seashells, and interesting rocks cairned along an overhang jutting out from the far wall. *Likely a crow's horde.*

I set out on my usual route around the property under the starlight, avoiding the disturbing locations and welcoming the calm of the landscape and the rhythm of my steps to still the urge to run mindlessly. Rounding the back corner of the house, I had a clear view of the western horizon and an impressive troop of gray-green clouds visible against the starry sky. They swirled and pushed toward me; I could feel the air pressure drop.

Heading to the forested parts of the property, Dr. Elsass' words replayed in my head like a stuck phonograph: "I'll call the sheriff…I'll call the sheriff."

I wanted this financial crisis to be resolved and dealt with. My father always said that if money could rectify a situation, then it wasn't really a problem. But I hadn't access to any money, so it *was* a real problem, at least for me. I reminded myself that I had a plan, and the head nurse knew the details. No phone calls, telegrams, or letters would reach St. Louis today. I'd done everything I could for the moment.

It will be well, I told myself. It will be well, it will bewell, itwillbewell.

Although I'd meant to take only a short walk and return before the sleet and snow started, I found my feet had led me to a grove of European ash at the rear of the house, inexplicably growing around a huge oak in the middle of the prairie. It was a place that tried to comfort me, ever since I came here in October, wrapping me in an aromatic cloud of green, even now, with the start of winter mere days away.

I'd recently learned from the caretaker, Finn, that his grandfather, Jürgen Osteen, had planted the trees in the 1830s adjacent to their log cabin, to remind him of his home in Germany. He called it Nerthus's Grove. While the ruin of the cabin still stood, as the family grew prosperous, they built the mansion that was now the Elsass Institute.

Anyway, his Grove was a comforting place. I could hear the trees whisper. Not always to me, I didn't think. They talked, in a language I didn't understand, to someone or something hidden in the soil, under the rocks, or in the stream.

"Come. Come, Come," echoed in my head. But it wasn't the trees; it was the voice that'd plagued me with obsessive tasks ever since I arrived here. The voice I'd just heard in my room. Did poor Berta hear it too? Had it inspired her to shout "Dagon?"

A freezing mist pattered softly on the bare branches of the trees, but I paid it no mind. I walked and walked, faster and faster, to strike a path out of the Grove. It wasn't a large area; I would clear the tree line by going straight in any direction. When I saw the artesian well's silhouette, I knew I was almost free; it was at the very edge of the circle of trees.

I was in such a state that I practically ran to the well, spooky or not. At least it wasn't in the Grove. Yet I never reached it. Instead, I came to the small spring, central to the Grove, gurgling as the cold air closed in on its warm waters, sulfur-laden steam rising from its surface. Somehow,

I'd gone in the exact opposite direction from my intention. I stopped, sweating in my excessive winter wraps, out of breath, with panic rising in my chest. It was full-on night; I'd been out walking for hours.

I heard rustling through the dried leaves on the ground—was someone running? Had they sent out a search party for me? Or was this person also trapped in the Grove? I started to call out, but a thought stopped me. Who would answer?

Did I want to know?

Just then, light trailed through the trees, illuminating huge snowflakes falling from the sky. It was gone just as suddenly, but relieved at the sign of civilization, I reasoned it must have been from a car in the parking lot.

I headed in the light's direction—and resolved to never take another evening walk alone as long as I lived—but somehow I got turned around again. Ahead was the well.

By now, my vision had grown accustomed to the dark, but the vapor rising from the warm water made the well difficult to see, and the scene felt wrong. A large, longish lump lay across my path, its clear menace screeching an alarm.

I tried to convince myself that the disturbing bundle was innocuous. Perhaps Finn had cleaned out some debris. But why would he care if the well was clogged? A modern pump, much nearer the house, supplied the Institute's water.

Something was wrong. Behind me, the Grove whispered. It was in the language of trees, soft, low, and slow, but I could feel their intent in my heart, "Don't look.

Come back to us. We'll keep you safe." I heard the other voice, too. "The water. Come to the water. The water is life."

"Shut up!" I screamed into the darkness. In that instant, I saw the truth: the lump wasn't a mound of wet leaves; it was a person.

I ran to them, my boots sliding across the icy ground. They lay curled on their side in the muck and snow, a handkerchief secured by a necktie against a bleeding head wound. I recognized the coat they wore. The person was Dr. Elsass. Kneeling, I shook his shoulder and shouted, "Dr. Elsass, Dr. Elsass." My hands came away bloody. I didn't think he was breathing, but in the dark, how could I be sure?

"Help, help," I called, rising to run back to the house. "Carrie, Dr. Cole, help!"

Sean

CHAPTER THREE

A Simple Locator Cantrip

*By this bone and by this blood/What was lost, now is found./
Hermes, speed its journey home.*

~From "A Working to Recover Lost Items," grimoire of
"Hector" (Taylor Avebury Humphrey), 1900. Marginalia:
"Ineffective. Perhaps needs more blood."

"I don't know that this is such a good idea, Mr. Joye,"
Malcolm Yates said. "Weather's bad, and just gonna
get worse." He'd scraped the ice off the repair shop's loaner
car for me, but seemed to be having second thoughts. The
garage was closed for the night, and its car park, covered in
a good six inches of the white stuff, was deserted.

"It'll be grand. See here, the snow's stopped." I held
out my hand to demonstrate, catching only a few stray
flakes drifting down from tree branches. I'd just left the
pay phone in the shop's office where I'd been trying, for
the sixth time that afternoon, to phone the asylum where
Violet stayed. By now, the operator recognized my voice.
She was quite sympathetic but said all the lines were down
in central Illinois.

Electric streetlamps reflected off the snow, which covered the ground, the petrol pumps, and the cars awaiting Yates's expertise. He was a young-looking fifty, a wiry Black man who'd recently made his way to St. Louis from the pecan groves and cotton fields of the Missouri Bootheel region. In November, he'd hired me to locate his missing best friend. My investigations business had been new, and I didn't have a whole lot of work. Since Yates was short on cash, I'd waved off payment until later. Later was now.

"Look your own self. To the west." He tromped through the snow into the vacant, snow-packed street and pointed at the western horizon.

"I can't see anything."

"Would you come on over here, sir?"

I sighed and followed him to where an enormous Standard Red Crown Oil sign didn't block the horizon. "I see the dark sky. It tends to do that by seven in the evening in December."

"Don't you see those clouds? More bad weather coming in. And strange weather, too. Those clouds ain't right. Shaped like summertime thunder clouds."

The degree of darkness to the west compared to that directly overhead was all the same to me, although I had to admit I sensed a threat in the air. "So, shouldn't I be getting along to the east, now? As soon as possible?"

Yates glared. "It's not that I don't appreciate you finding my dog, Mr. Joye."

"And I was glad to do it." I'd tried a little divining cantrip I'd read in a book, and, swear on my life, it actually worked. Or perhaps it was the walking about with bacon in my pocket. Anyway, I did find the dog, none the worse for wear, wandering around Forest Park.

"I'll take good care of the car. And have it back tomorrow." My hand itched furiously, and my pulse pounded in my ears. The feeling was to run. Run all the way to Normal, Illinois, if need be. The heebie-jeebies had been building all evening as I located Yates, bought him a round of hooch, and lured him over to the garage.

"Maybe I should come with you," he said. "Case you run into bad snow or a flat tire of something."

"Don't you got nothing better to do on a Saturday, the week before Christmas?"

Yates's face fell slack, his posture signaling defeat. He had work to do over the weekend, and I knew it. With all the snow, Saturday morning would be busy at the petrol station. "Well then, let's clear off a path for you," he said, "at least to the street."

We got to work with the snow shovels, which was good for me, 'cause my mind was going a mile a minute. Maybe not my mind, so much as my—I don't know—soul. Worry over Violet weighed me down and anger at her stirred me up. I put my back into it, but moving the thick, wet snow was a sore trial.

As I worked, I had a vision, but I didn't catch wise as to what was going on at first. I'd a sense of being in two places at once, a feeling that grew stronger and stronger. So, while I sweated in my new-to-me topcoat and slid about the car park in dress shoes shoveling snow, I was also in a dark grove, sleet pattering on the shriveled leaves, filling the god-awful silence of the country. Someone was whispering, low, intimate, and inviting. They weren't talking to me.

Violet. They were talking to Violet, all creepy-cajoling, like. I sensed a threat to her. She knew it, too. Scared, she reached out in every direction for help. The trees were sympathetic, but this problem was beyond their power.

I realized that it must have been her damn enchantment from this last September that still left us linked; I just couldn't manage to break free from her and her family. The itching palm and an irresistible urge to go to her made all the sense in the world now. Out of pure spite, I'd half a mind not to go—Yates would be happier, and I'd have a better use for my car-favor down the road, I was sure.

But Violet was in some kind of a jam. I was sore at her, but…I'm a soft touch. Bad memories scared her. Inner demons shut her down when she faced the sins she'd only committed to ease her pain. And now, a new threat was calling.

Yates scraped the last of the slush from the petrol station drive and threw out a few handfuls of cinders he had at the ready in a bucket. "There, now," he said. "That should do ya." He had a pitying look for me as I took off my hat and wiped sweat from my brow. "You seem tuckered out.

Young fella like yourself ought to be able to shovel a bit of snow now and then. Get gassed in the war or something?"

I started for the garage to return the snow shovel to its rack. "Or something," I muttered as I stowed it away and lit a cigarette, offering him the half-full pack. "I thank you, sir, for the use of the car. And clearing the way."

Now that I was free to leave, I felt reluctant to go. I was tired of playing patsy for the Arwald women—both Violet and her sister Lillian. They had expected me to come running anytime either one of them crooked her little finger. And Violet was the one who had witched me. Maybe the urge to tell her off was just another ploy. I imagined her saying, "Sorry about dragging you out in a snowstorm, Mr. Joye. But since you're here, could you…" I shook my head. No, Violet's nervous breakdown had left her in silence. I'd visited a few times; she hadn't said a word. I'd actually welcome some sass from her.

I had to act on the prickling sense of doom in the back of my brain and the scene that conjured itself up in my mind. Something bad was out there, in the snow, in the woods, in the country. It was bearing down on Violet, on a very broken Violet. Maybe she was deliberately reaching out to me—by choice or in a panic. Either way, I needed to put a stop to it.

Violet

CHAPTER FOUR

Death Doeth Become Her

Is another suspicious death dogging Mrs. Violet De Noailles Arwald Humphrey's high-society doorstep? Don't miss this "Daily Dish" exclusive: What does her former maid have to say about those black magic infant sacrifice rumors?

~From *The West End Bugle*, "Daily Dish" column, October 7, 1924.

"Out of the way, Miss Violet." A voice pierced the terrible scene by the well, playing over and over again in my mind. "Coming through with hot rolls."

I found myself in the kitchen, shaking uncontrollably. I had no memory of how I got there, but my boots were caked with mud and my stockings torn. Blood dripped down my knee from a fresh scrape. Cook and Lottie, her helper, bustled about with their final preparation and paid no attention to me other than to complain that I was in their way. I grabbed Cook by the shoulder. "I need Nurse Carrie. Or Dr. Cole. Where are they?"

"What's this, then? Can't you people see I'm trying to get the Director's fancy dinner on the table? I'm late enough as 'tis. Ain't seen any of 'um, all afternoon."

Her lemony irritation—sharp, acrid, and stinging—enveloped me.

I clomped off toward the dining room, still wearing the muddy galoshes. Surely everyone, including the medical people, would be gathered there. I ran up the stairs and through the back hall, a foul scent and wet, splatting noises against the hardwood floor pursuing me. *Just my boots. Nothing is following me.* I slid into the room.

As expected, the room was full of guests. The clock chimed the quarter hour as I entered. Fifteen minutes after seven.

Percy Emerson stood with his back to me. He was speaking with some old goat whose eyes grew round at the sight of me, taking a step backwards. Without turning around, Percy said, "'Bout time, Elsass. Starving your board of directors is no way to win friends and influence people."

The rest of the guests were chatting over drinks or watching the snow. Over drinks. Plenty of drinks. They all turned to me, food-expectation written all over their faces. I took a certain delight in how profoundly I was about to disappoint them.

Before I could speak, another voice piped up. "If you thought that was the Director's typical tread, you are even less perceptive than I'd thought." Ah, Dr. Cole's French lilt. I usually found its floral bouquet as soothing as the man himself was annoying, but tonight…not so much. He smirked at his joke.

My therapist, Ibrahim Cole, was a young African physician Dr. Elsass had recruited. I gathered his real interest was neurologic research, but he was required to learn the Talking Cure by practicing it on me. He had no interest in it and believed all mental illness had a physiologic basis.

He maintained that healing anomalies of the brain and nervous system would cure us, not endless discussions of our childhoods and sex lives. Yet he still made me talk of these things, ad infinitum. "Now, my dear Mrs. Humphrey, what have you done with our dear Director? The party awaits him."

"What?" I laughed. Giggled like a hysterical child, to be honest. "I've done nothing with the Director," I blurted. *I must sound insane.* I took a deep breath and started again. "I just now found him outside, seriously injured. I've come to get help."

"Where?" Cole set down his glass of fruit juice.

"Near the artesian well, beyond the Grove."

"Wait here, I'll get my bag." He bounded out of the room. At his departure, everyone started to chatter, their bright-beaked words flying about my head.

A board member, who was in conversation with Percy, guided me to a chair. I was sorry I'd thought he looked like an old goat. "What a shock for you. Here, rest a moment." He put a glass a water in my right hand just as Percy handed me a gin cocktail in my left. "Shock is right." Percy grinned. "Do you think he's dead?"

I gulped the water and shook my head. Really, I had no idea. But I wanted to think that he was merely injured.

Blanche Emerson was staring from across the room —not at me, but at the glass. Red fingerprints marked the tumbler. My fingerprints. I smelled of coppery death. I flinched and dropped it. Nurse Carrie materialized, her face red and perspiration-soaked curls tendrilled around her face.

"Give her some room, people. For goodness' sake." She took my bloody hands. "What's this?"

"He…his head…" I couldn't say it. I refused to become involved in this situation, squeezing my eyes shut. I could feel someone, most likely Carrie, easing me out of my wet coat and boots.

"Did she say he was in the well?" a voice floated out of the dark.

"Artesian well, wherever that is," said another.

They chittered in the dark like roosting finches. I shivered, and someone draped a blanket over my shoulders. I imagined I was going into shock. I didn't really care one way or the other. My feet and hands felt like ice.

"It's freezing in here," someone said. "Stoke up that fire."

Ah, maybe it's not just me.

In time, whether long or short, I couldn't say, Dr. Cole's voice boomed through the room. "Will you all please stay calm. Stop milling about, go into the parlor, and take a seat."

"Well, I never," someone murmured. I didn't recognize who spoke, but I knew the quiet voice of entitlement, always on guard to any threat to its position. Like when a

Black man takes charge of an emergency situation. "Who does he think he is?" I heard them shuffle out of the room. I stayed where I was, hoping to go unnoticed.

"What have you found, Ibrahim? It sounds like the director had a terrible accident." Carrie was using her head nurse voice, the one she unleashed on orderlies, maids, and her nursing staff daily. "And you need to report off to me directly—we can step into the other room."

With great effort, I opened my eyes, struggled to my feet, and went across the hall to the parlor. I stood on the threshold of the rear entrance, trying to focus on the scene before me. Carrie sounded normal, but she was shaking and her complexion an ashy gray. She stood in a shadowy corner of the room.

The parrot's green and purple feathers gleamed in the firelight. It was quiet, just staring at Carrie.

Dr. Cole ignored the head nurse and addressed Blanche. "This may be an unpleasant discussion for you. If you'd prefer to leave, I'm sure Nurse will see to it."

Blanche smiled winsomely and shook her head.

He then turned to the directors, perched on various loveseats and ottomans around the room. "Gentlemen." He straightened his bowtie. "I have some sad news. Dr. Elsass is dead. It is impossible to say exactly what has happened without a proper examination. I've dispatched Teddy to find Finn so they can pull the director out of the well."

I heard a gasp from someone, and the ozone scent of a lightning storm filled the room.

"The well?" I said.

That didn't sound right. I had a clear image in my mind, as much as I wanted to make it go away. Elsass hadn't been in the well.

"Finn's working on the boiler," said Carrie.

"No, he's not," said Dr. Cole. "I've already been to the sub-basement."

Percy strode toward the doorway to the front hall. "We need to call the county sheriff, that's what we need to do. We have a homicidal maniac here—" He jerked his thumb at me. I hadn't gone undetected at all. Then he addressed Dr. Cole. "You, boy, you best watch her." Turning to Carrie, he continued, "Don't you have a place to lock her up?"

Dr. Cole and Carrie both sputtered, their words piling up on the floor in front of them, malformed, reeking, and ugly.

Percy gave them a cold stare. "*I'm* the president of the board. Even if I weren't, I outrank a nurse and a colored orderly."

There's an old saying, "If looks could kill." Blanche's stare drove a dagger right into her husband's chest.

Dr. Cole stood tall and jutted out his chin. "Sir, I'm a graduate of the Sorbonne's medical school. I served in the medical corps alongside Dr. Elsass throughout the war."

"Can't you take a joke?" Percy grinned. "Still, it's not like you're a real American doctor. Let me just make this call, and then we'll talk." He stepped out into the hall. We could all hear him pick up the phone receiver and click the transmitter. "Operator?"

Words crowded the room. It's just people talking at once, I told myself. And I preferred it to Percy's voice ringing through my head, "Homicidal maniac."

"Operator?" Percy shouted into the phone as he clicked the transmitter over and over, the staccato clicks whizzing over my head. I had to make a conscious effort not to shy away from their sharp beaks and claws. They are not real, I thought. Not real. Perhaps none of this was real: Percy, the phone, the body.

"The line is down," Carrie said. "Has been for several hours." She turned to an elderly board member, "Can I prevail on you to add a log to the fire?" I'd been told this man's name recently. *Muttonchops. Dr. Muttonchops? No, that wasn't right.*

A hush fell over the room. We turned to Carrie to tell us what to do, what to think, what to feel. Except for Percy, still in the hall shouting into the dead telephone, and Dr. Cole, who'd marched across the hall to the dining room and grabbed a seat at the table. I could see him, scribbling notes in a small journal.

"Now, first things first." I wouldn't say Carrie was calm. She was obviously shaken. But equipoise flowed off her in teal waves, gently lapping at my feet. She'd summoned strength from some depth I couldn't even fathom and was planning to get us all through the night.

I hung on to her every word. The normal, healthy people all seemed to be in the same boat as me—adrift and storm-tossed, grateful for a beacon in the emotional gale.

Carrie continued, "Let's together count our blessings. We have electricity, indoor plumbing, and Finn will have the boiler fixed soon so the central heat will be back on. Meanwhile—a cozy fire!" She stretched her lips across her teeth in the figure of a smile. "And brandy. Blanche, dear, could you help us out with that?"

The directors nodded, falling under her crisp yet kind authority, as my fellow patient put down her sketchpad and picked up her cane, a souvenir from a bout with polio. Dutifully, Blanche poured snifters and carried the first across the hall to Dr. Cole.

He didn't drink alcohol, I knew—and I was sure Blanche knew it, too.

"Oh, you think to tempt me, my dear Miss Blanche, on this sad night." He laughed, a skittering giggle at odds with his usual melodious bass. "But, no, it is written in the—"

She interrupted him, her words indistinct from across the room, but her tone was charming.

In a moment, the two of them appeared in the doorway.

"Nurse," Dr. Cole said. "It's time to serve our guests their dinner."

Blanche left his side, brushing against his arm to get by, and found a taker for the brandy. Dr. Bertinelli, that was his name. *Muttonchops Bertinelli.*

"As soon as Finn retrieves him, I'll be in my lab with the body," Dr. Cole continued.

"No unpleasant talk before a meal," said Dr. Bertinelli. "Especially, in front of the ladies."

"Pardon me." Dr. Cole made a small bow to Blanche. "A gathering of medical men…Sometimes we forget ourselves."

"For goodness' sake, I don't need you to remind me that it's time to eat," Carrie said. "I know *I'm* tired of waiting around to eat—how long has it been? Over an hour, I think."

The thought of food made my stomach flop. The room spun. I staggered to the nearest chair, plopped myself down, and closed my eyes.

"Since before six," some man, another director, I suppose, chimed in. "The 'music' started right at six."

"So it did. I loved that first song," said Carrie. "My favorite, 'Nearer My God to Thee.'"

A moment of silence swallowed the room. Curiosity getting the better of me, I squinted at the gathered guests. Everyone was staring at Carrie, puzzled expressions on their faces.

A clean-shaven, slightly younger old man said, "I don't remember—"

"It's not as if the poor dears can carry a tune in a bucket, Abel," said Dr. Bertinelli. "Could have been any hymn you care to name." He lifted his brandy in a toast. "Here's to music therapy. Soothes a savage breast."

Carrie smiled at him, a real one this time. "We feel strongly about art's merit here." She pulled a bell cord. "I've just rung for the meal to be served. That will sort us out."

Percy stormed in. "All the phone lines are dead, and there's no heat." He turned to Carrie. "If you're in charge, what kind of place are you running here?"

"The situation is under control."

He smirked and reached out to pluck something from her hair, and offered it to her. It was a dead leaf, although it smelled like a dead mouse to me. "*Is* it under control? Where have you been?"

"Mr. Emerson, please escort your wife." She snatched the leaf and crumbled it into her pocket. "A regular routine is important to her."

Actually, sitting with one's spouse at dinner wasn't the way things are done in polite society, but I imagine party etiquette isn't part of most nursing school curricula. The guests stood and sorted themselves, then proceeded into the dining room, while a maid lit the decorative hurricane lamps that had been placed in the windows. Not moving from my corner armchair, I channeled all my efforts into not fainting nor throwing up.

"Cook will be serving our meal in a moment." Carrie attempted to herd them out of the room. "I must go make sure everything is ready."

Percy sidled up to me and grasped my arm. I squirmed under his touch but couldn't break free.

"Are you all going to chow down on Elsass' grub while his murderer just sits here?" He gave me a little shake.

Carrie bristled. "That is entirely uncalled for, Mr. Emerson. I can't allow you to manhandle our patients—"

At that moment, Finn, the handyman, clomped through the service entrance. "Teddy said you wanted me. I'm in the middle of rigging up a part for the stoker—the sooner

I get that done," he glanced around the room, "the sooner you'll have heat again. Then I can see to the phone wires."

Percy laughed. "Sounds like the whole place would fall down without you. Maybe you should be the director." He poured himself a second, or possibly a third, brandy. "We have another job for you. Dr. Elsass is dead. Drowned in the artesian well, he did, apparently."

Even in the dim light, I could see Finn's ruddy face drain of color. "Wh-wh-what?" He lowered himself into the nearest chair.

"I'm sorry, Finley," Dr. Cole said. "We are putting a lot on you, but I need to examine the body in my lab to determine the cause of the accident or—"

"Or deliberate death. That's called murder, isn't it, Mrs. Humphrey?" said Percy, his words sharp, pecking at my nerves.

"Mr. Emerson," Carrie barked. "Was that necessary, helpful, or kind? You may be the board chair, but I will not have you undermining our patients' recovery. The director obviously had an accident."

At least in that moment, I didn't care what Percy Emerson thought of me. I was transfixed by Finn: the fire's reflection in the tiny beads of sweat on his forehead, his ragged breathing, the acrid odor rolling off him. Coal dust and panic?

Percy laughed, raising both hands in surrender. "Of course. She's not the only suspect. Just the most obvious." He pulled a cigar from an inner pocket, cut it, and poked it in his mouth. "You, for example, I don't recall you being with us at the cocktail hour. That's the time Elsass must have died." He lit the cigar. "And this one"—he gestured at Dr. Cole—"strolled in long after everyone else had arrived."

The room erupted in a red deluge of voices, and all eyes fixed on the foreigner in our midst.

I could see Dr. Cole mouthing words, although apparently he had no voice against the rising tide. I thought he said, "That's ridiculous," then stood and raised his hand to call a halt to the chatter. "As the staff here is certainly aware, I've been in Chicago all afternoon. I stopped for prayers on my journey home at sundown." He strode to Finn's side. "The time of death is currently unknown." He glared at Percy as he tucked away his notebook. "First things first." He counted on his fingers, "Body. Lab. Examination."

"And by then we can phone the sheriff to come investigate," said Dr. Bertinelli.

Finn, who'd recovered some of his color, squared his shoulders. "Well, let's get the boss in out of the cold and snow then." He stood. "I'll round up some help."

The cook's assistant, Lottie, appeared at the door. "Nurse Carrie? Soup's on."

"Alright." Carrie shooed Finn away. "Go see to poor Henry—" her voice broke, "I mean, Dr. Elsass. Our guests can proceed with their meal if they wish."

Finn buttoned his coat. "Can someone show me where he is?"

I watched myself, a character in a play, as I stood up. My mouth moved, and words flew out. "I will." I had no desire to see that place again, it all felt so unreal. My need to reassure myself and connect to the here and now outweighed any fear of the well or revulsion at death. I knew death intimately. We were old companions, if not friends.

"Are you sure?" Nurse Carrie asked. She glanced at Dr. Cole, her eyes narrowed and forehead wrinkled.

I nodded. "I think I need to. It all seems like a dream." I was thinking of another dream-like death. I had no recollection of my husband's dead body. Taylor had a myriad of faults, sins on his heart, and crimes on the police blotter, but he was someone important to me and I'd let him down.

"I shall go, too," Dr. Cole said, lifting my wrist and then glancing at his watch to take my pulse. "Mrs. Humphrey is my patient, after all. And I must direct your efforts, Finley, so you don't destroy any evidence."

"If the chief suspects are all going to wander loose around the property, I'm going, too," said Percy.

"And if the—" Carrie sounded like she might throttle Percy Emerson, right there in the parlor in front of the whole board of directors, "—chief inuendo spreader must tag along, so will I."

Violet

CHAPTER FIVE

Incident note: Patient appears in lounge after outdoor exercise hour with torn gloves, hands caked with mud, and fingernails broken. Clutches yet another star-shaped stone. States has no memory of obtaining it. Staff confiscated stone and reported off to Dr. Elsass. ~G. Martin, RN.

~From nursing notes, Violet Humphrey, December 15, 1924, 1800 hours.

As my various keepers dealt with their coats and scarves, I hurried into the kitchen where Carrie had deposited my muddy boots and hung my still-wet jacket to dry. Comfrey Rouse came in the back door with a basket of freshly dug tubers and a heap of cut sage, the warm, earthy scent a comfort.

"The storm's getting bad, Miss Violet." A middle-aged woman with bright red curls and a face freckled from her long hours in the sun, I often encountered Miss Comfrey on my walks about the property. I had no idea what her official job was, but she always seemed to know if I needed silent company, neutral conversation, or to be left alone. She treated me like a sane adult even when I wasn't. "You'd best put on some galoshes."

I nodded, and for that moment, at least, didn't feel like the prisoner I actually was. "Thanks. I will."

"The earth has her ways, mind you, her seasons. Just stay connected. Listen to her."

I knew that, but tended to forget, caught up in dark moods and thoughts. "I'll try."

She grabbed my hand and held it for a long moment, examining my face.

"Is there something else?" I asked. "I won't be long, and I'm going out with Nurse Carrie and Dr. Cole. The director has had an...accident."

I couldn't read her clearly: Was Comfrey surprised at the news, or was something else on her mind? She nodded and released my hand. "None of your digging while you're out there, alright?"

I had no idea what she was talking about, but I agreed and left wrapped properly for the weather. The rest of the party joined me in the parking lot, which was taking on an icy sheen. We followed Dr. Cole, trudging past the septic tank and around the corner of the house, skirting the Grove. He approached the artesian well. Something floated on the surface.

"But he was over there." I pointed to the stone path, where the frozen rocks gleamed in the lantern light. "He was curled on his side. He's been moved."

I grabbed Nurse Carrie's hand, and she squeezed mine. "You must have been quite upset. Not thinking clearly."

I was upset, but I knew what I'd seen. And, making me even more nervous, I had a strong sense of being watched; it flowed over me like sticky sludge. I told myself the thought was ridiculous. Irrational. Who'd be out here in the dark and wet? I remembered Miss Comfrey's words and sent my intentions deep down into the earth, begging for support.

Dr. Cole was hunched over with an electric flashlight, examining the pavers I'd indicated. He stood, brushed snow off his trousers, and straightened his coat. "Perhaps, Mrs. Humphrey, perhaps..." He shrugged. "This was his position when I came out here a few minutes ago." He nodded to Finn and Teddy, who'd put on hip boots for the job. They unfolded a large canvas tarp and spread it on the ground.

A young orderly gave Dr. Elsass a wide berth, holding the kerosene lantern high, illuminating the body. I didn't want to look, but did so anyway to distract myself from the low murmuring of the Grove and the residual sticky sensation of being watched from afar.

What I saw was the medical director floating on his back in the well's overflow basin. His jaw was slack, and his eyes were wide open, glassy, with a cockeyed gaze, the necktie still tied around his head.

"Wait for the sheriff," suggested Percy. "Don't move him—"

"On that we agree," said Carrie. "As acting director—"

"Nurse," Dr. Cole said, "Don't be ridiculous. The sheriff won't be available for days. With the phone lines down, we can't even inform him of the death."

"Pretty quick to destroy the evidence, aren't you, doc?" Percy said.

"Evidence of what? Most likely, the man slipped on these wet stones and fell into the well." He regarded me for a moment. At last, he said, grudgingly, "Or fell, as you found him, Mrs. Humphrey, then recovered enough to crawl in his confusion into the water and drown. The postmortem exam will show me more."

Sleet pattered off the leaves overhead, a cool blue sound, strangely comforting. I wanted the rhythm to fill my thoughts as I tugged on my connection to the earth, but the voice only I could hear was loud and insistent.

Leave the offering in the water.

I was generally alone when the voice spoke to me. Didn't Carrie hear it?

The water shall free him.

But Carrie didn't react, nor did the men struggling with the body. I was trembling.

"He can't stay here," I said. "It's not safe for him. Something is in the woods. Or the water. They'll…" I didn't know what the whispering voice would do, but it wasn't good.

Emerson laughed. "Setting up the cuckoo defense again, I see." Nurse Carrie and Dr. Cole exchanged knowing glances. *God damn them and their smug attitudes.*

Nurse Carrie wrapped her arm around my shoulders. "You're shaking, Violet. I'd say it's shock. We should go in."

"Yes," said Dr. Cole. "Mrs. Humphrey's presence isn't required. And I have an idea that will address your concerns, Mr. Emerson." He tapped Teddy's shoulder, then looked him square in the face, the lantern light casting his profile in sharp shadows. Dr. Cole pointed to the house, then mimed taking a photo. "Bring me the camera from the director's office."

Understanding dawned on the boy's face. "Camera? Yes." He started to dash away, then turned back. "Where?"

The trees were making a dreadful racket, "𝕽𝖚𝖓 𝖆𝖜𝖆𝖞, 𝖗𝖚𝖓 𝖆𝖜𝖆𝖞. 𝖂𝖊 𝖜𝖎𝖑𝖑 𝖍𝖎𝖉𝖊 𝖞𝖔𝖚."

Dr. Cole pointed at Dr. Elsass's body and spoke louder. "The director's office."

"Interesting." Percy grinned. "I like your style, doc. Since we're going to do the sheriff's job for him, we might as well do it right."

"Sorry, it's really noisy out here," Teddy said. "Can you write it?" He held out a notebook and a pencil.

"Sure." Percy grabbed the notebook and jotted something in it, handing it back to him, along with a coin. "Off with you then."

Teddy grinned, glanced at the notebook, and dashed off through the wet snow.

I didn't like Dr. Elsass, but I couldn't leave until I knew the director was safe from the greedy well. I hushed the trees, ignored the voice, and shrugged free of the nurse. I needed to pace, so I took a few steps toward an old log cabin that was quietly decaying nearby, a relic of the property's early settlers. Something on the ground caught my attention, barely visible in the wild swings of the lantern light. "Dr. Cole. Over here." As soon as I spoke, the cold whispering quieted, the sleet tapping against the leaves even harder.

He came to join me, walking along the flagstone path.

"No, no—walk around. See that? Footprints in the snow."

"I do see. And more over here. Do they come from the cabin? Or go to it?"

"What are you looking at?" asked Nurse Carrie, marching toward us.

"We were looking at a number of footprints, nurse," he said. "Before you blundered through them."

"People walk through here all the time," Carrie huffed. "And you said it was an accident."

Just then, Teddy ran up, camera in hand, and passed it off to Dr. Cole. "Ready. It has film." He reached into his pocket and retrieved a handful of flashbulbs.

"Thank you." Dr. Cole patted him on the back, then set to work photographing the tracks, the body, the path, and the well. The rest of us stood around, shivering and glaring at each other.

Eventually, Percy said, "My feet are freezing." He stomped his bespoke Italian wingtips on the ground to emphasize the point. "We should wrap this up."

"Since that's all the flashbulbs I have, it will have to do," said Dr. Cole. "Alright, boys, heave him out—gently—and get him to my lab. And what's that? Strange." He pointed at something in the dim light. "Watch out; don't trip on the conch shell. Someone's idea of décor, I suppose."

Violet

CHAPTER SIX

Chief complaint: Catatonia.

Informant: Patient's sister, Lillian Arwald.

Proximal Cause: Manic episode, which included threat of harm to Miss Arwald's young child. VH believes herself to be a "witch" capable of summoning a "monster." Death of VH's husband due to gunshot wound during this manic episode. VH's responsibility for that tragedy is under police investigation.

~From Elsass Institute intake summary,
Violet Humphrey, October 5, 1924.

While Dr. Cole remained to supervise the men removing Dr. Elsass from the well's overflow basin, Carrie, Percy, and I returned to the house, crunching over the sleet-encrusted snow. Contaminated by blood and death, I was desperate for a bath. My heart pounded in my temples as the trees chattered their alarm, the voice in my head calling me back to the water. I ignored them all, filling the air with every inane question about the evening I could think of.

Clearly, events had shaken Carrie; she gave the briefest of answers as to the menu for the weekend, how long the board members would stay, and from where the Christmas tree had been harvested. In a bout of chivalry I certainly didn't expect, Percy escorted me across the ice-covered parking lot, then returned to assist Carrie.

By the time we had all reached the kitchen stoop, the sleet had stopped, and patches of starry sky began to appear among the shredded clouds, although the western horizon remained ominous. Random lightning strikes painted the sky with broad green and purple strokes. I'd never felt so cold in my life.

We shed our boots and wraps in the empty kitchen, still blessedly warm, and made our way to the front hallway, where we encountered the other board members. They'd already finished eating and appeared intent on heading home, the late hour and icy roads notwithstanding. Both maids, an orderly, and one of the junior nurses were either carrying bags down the stairs or finding coats and wraps for the elderly gentlemen.

Was it the lack of heat or fear that drove them? Fear of me, for instance. Or could they smell death in the air, too?

"I'm going for a warm bath," I whispered to Carrie.

"Dear, you know the rules; there's no one available to watch over you. And I doubt we have any hot water, with the boiler on the fritz."

As I blinked away tears, Percy took in the signs of mass exodus, then laughed as he winked at me.

I could feel Elsass's decay creeping under my skin and bolted off to warm myself by the parlor fireplace. I didn't care if a nurse was available to assist me or not;

I'd scrub off with ice cubes if I had to. As soon as Carrie was busy helping with the others, I'd sneak out to the washroom.

Blanche was still sketching, oblivious to it all. The parrot preened its feathers, then squawked and flapped as a clunk from the furnace reverberated through the ductwork. I heard Percy's voice. "Blanche, honey, go pack your bag."

"Everyone, please," Nurse Carrie said, her eyes shooting daggers at Percy as she blocked the front door. "This board had important matters to discuss at the meeting scheduled for tomorrow." She gestured at the open parlor. "And surely, you'd like to know what Ibrahim has to say about the accident. If you could wait in there, he'll be along presently."

The staff, at least, stopped the luggage brigade and filed into the parlor. But the old doctors harrumphed and stood their ground. Meanwhile, Blanche asked her husband, "Why do we have to leave right now?"

"Because I said so. Hurry up and don't forget your mink. It will be a cold ride home."

As Blanche struggled to her feet, she grabbed for my hand, her expression begging me for something. Help? We stood together, transfixed by events and the stream of people flowing through the room. I had to get a grip on this situation.

And that task would start with me getting a grip on myself. I took a deep breath, ignoring the putrid, green panic that filled the air and my own reek of decay.

"Mr. Emerson, please. A moment of your time," Carrie said.

Percy laughed. "Since you said 'please.' You do seem to have your 'patient' under control, for the moment," he said as he pointed at me. "I'm going to lay it out for you: I'm worried about what Mrs. Humphrey will do when she's not in her right mind. Such as bashing Blanche in her sleep." He was oblivious to the fact that, far from being afraid, Blanche clung to me like I was her last friend on earth.

"It's such a long drive to the city," I said, watching Blanche's face. Had I guessed correctly that she wanted to stay? She nodded. "Hours and hours on icy roads," I continued. "Do you really want to have a passenger along, distracting your concentration?"

"Everyone, please," Carrie said. "This way, Dr. Lieberman. I'm sure the boiler will be operating again once Finn can get back to it. Your rooms will be warm soon, and we have no shortage of quilts. I've ordered hot toddies."

As if on cue, Lottie, the cook's assistant, appeared in the doorway with a tray laden with cups, saucers, and a steaming carafe. "Dr. Cole said for me to tell you he went over to the caretaker's house across the way to try their phone."

Carrie stared at her and the tray. "Ah, and where is Cook?"

"Mrs. Holmes said she just remembered she was supposed to deliver a message and dashed off. Not sure where or what. You know how she is sometimes." Lottie moved into the parlor with her heavy tray.

Carried nodded, then addressed the group. "Now, settle down, everyone. Girls, will you two please serve the drinks? Robert, return all the bags to our guests' rooms."

Percy wavered, then took a swig from a hip flask. "No, I don't think I want to wait around," he said, pulling on Blanche's arm. She clung to me more tightly. "We're getting *away* while the getting's good. If any of you gents want a ride to St. Louis, come on along." He gave Blanche a rough tug, and she released me, defeat written on her face.

The men looked at each other, then Percy, his flask, and each other again. "Thanks, but I live in Mount Vernon," said one.

Dr. Bertinelli added, "I have my car."

"Now, Dr. Abel, Dr Bertinelli," Carrie said, "you don't want to drive in these conditions." She took the arm of the Mount Vernon resident, Dr. Abel, apparently, and steered him to an easy chair. "At least have a hot drink first." I went to help Lottie. Anything to distract myself.

The sound of heavy boots treaded up the backstairs, then creaked through the service corridor. Finn appeared. "The director's in Dr. Cole's lab, and the stoker's fixed. For the moment. I need a new part, but I've jerry-rigged the conveyor screw. Will do for us through the night, anyway."

"Thank you, Finn," said Carrie.

Percy poked him in the chest. "What about the phone?" He didn't seem to notice Blanche slipping out from under his grasp.

Finn glared at him. "If you can give me a moment to grab a sandwich, I'll see to it, but it's most likely wires down from the wind and ice. Sheriff ain't gonna come out here in the middle of a storm, anyway."

"That's fine. Take your time, get some food, and sleep." Carrie turned to the board members, now seated in the parlor. "Hear that, gentlemen? We have heat. So, a nice hot toddy and then to bed."

"Bed?" Percy blustered. "We need the sheriff out here. Now."

Blanche made a beeline for me and took over pouring the hot water over lemon slices in each cup. "If you don't want to go with him," I whispered, "Don't. I'll back you up." Lottie topped each cup with a generous glug of whiskey and a spoonful of sugar, and I passed them around.

We heard the front door open, and a blast of cold air chilled the room. Feet stamped on the mat, then footsteps. We all waited expectantly. What we expected, I couldn't say.

Dr. Cole hurried in, brushing snow off his shoulders. "Starting to snow again," he said, "very hard. And the wind blows in all directions. I almost got lost, just trying to walk across the lawn. Luckily, my sense of direction is good."

Now that I was feeling a little more in control and focused, I noticed an odd sensation about the weather that I'd had all evening. Call it intuition, or perhaps I'd begun to remember what I once knew of the craft, but this storm had a decidedly unnatural element: not just the phenomenon of lightning in winter, but also its green and purple flashes against the dark clouds.

Dr. Cole scanned the room. "Excellent. You're all gathered."

And they were. Even the recalcitrant Percy Emerson was now deeply into Dr. Elsass' whiskey, imbibing it straight from a coffee cup. He marched over to a window to judge the snow's progress, perhaps. Thunder taunted me from a distance.

Dr. Cole shed his topcoat and hat, handing them off to Carrie, who trotted off to hang them up somewhere. "Gentlemen, your attention. Please."

Blanche offered him a cup. "Warm yourself, doctor."

"Thank you," he said, smiling at Blanche as he waved off Lottie's offer of supplemental whiskey. "Just the hot lemon drink." He gulped it, then set the cup and saucer on a table. "I've several bits of news that will interest you all. One: I've just come from the caretaker's house—that phone isn't working either. Mr. Maderia told me—"

"Who?" asked the director with the neat goatee, the ancient man who'd offered me water earlier. Lieberman, I thought Carrie had called him. "Speak up, young man." He proffered an ear trumpet.

"Tomás Maderia," Dr. Cole raised his voice and spoke directly into the device. "He rooms there with Finley. Tends to the vegetable garden and the chickens. He says the lines are down from here to the highway. So, we are unable to call the sheriff this night."

"So I'llss drive to the…sh…sh…town," Percy said.

"Yeah, so the director had a bad accident," said Finn. "I'm sure the sheriff has better things to do—"

"While the head injury is consistent with misadventure," said Dr. Cole, "This—" He removed something from his pocket and held it up. It was a lidded laboratory glass dish, small, flat, and clear. "—contains a note I found on the director."

Percy and Finn crowded around him, while the room erupted in cries of "What's it say?" and "So what?"

Percy grabbed the container from Dr. Cole and peered inside. "The ink's all smudged. Illegible."

To me, Dr. Cole asked, "And you, Mrs. Humphrey? Can you see this any better?"

I was more than a little surprised that he'd ask my opinion. I shrugged and took the dish over to a lamp to examine it in stronger light. "It's waterlogged. The ink has run."

"But it was folded," said Dr. Cole, striding over to retrieve it. "The creases protected a few letters. I can make out a looped capital, possibly a M or N. Then E-E, followed by a smudge and a space." He tapped the glass covering the wet note. "Here is clearly a lower case T and perhaps another smudge. Then…is that two Ls?"

"Or a L and a K," I said, drawn into the puzzle despite myself. "Or a B, possibly? But at the end of a word. Some letters before the L are hopelessly blurred."

He took the dish from me and pocketed it.

"So?" said Percy.

"My English is not nearly as fluent as yours, Mr. Emerson. But I can guess. 'MEE—' could be 'meet.' Then, obviously, 'at the—'," he glanced at me, "Double L as in —well."

Percy, suddenly clear-eyed and sharp-witted, locked me in his gaze with tiny silver keys that rattled against a slamming jail cell door. "Which is exactly what you did, didn't you, girlie?"

Panic clawed my chest as I scanned the room. For what—Support? Protection? I needed Carrie. Until that moment, I hadn't realized how safe the head nurse made me feel. Where was she?

More than a whiff of judgment hung in the air like musky incense smoke. These people were strangers, but they knew all about me, I was sure. They *had* to know every word printed in the newspapers and perhaps more. How private would my records be in a place like this? Obviously, my sister had shared the whole story—her version of it—in my medical chart, which also held the details of anything I had confided to the doctors and nurses since then.

Blanche blinked, wide-eyed and confused. At least she wasn't in on it. Dr. Cole had a bright, eager gleam in his eyes; if I had attacked Dr. Elsass, he could justify who-knows-what sort of exciting new treatments for my derangement. As if ice-water baths weren't bad enough, I'd heard him talking up electric shock—galvanism—to the director, and even inducing fever through hot swaddling blankets or deliberate infection. I couldn't bear it; I simply could not.

The voice in my head muttered, but I couldn't make out the words. Shut up, I thought. "I—I—just found him there. Like I told you before." I turned on Percy. "I'd been out walking for almost an hour."

"In a sleet storm?"

"Stop it," Carrie said from the doorway. "I will not have you bullying our patients." I thought she was even more flustered than I was, her chest heaving in rage over my ill-treatment.

I breathed in softly through my nose and expelled the air in a deliberate shove. "I don't have to answer to you," I managed to say, my words coming out in tiny squeaks. "But I will point out—" I felt a little stronger, "—I had just spoken to Dr. Elsass in his office, and I saw that note on his desk, the one Dr. Cole just showed us. At least one of the same size and color. What could I possibly gain from another meeting a few hours later?"

"OK, lady, I don't know or care. It's a police matter, but we're not going to get any law out here tonight. You're the prime suspect in my book, and I don't know what you'll do next." Percy wheeled around to address Carrie, "You have a padded cell here, don't you?"

Carrie spluttered, "Hardly."

I felt fear rising as a tendril of a voice whispered from somewhere nearby, "Come."

Get out of my head.

"This is a progressive institution. We have a quiet room."

"As long as it has a lock." He poured himself more whiskey. "I do suppose we're stuck here for the night, but I won't have my wife at risk—"

"That's a preposterous idea," Carrie said. "Mrs. Humphrey—"

Although my body remained in the parlor, my mind spun away. But rather than the crisp, cold, comforting blankness of my recent catatonia, I had thoughts —a vision, perhaps. I was back at the well, its warmth feeding a creeping layer of fog across the path. The bare tree limbs swayed in the west winds. The sleet had stopped. "Come to me," the whisperer said. In my mind's eye, stars shone, and they were brilliant, cold, hard diamonds. Watching.

"Where are you? Show yourself." I took a hesitant step toward the well. "I'm not afraid of you," I said, my heart pounding in my chest.

"You are afraid. But you need not be. I can help you."

"I'm—" My words stuck in my throat. What was I, really? I thought about death's appeal. Especially since—

Noise crashed through my shield—the caged parrot sounded an alarm. The parlor had filled with a chattering flock of sparrows, intent on picking me to pieces. Choking back a scream, I opened my eyes to see a free-for-all debate raging around me.

"It's a reasonable precaution," Dr. Bertinelli said.

"Didn't I read about her—" began Dr. Lieberman.

From the rear of the house, a door opened and slammed shut. I latched onto the sound, something, anything, to distract me. Someone ran up the stairs as cold air blew into the room. "Need Finn—is he in here?" It was Tomás, the man who lived with Finn and Teddy in the cottage. "The generator's making an awful noise."

As if to illustrate the machine's distress, the electric lights flickered once, twice, three times, and then went out.

Sean

CHAPTER SEVEN

You've neglected your duty to your husband long enough. It's time to make immediate amends.

~From anonymous letter, postmarked Normal, Illinois, December 16, 1924.

I crossed the McKinley Bridge into Illinois and wasn't making bad time, but caught up to the storm that had dumped snow on St. Louis a few hours earlier. Out here on the prairie, it was colder, and the wet stuff came down as fine ice crystals, plinking against the roof, glazing the windscreen, and, most importantly, slicking up the asphalt road. I slowed the car to a crawl.

Creeping along wouldn't do at all; I wanted, no, needed, to talk to Violet. She was playing me for a sucker. Again. And using magic to do it, which was pretty low. Some reasonable corner of my brain chided me to not cast stones about magical misuse, but I chose to ignore it. I'd tried a spell or two to help somebody out, but that's not the same as summoning me in a blizzard for some errand or other.

My brain said Violet was way out of line, and it was time to warn her off. My gut told me something else. I worried she was in trouble, my concern rising the closer I got to the asylum. It was near a town called Normal.

Generally, to settle my nerves when I was feeling anxious, picking an option and getting on with it was all I needed. But this trip to see Violet wasn't calming me at all. And worry can wear a body down. After a couple of hours, the road started swimming before my eyes. I blinked, yawned, and sang aloud every song I could think of. The window cranked open, cold wind blasting my face.

Suddenly, I felt the front tire of the driver's side jolt over the stony shoulder, and the car's rear end fishtailed across a frozen patch covering both lanes of traffic. I followed the front end, steering along the shoulder and tapping the brake as resistance slowed the car. Rolling to a stop, I stared into the darkness for a minute. Stuffing my heart back in my chest and breathing a sigh of relief, I cranked the engine to life and resolved to pull over at the next likely place for coffee, a smoke, and a visit to the jacks.

A few more miles brought me to the outskirts of Springfield, where I found a tiny but brightly lit truck stop called Honest Abe's Gas and Grub.

Ice on the building sparkled off the electric lights blazing through the windows. A stiff breeze flapped the sign by the road, advertising cheap petrol and hot food to the oncoming traffic. A motor coach was parked out front—its placard declared it was headed to Chicago. I parked as close to the diner as I could, then slipped and slid to the entrance. Wouldn't it have been grand now if I'd thought to borrow some wellies, too?

The windows were steamy in a cheerful way, and I could smell coffee and greasy fried things from outside. A little bell rang as I opened the door, and everyone in the room turned to me. Crowded with exhausted men, women, and even a few children, every booth and table was full. So I grabbed an empty stool at the counter. The big man next to me wore a bus driver's uniform. He glanced up from his newspaper and passed me a menu.

"Pulled over out of the storm for a while, have you?" I said.

"Yeah, company policy," he said in a bored sort of way, as if it was all one to him. Probably was. "You?"

"I spun out a few miles back. Thought I could use a break."

He nodded at the wisdom of my decision. "Gotta pace yourself."

"See here, sir," a short man said, wiping away a circle of condensation on the window glass and peering through it. "The sleet has stopped."

"So what?" said the driver, not looking around. "You seen a county truck come by spreading cinders? It'll snow some more within fifteen minutes. Better to drive on the fluffy stuff than this ice." To me, he said, "Which way are you headed?"

"Normal."

"You're in for some rough weather." He returned to his newspaper. "Hope you got good tires."

I headed to the jacks as the waitress brought me coffee, and when I returned, it appeared the driver and the little guy were about to come to blows. "Get this through your thick skull, mac," said the driver, "I'm responsible for the lot of you. I'll get you safe and sound to Chicago. It might be tomorrow, but we'll get there. It's warm and dry here. Food. Facilities. You could do a lot worse."

The little guy huffed over to his booth, where a lady had just helped a child fall asleep, curled up on the bench.

The diner was out of just about everything on the menu. The bus passengers had cleaned them out.

I ordered the last piece of pie in the place—pumpkin. I'm not a fan, but it goes alright with some ice cream, which they had. At least the coffee was hot and strong.

Someone tapped my shoulder: a trim woman in a smart blue coat with a hat to match. She had short, blonde curls, and I'd guess she was about forty. I'd wager she was even more beat than the rest of them, as if somehow this journey had taken an extra toll. "Excuse me," she said, "I couldn't help overhearing that you're headed to Normal. I'm Evelyn Elsass."

"Sean Joye."

She held out her hand, and I gave it a squeeze. "Mr. Joye, I'm rather desperate to get to Normal as soon as possible. This fellow—" she jerked her thumb at the bus driver, "doesn't know how to drive in the snow."

"It ain't snow, lady, it's ice." His attention was fixed on his crossword puzzle. "And if I flip the bus over with youse all in it, I lose my job."

Mrs. Elsass rolled her eyes but kept her attention on me—I was obviously the mark for this little scam, whatever it was. "Could I prevail on you to give me a ride?" She tried to look—something—I didn't know what. She wasn't flirting with me. I didn't think so, anyway. And she was kind of pretty. Old enough to be my mam, although that didn't always make much of a difference. No, she was trying to be sad. Or helpless, maybe. Her blue eyes glistened with fake tears.

"Sorry, Mrs. Elsass, I'm in a big hurry. I wouldn't want to be responsible—"

"Oh, a hurry is perfect. I'm in a hurry, too. My husband—she put a lot of emphasis on the word "husband," so I wouldn't get the wrong idea, I suppose, "—is working there, and I need to join him."

I closed my eyes. The ice cream was giving me a headache. Or possibly Mrs. Elsass.

"He's opened a…sort of hospital there, and…"

OK, I had to bite at that. "What sort of hospital?"

"A rest home."

"For old people?"

"Some are old. It is for nervous people."

The bus driver stopped pretending to care about his newspaper puzzle. "That looney bin they put in the old Osteen mansion? Just off the highway coming into town?"

Mrs. Elsass threw back her shoulders and glared. "It's a private asylum. The Elsass Institute."

"Yah," he said, oblivious to her ire. "That's the place."

She grew a little weepy around the edges. Not good. "Anyway, I have to get to him." Digging around in her bag for a hanky, she came up with a piece of paper and waved it at me. "He's…in trouble."

They find me. They always find *me*. Usually, my first impulse is to avoid obligations like this, and given the course of my life, it's been a pretty sound policy.

I had recently taken up magical studies, and made up my mind to see beyond the obvious, at least, for what I could learn about a situation.

First step: pay attention to the right-now. The paper she showed me, for instance. It wasn't stationary, but rather from a cheap tablet. And it was covered in a feminine scrawl that tickled some corner in the back of my memory. Interesting.

Then I really looked at Evelyn Elsass. With the mind's eye, as it were. Her anxiety made my skin crawl. Worry and—something else—hurt, anger, or whatever it was, wrapped her tight. Her eyes were red, her fingernails chewed, and her face was blotchy. And that paper —it glowed faintly, with a pale golden sheen. I started to take it from her, but she wouldn't let go of it.

"He says that in your letter there? Can I see it?"

"No, he…" Her voice dropped. "It's private." She shoved the letter back into her bag. "I can pay you. Please take me there."

I sighed, defeated and curious. "You don't have to pay me. I'm going there, anyway." My hand was itching again.

Best be on my way. "Be out by the Haynes—parked out front—in ten minutes."

I thought she was about to hug me, but she restrained herself. "Oh, thank you. I'll be no trouble at all. I'll get my things and freshen up."

I finished my pie and ice cream and left fifty cents on the counter.

The driver grinned like a man pleased to offload a problem onto another. "Her suitcase will be at the Normal bus station. Tomorrow."

Mrs. Elsass and I crawled along Route 4 the rest of the night, her nervous chatter filling the frozen air. I concentrated on my driving and paid her little mind.

At least the Haynes was a heavy car; that was something. Even so, the clouds stalled right overhead—I'd swear they kept pace with me. There were even the occasional crack of lightning and rumble of thunder. No, the weather didn't let up at all, the wintery mix packing the road with ice before changing to fluffy white snow around three in the morning.

The snow stopped as the horizon turned a morning shade of gray, just in time for Mrs. Elsass to notice a signpost for the Elsass Institute. We turned down a lane between a forest and bare fields.

"There's the old log cabin," she said, pointing to a shack barely visible under the snow-draped pines. "At first, Henry sent interesting letters about the property—including some sketches."

"Uh-huh." I didn't take my eyes off the road. The pavement had yielded to a rough gravel road, which likely would have been worse without the cushion of snow and ice.

"Built by the first German settlers to the farm."

"Isn't Elsass a German name?" Americans hadn't been exactly kind to their German-heritage citizens for a while. Things were maybe getting a little better now, but the armistice was just six years ago.

She sputtered, then said, "Henry's people are practically French. From the disputed territories."

We slid across a small bridge spanning a frozen creek. A low stone wall lined the road, and behind it was a lawn of snow and a huge Victorian mansion surrounded by a high chain-link fence. We came to a stone archway inscribed "Osteen. 1834." We could plainly see the house ahead and a likely route for the driveway right up to the front steps, but a padlocked gate in the fence halted our progress.

I got out and took a walk around. The place had that silence of new snow. It was seven in the morning, and the snow had stopped, but dark clouds still covered the sky. Greenish lightning flashed in the distance, and a few raindrops splashed across the car's hood. Dim lights moved through the mansion.

"Hallo?" I yelled at the house. "Come unlock the gate." Snowdrifts covered the driveway ahead. "I got the boss's wife here to visit," I shouted. The rain stopped briefly, and an icy wind slammed at us from the north.

I heard the car door slam and a gasp. "My, it's deep."

"You might want to stay in the car, ma'am." I continued shouting at the house.

She ignored me, stomping about in her galoshes. "Goodness, what a place. He said it was a fine house, in need of some maintenance, but…"

"Wait in the car. I'm going to explore a bit." I turned up my coat collar and walked down the road, my eyes peeled for another driveway or maybe someone out and about who could help us. After about five minutes of trudging through the snow, I spied smoke from a chimney in the distance. I decided to drive over to this hypothetical farm and started back to the car; I'd had it with walking in the bitter cold.

"Any sign someone's coming down from the house?" I called out as I approached Mrs. Elsass. "I see another house, about a quarter of a mile away." She was up by the gate, bent over the padlock. I heard the clunk of the lock opening and saw it swing free.

"He sent you a key?" I struggled to open the gate against the pile of snow behind it. "You might have said something."

"Nothing like that." Her laugh rang out in the silence. "I'm a little rusty at it, but I've broken into a few diaries in my time." She brandished a hairpin and a thick sewing needle before returning her improvised lockpicks to her bag.

"Diaries, ma'am?"

"I've three older sisters. Please call me Evie."

Violet

CHAPTER EIGHT

Maintain safe environment, avoid overstimulation.

Monitor closely when outdoors to redirect from behavioral tics such as digging.

Address reported auditory hallucinations with reality redirection.

Encourage brief supervised family/friend visits, as tolerated.

Commence twice-daily sessions with attending physician. Patient assigned to Dr. Cole.

~From Elsass Institute care plan,
Violet Humphrey, December 1, 1924.

"You on guard duty?" The voice, coming from the hall on the other side of the locked door, sounded like Lottie, the cook's assistant. I tried to ignore her words, but they slithered through the keyhole.

"Yeah. Been sitting here all night. Making sure Miss Violet don't hurt herself." The head orderly, Robert, had shoved me into this room after a nurse made me change into an appropriately institutional garment for my confinement.

I heard a rustling sound, then Lottie continued, "Whadda ya think? Did she do in the boss?"

Even in the closed, interior room—a closet, in the mansion's former life as a farmhouse—I somehow knew it was morning. Saturday morning. I hadn't slept, not really, the whole night. My cell had no electric light or radiator. For safety, I suppose. They might call it the "quiet room," but it was a cell.

Although Finn had repaired the coal stoker—I could hear its rhythmic clunks deep in the sub-basement, cold crept through the walls. I lay huddled near the door all night. It was warmer there.

"Not likely." Robert shone a flashlight in on me every fifteen minutes all night long, with the effect that I never got to sleep properly. "She's nice. Don't never make any trouble."

"Sounds like the swells might be starting to agree with you."

"Oh, who does Mr. Emerson blame now?" Robert had missed out on a lot of gossip in his devotion to duty. I was impressed he'd stayed by me, despite the cold, boredom, and the very many more interesting things going on in a house filled with sudden death.

Lottie laughed. "You got his number. Yeah, he's rethinking the whole thing. Our African doctor is looking guilty to him now. More so than the society lady."

Well, that was interesting. Although Percy had easily turned the board against me, which was frightening , I didn't believe a murder accusation would stick for long.

I heard mumbles and shuffles, and the floorboards creaked. "So, young lady, you here to relieve me? Or relieve my boredom?"

"Why, Mr. Reynolds," Lottie shifted to a most flirtatious tone, "whatever do you mean?"

"Nothing, nothing, Miss Lottie," Robert sounded alarmed. I guess he'd overstepped his own idea of propriety. I didn't think Lottie minded. "Guess I'll go get some shut eye. Ain't heard a peep out of her, and she was just lying there every time I checked. Likely asleep."

I smiled at the young people sparking just outside my cell and thought on my own path. Maybe it was just my life—the bumps in my road were always smoothed out, sooner rather than later. Even my confinement at the Elsass Institute, while harsh, was infinitely better than answering police or press questions about that night back in October. That night my husband tried to kill us all in the course of a summoning ritual gone wrong. *And who else aimed for a blood sacrifice that night?*

"I wasn't...myself," I shouted into the dark. I'd forgotten...so much.

"I stand corrected," Robert said. "You alright in there, Miss Violet? We disturbing you?"

"I'm fine. Yes, you two woke me up. Take your courting elsewhere."

Lottie giggled.

Desperate for distraction from a guilty conscience, imaginary voices, and worry over my future, I turned the puzzle of Dr. Elsass's death over in my mind. The note on his desk when we last talked was important, I was sure of it. Was it the same one found with his body? Someone—*could* it have been Dr. Cole?—had lured him out to an inconvenient, yet private setting, at an inconvenient time. And he'd gone—due to a threat. Orr perhaps a promise. What leverage could his young subordinate have over him in this situation? And why would he take such pains to show us the note? If he'd written it, wouldn't he have destroyed it?

The doorknob rattled, and the door swung open, nearly hitting me as I crawled out of the way. Dr. Cole stood on the threshold. "May I come in?"

I glared. "Excuse me for not getting up. I'm conserving body heat."

"My, it *is* brisk in here." He addressed the servants behind him in the hallway, "Lottie, find a blanket, please, for Mrs. Humphrey."

Dr. Cole handed me a warm tin cup of tea and a few oatmeal cookies wrapped in a napkin. He settled himself on the floor as Lottie came in with a quilt and draped it around my shoulders. The glow of a lantern spilled into the closet.

"Don't leave her alone with that wrap, doctor. Policy. Nurse Carrie will have my head."

He nodded, dismissed her with a wave of his hand, and said, "You can keep the quilt. I'm releasing you."

"The board might have something to say about that," I observed, enjoying the blanket's heft and warmth. "I'm persona non grata."

"Something has happened, which I think exonerates you. You alone, of everyone in the place, couldn't possibly have—"

"Is someone else dead?" Cold clutched my heart, and I heard a murmur of laughter in my head.

"Not dead but attacked. And the prognosis isn't good for her."

"Shouldn't you be with—who is it?"

"I've examined her—it was Mrs. Holmes, the cook— and left orders. Nurse Carrie is seeing to her now."

"So, I'm free? What happened?"

"Yes, you are free," he said, stretching out his long legs. He pursed his lips and ignored my request for details.

"Something on your mind, doctor?" I bit into one of the cookies. In all this, I'd forgotten to be hungry. At its sweetness, indigo glints flashed behind my eyes. The cookie's satisfying, toothsome sensation in my mouth— chewing it, swallowing it—made me suddenly aware I had a body, grounding me in the here and now.

"Mrs. Humphrey, may I speak frankly? Not as your doctor, but as a person, a stranger here, a person thought of..."

"With condescension? Suspicion?" I finished the cookie, then suddenly felt stuffed. I sipped the tea. Soaking in the warmth of the quilt and my hot drink, I stretched out my legs, too. I had no idea of the modesty protocol for this situation. They'd put me in a sort of union suit for the confinement. So, technically, I was lounging about with my doctor on the floor in my underwear. He didn't seem to notice or care.

"America is a horrible place in which to be a Black person." I wrapped the other cookie in the napkin and handed it to him. "I hope someone told you that before you came here."

He grimaced. "Dr. Elsass mentioned that attitudes in this farm country were different than Paris, but then minimized its importance."

"But things turned out differently?" For most of my stay, I'd been so focused on my own inner demons that I had little thought of others. Only in the last few weeks had I noticed the constant, minor, needling disrespect the nurses and the staff inflicted on him. I didn't much care for his attitude, either, but it had nothing to do with him being a Black African. "Where are you from, anyway?" I asked.

"Originally, Sierra Leone, although I've lived in Paris since before the war."

"School?"

He nodded. "I think the board members...They should be turning to me, as the only physician on site, to lead the Institute, at least for the moment, but instead..."

"They're looking to pin a murder on you."

In a puzzled tone, he said, "Pin? Like a...sewing item?"

"No, like accusing you with little or no evidence. Citing facts picked out and twisted or even lying about events."

"Ah. Yes." He faced me directly. "I sense danger, and I feel that my situation is being... what did you say?

'Twisted.' Yes, bent out of all meaning." I realized he was both very young and frightened. A burnt electrical sort of smell assailed me.

Did he think I, a mental patient, could possibly help him? And why did he think I would want to? "Like you twist things about me, in our 'cure talks'?"

Dr. Cole's eyes grew wide, and then he smiled. He had a good smile, I had to grant him that. "You should know Dr. Elsass's Talking Cure has very little evidence of efficacy. If you came to me—for example, at the hospital where I studied in Paris—we would have addressed your issues properly as the chemical imbalances and nervous system malfunctions that they are. Physical problems with a physical treatment."

"Are you saying you don't believe those horrible things you said about me?"

"I'm most sorry, Mrs. Humphrey. I was under Dr. Elsass's direction here. He had a strict protocol and reviewed my notes almost daily."

I took a deep breath to calm the anger suddenly boiling up, the cookie a nauseating lump in my stomach. "You said I was…frigid. The source of my…neurosis, entirely sexual."

"I could show you his written instructions for your care, which outlines the treatment plan."

I drew in my arms and legs under the blanket. "It doesn't matter."

"But it does," he said. "I don't want you to be angry with me. I… I think I'll need a friend here, someone on my side."

Incredulous, I said, "I'm a crazy lady. I can't help you."

"You are not. You've suffered traumatic losses and deep grief. Your brain chemistry and nervous system have manufactured many delusions to protect you. Compulsive behaviors for comfort. But you are a respectable widow from a good family. An upstanding woman. Allah has been good to me for making your acquaintance in this land." He bowed stiffly, without getting up. "I'm sorry for…not being braver about your diagnosis and treatment."

I eyed him, still miffed. I only then realized how miffed.

They attack you when you're down; when you haven't the strength to defend yourself. And I had just accepted it all. Dr. Elsass through Ibrahim Cole—or so he claimed—had insisted my delusions stemmed from sexual issues rooted in my childhood. That my psyche was abnormal, diseased even, as indicated by a lack of physical urges and longing to mate.

"I've always felt perfectly normal," I said. The voice in my head laughed. "About sex. Though obviously I was… not myself…a few months ago."

"Your depression would be better treated with hydrotherapy. Or the new electroconvulsive treatment, perhaps. We've wasted so much time."

I thought it funny he called me 'respectable.' "I wasn't delusional the other day, when I told you I was a witch."

His mouth dropped open as I stood, held my head high, and sauntered out of the room in my union suit, the quilt flowing behind me like the train of my debutante gown, so many years ago.

Sean

CHAPTER NINE

I can't stop thinking about you, doll. Next time you're in St. Louis, give me a holler if you can spare the time. Love to take you out for a meal or dancing. Just let me know where and when. My brother's got a phone: Mohawk 5724. Merry Christmas, Sean

~Christmas card received by head nurse Carrie Bartowski, December 17, 1924.

I leaned on the mansion's doorbell long enough to be annoying. "Stop that, Mr. Joye." Evie slapped my hand away from the buzzer. "Henry won't be best pleased with us rousting the whole household at dawn."

I was dead on my feet, and she looked about as bad as I felt, her case of nerves the only thing keeping her upright. And as if the long, miserable trip hadn't been bad enough, the car was stuck in the snowy driveway. We'd hoof it through the drifts and up to the porch.

I was about to ring the bell again when the door flew open. Filling the entrance was a tall, broad-shouldered man reeking of bourbon and cigar smoke. His well-tailored suit tried and failed to conceal a paunch around his waist. A prosperous, civic leader type. My favorite. "You're not the sheriff," he said.

"Never claimed to be." I stuck my foot in the door. "This here," I took Evie's elbow with one hand and started to shoulder past the swell, "is the boss's wife, Mrs. Henry Elsass. Evelyn. She's been traveling all night."

He put both hands on my chest to stop me. "Wait, wait, wait, friend. Let me get this straight. You've brought Elsass's wife here?"

"That's what I said, Mac. And she's cold and hungry."

He beamed, as if he couldn't be more pleased at this turn of events. "Of course, come in." He led us into the foyer. A steady stream of uniformed young people—orderlies and nurses in starched whites and maids in frilly caps and aprons—toted suitcases down the staircase behind him.

"I'm Percy Emerson," he said to Evie. "President of the Institute's board of directors." He took her hand. "I'll get one of the girls to attend to you." He glanced at what appeared to be the entire household staff involved in an evacuation. "Ah, we need to find the head nurse." He thumbed at me as he said to Evie, "Your driver can go around to the servants' entrance. There's a parking lot there."

I'd just opened my mouth to tell the stuffed shirt where he could get off, when Evie latched onto my arm. "Mr. Joye stays with me. He isn't my driver. He rescued me from a roadside diner when my bus got stuck."

Emerson shrugged as he gave me some side-eye. "Mighty white of you."

"I was coming anyway—" I'd almost forgotten why I was out here in the middle of nowhere. *Violet.* Violet was pulling my strings, and I was sick of it. "—to visit a patient."

"This isn't a good time. The Institute is a mess for…a number of reasons." He was shoving me out the door when he noticed how very stuck the Haynes was. He paused. "I'll send a man to help you dig out the car. You can leave off Mrs. Elsass and come back for her in a few days."

"Wait just a minute, Mac," I said. "I gotta speak to Violet Humphrey."

"Oh?" That interested Emerson for some reason.

"Yeah." I weighed various lies and versions of the truth. "She's in some sort of trouble, isn't she?"

He raised his eyebrows as his jaw went slack for a moment. *Bingo.* "What's that to you?"

"Sean Joye," I said, offering my hand. "I'm her sol… attorney." Not solicitor. Americans have a different word for everything. Of course, I was lying. I wasn't a solicitor, attorney, lawyer, or even barrister to her. Just a chump.

Why did I lie? My read on Emerson was that a business relationship would pull more weight than simple family ties or friendship, a couple of other lies I could have tried. Well, maybe that last one wasn't a lie: We were friends. Or could be friends of a sort. If only she'd stop witching me.

Emerson led us into a big dining room full of people and Christmas decorations, smelling of bacon and pinecones. I removed my hat and nodded to the guests at the table, searching the room for Violet.

"Conveniently enough, this is Mr. Joye, Mrs. Humphrey's lawyer. So he says." Emerson pointed to Evie. "And this is someone we all should meet. Gentlemen—" he raised his voice at a trio of geezers hunched over bacon and eggs and then glanced at a couple of women "—and ladies."

One was a real knockout; a cool blonde pushing apple slices around on her plate with a fork. The other I already knew—she was the head nurse for this place, Carrie Bartowski. She stood near the sideboard and looked up from her conversation with a maid. Emerson flashed a smile. "May I present Mrs. Dr. Henry Elsass."

Carrie flopped in a chair, her pale, freckled face now ashen. The other woman didn't respond. Evie paid no attention to either of the females and addressed the old men. "Please to meet you. I'm Evie Elsass. But where is my husband?" She turned to Carrie. "And do you think I might have something hot to drink?" Interesting. Evie *had* noticed the head nurse, but didn't see the need to acknowledge her until she wanted something.

Emerson grinned like he'd won first prize. "Of course, of course. Carrie will fix you right up." He pried Evie off my arm and settled her in a chair. "She's the head nurse." He draped one arm around the other woman's shoulders. "And this is my wife, Blanche."

By the way she was acting, I'd never have guessed the looker even knew who Emerson was, let alone be married to him.

I'd stood on the threshold through the introductions, watching Carrie's reaction to all this. She cleared her throat a couple of times and drank a glass of water. Finally, she locked eyes with me and beamed. I'd begun to think she'd forgotten she'd ever met me. Which was a letdown; I'd fancied I'd made at least a bit of an impression during my past visits.

"Come in, Mr. Joye." Carrie stood and walked around the table to join me. "Nice to see you again. I'm glad Mrs. Humphrey was able to reach you. She has some concerns, and our phone service was on-and-off yesterday afternoon." She glanced around the crowded table, as if just realizing we weren't alone. "Certain matters have come up, but we can discuss them in private."

I smiled as charmingly as I could muster with no tea or grub after a night of icy roads. "Ah, but ain't we old friends now, Nurse Bartowski? You can call me Sean. But yes, you're right. I got a…message from Mrs. H."

"In that case, I can take you to her." It appeared that she wanted some distance from the people gathered around the table and led me away. A grand breakfast was spread on a sideboard, and my stomach growled. We went into the parlor-library where I'd visited with Violet the last time I'd been at the Institute. A Christmas tree, half decorated, stood tall near the front windows. The Institute's handsome green parrot greeted me, but I'd no bit of biscuit or veg for it today.

"Give me your coat and hat." Carrie's voice dropped as she opened a large coat closet. "We're all at sixes and sevens here with the storm and—"

I yielded my overcoat and hat to her shaking hands, giving her ice-cold knuckles a little squeeze as I did so. "Yeah, you folks all seem a bit on edge. Except for that Emerson fella. He's having a good time."

We were still holding hands, and she pulled me in closer. "Excuse me, but how do you know that woman? The woman in blue? Is she really—" Carrie choked on the words, and her eyes glistened with barely controlled tears.

Plainly she was shocked Dr. Elsass's wife had shown up at the Institute. I suspected she didn't know Evelyn Elsass even existed. And she was taking it very much to heart.

"I don't know her at all," I said. "Met her at a truck stop near Springfield where her bus was stuck in the ice storm."

"How odd. And fortuitous for her." She let go of me just as a dark-complected Black man passed through the parlor. I guessed he was about thirty, with close-cropped hair and wire-rimmed glasses. He wore a decent suit but appeared to have been up all night doing chores in it. Mud speckled the trouser legs, and drops of blood soiled the cuffs of his wrinkled shirt. I'd no likely guesses as to what his job at this place might be.

"Ibrahim," Carrie said. "What news?"

"I was on my way to change clothes, Nurse."

"I just need a moment of your time." She nodded toward me. "Violet has a visitor."

Looking distinctly uncomfortable, he approached. "I've released Mrs. Humphrey," he said to us. "How did you get here, sir, with the storm?" He had a foreign accent, quite musical. Sort of French. Maybe. And definitely an air about him. He had my attention.

I held out my right hand. "Sean Joye. I've just arrived. Been creeping along the highway all night." I turned to Carrie. "'Release?' That must mean you had Mrs. H. confined. She not doing so good?" My instinct was concern and sympathy. *Naw, that's just her witching you.* I hardened my heart. I was there to tell her where to get off. Time for her to leave me alone; I owed her nothing.

"She had a terrible shock last evening and needed an… enforced rest," the man—Carrie had called him Ibrahim—said. "At least that's the medical necessity I saw, whatever others might think." He shook my hand. "I'm Dr. Ibrahim Cole, Mrs. Humphrey's attending physician."

"Pleased to meet you, doc," I said. *A doctor.* His dirty clothes made even less sense.

Ibrahim eyed me up and down. "What could be so important to drive all night in a storm?" He wasn't giving up much. Likely a hell of a poker player. Alright. I might just have to call that bluff.

"Mrs. Humphrey called Mr. Joye. Apparently, he's her man of business," Carrie said before I could answer. "And I didn't know that you had that role." She caught my eye, "I took you for one of her old…friends."

I wanted to laugh at that idea—me, someone's man of business—but let it lie. "And along the route, I acquired a passenger who was anxious to get here as well."

Ibrahim looked expectant, like awaiting the punch line of a joke.

"Did Henry ever mention a…wife to you?" Carrie said.

He didn't act surprised but thought that one over. "No, not that I recall. But we didn't really share social conversations. And he's—was—of an age and position in society to have a wife."

Was? I forgot whatever amusing line of repartee I'd come up with. "Did you say the director 'was'?"

"I was about to explain." Carrie bit her lower lip. "That's part of why we are so scatterbrained this morning. Dr. Elsass had a terrible accident last night."

"Mrs. Humphrey found him dead," Ibrahim clarified.

My first thought was of Evie and the misgivings she'd shared on the long ride. She thought her marriage was in trouble. But not a hint of worry about her man's health. "Ah." I had no words to say to these two. Thinking of Violet's witchy hold on me, the director's death explained a hell of a lot. Maybe Violet hadn't summoned me on a whim after all. "Rough for Violet." Maybe she hadn't even consciously reached out. It had just happened.

"It was yet another traumatic experience." The doctor clapped me on the shoulder. "A familiar face will do her good." He turned to Carrie, "Nurse, could you see to that? Mrs. Humphrey went to her room to dress, I believe."

"I was just about to take him to her," she snapped. "This way, Se—ah, Mr. Joye."

I grabbed her by the arm. "Go to Evie—Mrs. Elsass— with this news right now, before that buffoon springs it on her."

She stared at me, long and hard, totally puzzled. Finally, recognition dawned. "She doesn't know," she whispered. "How could she know?" She pointed me toward the stairs down to the kitchen. "Would you mind taking up some tea and toast to Violet? Lottie will help you."

"I'll manage." My stomach growled.

Violet

CHAPTER TEN

Passing the mouth of the Illinois, we soon fell into the shadow of a tall promontory, and with great astonishment beheld the representation of two monsters painted on its lofty limestone front. Each of these frightful figures had the face of a man, the horns of a deer, the beard of a tiger, and the tail of a fish so long that it passed around the body, over the head, and between the legs. It was an object of Indian worship…

~From *Journal of the Mississippi Voyage*, Father Jacques Marquette, July 1, 1673.

I stared out my bedroom window at the back parking area; Finn, a snowplow attachment on his tractor, was attempting to dig out an exit, while a couple of men were clearing off some of the cars. It seemed the guests were intent on leaving, despite the dangerous roads and the day still dark, although it was eight o'clock in the morning.

Hard to blame them for wanting to get away from a house full of crazy people and a "homicidal maniac." I was sure at least a few of the board members and staff would blame me for the attack on the cook, even though I'd been locked up all night. Or think that I had a colleague in crime.

I didn't feel very maniacal at the moment. I was exhausted. It took all the will and energy I had to shiver into my warmest clothes. What I wanted was to curl up in bed under a pile of quilts. Or walk out into the woods, following the voice in my head's advice to find the water and lay down my burden.

I heard a knock—it was forbidden to ever close our bedroom door, but the nurses and attendants were too busy to notice, and I was desperate for some privacy. I watched the handle turn, and Sean Joye, about the last person I expected to see that morning, poked his head into the room. A memory, tamped down for months, jolted through me. I gasped, heartsick. Bile, real bile, burned as it rose in my throat.

Today, he carried a breakfast tray, not a revolver. "Carrie thought you might want a bite to eat."

My stomach flipped, and I edged into a corner, acutely aware that he blocked the only escape from the room. "How…When…Why are you here?"

Suddenly scorched into my mind's eye was a scene of smoke and terror. I saw a cramped ritual room, all odd angles and curved walls, the air too thick to breathe.

"As if you didn't know." Sean took in the bedroom I shared with Berta and Blanche, and set the tray down on my desk. "Nice room."

So deeply was I in my memory of the past—or vision, considering its vividness—his words confused me for a moment. The room I saw wasn't nice at all. The floor was inscribed with summoning glyphs, the place the summit of my husband's ceremonial magick practice; the perfect alignment of universal forces to Taylor Humphrey's own considerable will.

Sean glanced at me, then looked away, his jaw clenching and nostrils flaring as he took a deep breath. "My hand itches."

I'd no idea what he was talking about. I shook my head as if that would clear my mind of the horrible memory in which I felt trapped.

Another memory floated to the surface. I'd worked a spell into his palm in September. Warmth rose to my cheeks. I've done plenty of terrible things of late but working a spell on someone—this person—without their consent…it wasn't the worst thing legally, objectively, but in many ways, it had been the start of my descent. The fall was my responsibility, mine alone. And it was in play, I realized, when he shot Taylor dead. Protecting us all from the man I thought I knew so well. Sean's instinct to save me was heightened by my spell work.

Anger radiated off Sean in blue-gray wisps of smoke. The smell of burnt wires filled the space.

"This place is not a room." I leaned against the wall behind me, desperate to establish a connection to real time and space. "It's a cell." Which wasn't true; my lodgings were simple, but spacious and homey. I was just filling the air with words as I tried to think of what to say.

Sean's eyes blazed before he turned his back on me and walked over to the window. "You know," he watched the activity in the parking lot, "this shite," he scratched at his right hand—red and raw, I noticed—"makes me wonder." He faced me again and said, "I know you played me from the very start, but were you using magic to do it the whole time, too?"

I glanced about, desperate for a place to hide. We hadn't spoken since the night…it all happened; when I'd apparently slipped into a catatonic retreat. I'd been aware of Sean coming to see me at the Institute, but felt so far away, lacking the energy or means to even try to communicate with him.

"No," I said. "I'm sorry. I thought…" That was the trouble. I hadn't thought at all. "What do you want me to do?"

"I dunno." He shrugged. "Maybe, for starters, remove the spell."

I bit my lip. "I have." It should have dissipated long ago without my will holding it in place, at least if I remembered the wording correctly. So much from that time was a jumble.

"You've got to mean it for it to work. Even I know that."

I had no answer. "I *do* mean it. You *are* released. It was wrong of me, very wrong, to do that to you. My first lesson in the craft was to do no harm. The second was to do no workings without permission. I forgot them both. People died. Because I…"

Sean sighed, a scratchy, damp tweed sound. "Your little binding spell didn't make me a killer. Ease your mind on that score. I decided shooting Taylor Humphrey was everyone's best bet to get out of that place alive."

"But I made—"

"Stop it." He offered me his hand to shake. "Truce, for now, at least. What's going on here, anyway?"

The confrontation left me drained and lighter. Like I could simply float away, a snowflake on the December wind. The problem between us wasn't solved, but at least he'd perceived I had more pressing problems on my mind. "They think I murdered Dr. Elsass—the director here. I found him dead outside last evening."

"So, I heard." He patted my shoulders.

I'm not much of one for hugs, but his touch pulled my spirit back into my body and my mind into reality. I grabbed him and latched on tightly around his neck. He held me steady in a loose, comforting embrace.

"Who is 'they'?" he said into my hair. "That blowhard, what's-his-name?"

"Percy Emerson."

And why are they so sure he was killed? Couldn't he have just died in a normal way?"

I couldn't speak to other people's wild conclusions and suspicions. But I *had* burst into a dinner party with blood on my hands. I continued to cling to Sean like I was drowning.

"That head nurse…" the timbre of his voice changed, and a ripple of tension passed through his body, "seems like a straight shooter, the times I've visited here."

"Carrie. Carrie Bartowski." I pulled away to better see his expression.

"Yeah—" His face had a far-away look, his mind clearly elsewhere.

I laughed. "I believe you have a crush on her."

Sean blushed. "Me? Nah, 'course not."

"It's alright. She's a very nice, single woman. She's been a real friend to me here."

"It's a matchmaker you're being, now? I've sworn off romance. I haven't the stomach for it."

He struck me as very sad, and I was sorry I'd brought up the subject. I'd been too self-absorbed to understand how far things had gone between him and my friend Kyffin, a prominent attorney in the city. Another of my sister Lillian's victims. Kyffin had survived, but with serious brain injury.

"The only reason I brought her up," Sean said, "is that Carrie keeps tut-tutting and aiming to impose order on the mess. Everyone is leaving right after breakfast."

I disentangled myself from him and smoothed my dress. "Makes sense."

Sean went to the tray on the desk, poured a cup of tea, and offered it to me. "You're not entirely off the hook about the magic." He held up the sugar bowl with a questioning look. "Everyone clearing out is convenient for the real killer, assuming—"

"Black is fine." Sipping it, I felt thirsty and hungry, and tired of thinking about death. I nibbled a sliced apple.

He sat on a bed and stared out the window.

I'd expressed an opinion about his personal life, so he'd retreated behind the barricades again. *Fine.* "That's Berta's bed. She'll be none too pleased you sitting on her quilt."

"Then we won't tell her."

I pulled out the desk chair to sit across from him. "If you don't want to talk about your crush on Carrie, we can talk about me."

"Alright." He helped himself to a couple of apple slices off the breakfast tray. "Do you think this place is doing you good? You're talking again. That's a good sign."

I began with the past. "I heard a voice…back then. You know." I wanted to talk to him about the voice—the new voice—but the words stuck in my throat.

He nodded. "In September."

"The voice suggested a ritual…one requiring…death." *How could I live with the guilt—my crazy idea to sacrifice my baby niece to an ancient Mississippian god?*

The legend of Piasa, its beastly winged image, enshrined on the Mississippi River's bluff, had been the stuff of my childhood fairy tales. But what perversion of the old stories had I devised to believe human sacrifice would restore my own child to life? What monster had I become myself?

Come to me, the voice in my head gurgled. You'll forget it all.

Sean nodded, "I remember that night." As if there was any doubt that he could forget what he'd seen me try to do. "What do you make of it?"

"Dr. Cole says—" I laughed at the memory of my doctor's startled expression as I related the story. "He's the worst psychiatrist ever."

Sean looked quizzical as he munched the fruit.

"He says the voice telling me that I could bring back my little Tony through a sacrifice—urging me to…you know…"

"I imagine it's important for you to say it aloud."

"Alright. To sacrifice my sister's baby to resurrect my own. Dr. Cole says the impulse stemmed from internalized jealousy related to our childhood. An urge to rid myself of rivals. At least, he says that would be Dr. Elsass's theory." I half choked on another laugh.

"What did your doctor think, himself?"

"The chemicals in my brain are out of balance."

"Are you still hearing a voice? Or hearing it again?"

"I don't know. Last fall, I believed… I thought it was Father's voice, although now, of course, I realize Father would never say such things." Needing to feel grounded, I reached over to take his poor, red, swollen hand. "Are those people downstairs talking about me?"

He squeezed my hand, but his expression was glum. "Just what you told me—you found a body. In shock over it."

"I didn't hurt Dr. Elsass," I said. "You believe me, don't you?"

"Of course, I believe you. I never thought you'd hurt baby Susan, either, when it came right down to it. For all the daddy-shaped devils that might have been whispering in your ear."

"Thank you." I squared my shoulders. "That helps. I can't tolerate Percy Emerson libeling me. I may have to bring legal action."

"Oh, he's doing that, is he? He likes to stir things up for the hell of it, it seems. I'd say that Ibrahim—Dr. Cole, I mean—has a good head on his shoulders."

As if summoned, Dr. Cole opened the door. "Would you both care to join the group in the parlor? I've a few things to say about my post-mortem exam. And the attack on the cook. I'll be along presently."

He left without waiting for an answer.

"If he's concerned about who likes him," Sean said, "he don't act like it."

I thought about my earlier conversation with Dr. Cole. "He has concerns, I think. But maybe doesn't understand the precariousness of his situation here."

"If it is a murder, or even just a messy accident, they'll go for the Black man. Or the outsider. And he's both. Is he a friend of yours?"

I thought about that one. "I wouldn't have said so until this morning. I still don't know. He's been my main doctor here and has generally been horrible to me. Under Dr. Elsass's instruction, he now claims. I'm not sure how I feel about that. And if allowed his own treatment style, I don't know that it would have been any better."

"Don't you think it's time to get out of this place?" Sean said. "I could have you back in the city by evening. We could talk on the way about how you've been witching me."

Sean

CHAPTER ELEVEN

Soldiers are we,
whose lives are pledged to Ireland.
Some have come from a land beyond the wave,
Some to be free,
No more our ancient sireland
Shall shelter the despot or the slave;
Tonight we man the Bearna Bhaoil [gap of danger]
In Erin's cause.
Come woe or weal;
Mid cannon's roar and rifle's peal
We'll chant a soldier's song.
We'll chant a song, a soldier's song.

~From "A Soldier's Song" (The Irish National Anthem),
Peadar Kearney, 1907.

I'd had not a morsel, apart from a stale piece of pumpkin pie, since yesterday's cuppa with Mrs. Mac. So, I finished the breakfast nibbles the kitchen maid, sweet young lady named Lottie, had sent up for Violet, then we headed downstairs. In the parlor, Percy Emerson was holding court, complaining loudly to the room about the delay in leaving for home.

I found Violet a chair. Pale and thin—and hearing voices—she worried me, and I didn't think my concern was the effect of some spell. I glanced about for Evie, worried about her, too, and I felt like a heel that she'd heard the bad news from strangers.

Don't flatter yourself, boyo. You're a stranger to her, too. It likely made no difference at all who told her; there's no good way or good time to hear your spouse is dead. But I didn't see her and thought perhaps the nurses had put her to bed somewhere.

As is my habit, I noted the exits: The front door, just beyond the main parlor entrance, was my best bet for a hasty retreat. A couple of intersecting hallways were off the parlor, and right across the way was the dining room, where Emerson had not offered us breakfast when we first arrived. I noted a service entrance in there, presumably leading to the kitchen, which I'd visited earlier via a short flight of stairs. It had a back door that would serve in an emergency, too.

The parlor had plenty of windows and shared a fireplace with a library area, home to the green parrot that, I was given to understand, came with the house. Near its cage, I found Evie tucked up in an overstuffed chair away from the rest of the group. She was lost in thought and didn't notice me. I decided to leave her be for the moment and took a mental inventory of the people gathered in the parlor.

Percy Emerson, of course. No missing him. Laughing, smoking a cigar, and drinking a brandy at nine o'clock in the morning. I thought I could likely take him in a brawl, but he seemed the type to own a gun, although I didn't spot any telltale bulges. Probably left it in his car or luggage. An interesting choice, given his previous panic over the danger Violet presented to his safety. Made me doubt his sincerity on the topic.

Then there was Blanche—Mrs. Emerson. A cool blonde with a leg brace and cane at her side, watching the doorway with an intriguing smile on her face, which had vanished when Violet and I entered. Likely, she hoped for someone else to appear. She seemed entirely harmless; always a sign to be on guard.

Three elderly White gents, prosperously dressed. Each illustrated with a different beard style, like an advert in a barbershop: "The Smooth-Shaven Look," "Manly Muttonchops," "The Continental—A Dashing Goatee." The asylum's board of directors, I imagined. Obviously, a bunch of doctors. If provoked, they'd represent their own sort of danger. Speaking of doctors, "Dr. Cole not here then?" I asked the room.

At just that moment, Carrie rushed into the library end of the parlor, a maid behind her with a tray of coffee fixings. "Does anyone *ever* know what he's up to? We're all patiently gathered, though." She pointed to a low table, and the maid set down the tray. Carrie addressed the room. "Have a nice, hot drink before you start off home."

"I, for one, will be glad to get away," Emerson said. "Get some police protection." He turned to Violet. "So, they say you're in the clear. Not sure about that, but

I've been thinking this whole situation over…I've got it figured out."

"Do enlighten us,"Violet said. My heart bloomed with pride, her old condescending spunk in evidence.

"Well, who stands to benefit the most? Who's obviously jealous and itching for a chance to try his own ideas on all of you?"

"I'd like to see my husband now. Please." Evie, tiny as she was, appeared even smaller in the overstuffed chair in the corner. To Carrie, she said, "I can find my way, if you'll direct me."

"Don't be ridiculous. You can't be wandering about alone." Carrie took a seat herself and dismissed the maid with a wave of her hand. Her gaze caught me, a fish in a net. "Mr. Joye, would you be so kind as to escort her? The lab is in the basement."

"Me?" I said. "Nurse, I'm not—" *Keen to visit with a dead body this morning.* Of course, I couldn't say that. I had a certain reputation to maintain in her opinion—tough, reliable. A bloke who gets things done without a lot of fuss.

"Of course," Emerson interrupted, "you could do that. Right, counsellor? You're as close to a friend as Mrs. Elsass has in this place." He glanced at Carrie. "No reason not to."

Yet, I'd really rather not visit with dead Dr. Elsass. Especially with his widow on my arm. "Dr. Cole is coming right back to tell us—" I protested.

"A bunch of unpleasant medical things to cover up the crime. That is, if he shows up at all." Emerson went to Evie and made a small bow. "I'd take you down there myself, but

I need to keep an eye on the help. And make sure no one slips away. I'll give Cole another five minutes, then assume he's made a run for it."

Violet gave him a long, hard stare. She shifted in her chair and cleared her throat. *Oh, boy. This is gonna be fun.*

Apart from the initial shock, Dr. Elsass's death—murder or whatever it was—had done her a world of good. God rest his soul and all that, but I had high hopes of getting her home and into her old life. But no, I guess her old life wasn't possible. A new life of her own choosing.

Emerson and the other men seemed to have decided, despite their prejudices and wishes, that she was no longer a suspect. What would Violet owe Henry Elsass in death? He hadn't helped her much at this fancy, expensive hospital. And if his death was murder rather than an accident, why should she care if someone might escape justice?

Our eyes met. I'd wager she was biting her tongue, ready to blurt out something, but thinking better of it. I winked. *Let's have at it.* "What do you think, Mrs. Humphrey?" That'd learn her. "You appear to have something to say."

She drew in a breath as she returned her gaze to Emerson. "I'm not really surprised you blamed me, because that's the way your tiny mind works. But Dr. Cole? He wasn't even here yesterday. Not until the evening."

The room buzzed with harrumphs and whispers. Then Evie stood, reminding everyone of how very rude they were being with this discussion right in front of her. She marched over to me and took my arm.

I could see I was beat. I turned to Carrie. "And where would we be going?"

Carrie stood. "On second thought, perhaps you should wait, Mrs....Elsass. There *is* a procedure to be followed. The doctor wishes to share some information about the accident—" she paused to glare at everyone, "yes, accident. No one is guilty—" she choked back a sob, then cleared her throat. "It will save time and stop wild rumors if Dr. Cole speaks with us all at once." She glared around the room, serving up each and every one of the men with reproach. "Tales grow more and more ridiculous in the retelling. Two unfortunate accidents have happened over a brief period of time."

Muttonchops pounded his cane on the floor. "Here, here. The girl makes a good deal of sense. Accidents do happen, especially in foul weather and when the electricity and heat go out."

Evie sniffled, and I handed her a handkerchief. "You all are too cruel. I traveled all day, then all night to get to Henry, and now…" She blew her nose. "I just need to see him. And then…" a thought appeared to have just struck her, "you're an attorney, Mr. Joye? Perhaps you could help me examine his papers, find the will, and so forth. I need to think about what I'm going to do with this place."

Carrie gasped and reached out to steady herself on a chair.

As much as I'd have liked to stick around and watch the fireworks, my conscience got the better of me. I'd taken Evie on, and I had to see it through. And since she'd brought it up, I *was* curious about the inheritance situation. "Mrs. Elsass's got a point," I said. "Actually, several points. You're all a bit wrapped up in your own need to get home, if you don't mind me saying so. Give the woman five minutes with her poor man, for the love of Christ."

Carrie frowned, then shrugged. "Go on. Suit yourself. He's in the basement, Dr. Cole's laboratory. The steps are right behind the grand staircase." I wasn't winning any hands with her this morning. Likely, I'd just forked over whatever chips I might have accumulated in my past visits here.

"I know the way," Violet said. "Shall I come too?" she asked Evie as she approached us. "I'm...a widow myself."

"Please do," I said, giving Evie a little nudge toward her. "I'm sure another woman would be a great comfort to you."

"Then you should really lie down and rest," Violet continued. "Is there a guest room available?"

"What?" asked Carrie, her mind clearly elsewhere. "Oh, resting. Yes. We'll make up a room for her."

"Surely, I'll take the master suite," Evie said. "Henry's apartment. That would be a comfort, I think."

Carrie looked a lot like Evie had slapped her, her freckled face flushed and frown lines showing around her mouth. "Certainly." She sniffled and blew her nose on a handkerchief she had tucked up her sleeve. "He remodeled the stable into his residence. Someone will show you the way later. After a proper path through the snow has been shoveled."

Violet

CHAPTER TWELVE

The Order for the Burial of the Dead

Opening Hymn: "All Things Bright and Beautiful"

Chapel Choir

Welcome and Opening Prayer

Bishop Frederick F. Johnson

Scripture: 2 Corinthians 4:18: "We look not to the things that are seen but to the things that are unseen."

A reading by Miss Lillian Arwald

Homily: "Drink Ye Deep, the Elixir of Life"

Revd. William Alexander Ayton

~From Memorial Service, Taylor Avebury Humphrey, Christ Church Cathedral, St. Louis, Missouri. October 18, 1924.

I led Sean and Mrs. Elsass down the hall. After a detour into the kitchen to pick up a lantern—the electric power was still out—we descended the basement stairs through a plain wooden door on the backside of the grand staircase. Then we walked in silence through the dim hallway, past the female servant dorm and various rooms for the physiologic treatments Elsass allowed Dr. Cole to experiment with in his free time: magnotherapy and hydrotherapy, mostly. Now that I was at least verbal, he'd been talking to me about giving them a try, but I couldn't bear the thought of spending time in this dank basement.

What on earth was I doing here? Yet I felt compelled to do this hard thing. Maybe facing my fears was important to my recovery, or perhaps I needed to prove my humanity to myself by helping this wretched woman.

When we reached the lab, Sean knocked. *Dr. Elsass sure wasn't going to get up and answer it.* "Who do you think might be in there?" I asked. "Dr. Cole is probably upstairs by now, wondering where we are."

He rattled the doorknob. "Just making sure no one is home."

I glanced at the widow, her fingers gripping Sean's arm so tightly they'd turned white. This poor woman needed some sort of preparation for what she was about to see. "Mrs. Elsass—"

"Please call me Evie. This tragedy makes me feel so close to all of you." She clung all the tighter to Sean's arm by way of illustration, watching him with doe eyes.

A pink and sparkly aura hummed around her. *Damn.* Her husband's body wasn't even cold. I glared at Sean— he was doing it again. He shrugged. *And he knows it, too.*

Knocking louder, he shouted, "Dr. Cole, are you in there? I've got the doctor's missus with me."

No reply.

He untangled himself from Evie and handed her off to me. "Why don't you talk to Mrs. Humphrey for a while. Such as, how you came to make this trip." He leaned over the knob.

I understood what he wanted me to do, at least I thought I did, and took a few steps down the dark corridor, drawing her away. "Yes, how did you happen to come for a visit today of all days?"

Evie choked back a sob as she followed me. I noticed that she kept glancing back at her knight in shining armor. Stop it, I said to myself. Don't be so catty. Grief and worry trigger odd reactions. Carrie had told me that once.

"I received a letter," she said. "A…disturbing letter. I'd hoped to convince Henry to come home for Christmas. The children, our families—no one has seen him in almost a year." She pulled an envelope out of her pocket. The Institute's embossed return address hummed and glowered at the strangely familiar Spencerian handwriting.

"Did he write…hurtful things?" I had received a few such notes through the years, carried them around, frequently probing the wounds they'd left. "That would be hard."

Sean swung the door open. "Ladies."

"Oh, I thought it was locked," Evie said.

"No, just a bit stuck. Shall I go in first, then?" Daylight from the high basement windows cast the room in deep shadow. He held up the lantern.

Now that we were at the threshold of the creepy lab, Evie was decidedly less eager to pay her respects. I took her hand as she lingered on the threshold. "The letter wasn't from him," she finally said. "Hurtful things would have been better than the silence. The note was anonymous. I didn't want to believe it, but...I hadn't heard from him since last winter." Evie clutched the letter. It oozed a thick purple slime.

It's not real, I reminded myself. "Did you not want to move here, too?" I stepped into the room as Sean went around lighting additional lanterns and candles.

"I can't say I was looking forward to living in a mad house—"

"You *do* know that Mrs. Humphrey is a patient here," Sean said as he joined us. I gave him a little kick in the shin.

Evie's lips quivered, and she sniffled. "At the time—"

"No one wants to live in a mad house," I said. "I don't. But I'm sure I wouldn't have bothered you a bit; I was very quiet when I first came here. Shall we go in?"

Evie nodded and followed me into the room, where she grabbed Sean's arm. "I was ready to serve. To do my duty. A doctor's wife has obligations to the community where he works. I should have had a role here. And now it's too late." She took her eyes off Sean long enough to glance at the place and gasp.

Dr. Cole's lab was about as dreary as a basement room could be, full of gray, damp cold that smelled of disappointment. The furnishings were salvaged bits and pieces of the farm that the Institute once was. Old kitchen tables, cabinets, and rough plank shelving filled the space. It smelled of cedar, trying and failing to mask a distinct ammonia odor. Half a dozen cages held rabbits, which meant it was a real smell, not my imagination attributing odors to random objects. I was pleased at that bit of normality. But the poor things were afraid, their little squeaks of terror flitting about the room as they cowered, burrowed in their cages' straw bedding.

Dr. Cole's autopsy area was sized for small animals and adjacent to a sink and water tap. I couldn't imagine—didn't want to imagine—how he'd manage a human postmortem exam here. Surely, he wouldn't have...cut him open. Bringing Evie down here was a terrible idea.

She clung to both of us as she took in the sheet-covered corpse on one of the battered old dining room tables. "Oh, dear," she murmured. "I'd best get it over with, don't you think? And I need to see him. For my own peace of mind."

I tried to remember my husband's funeral, a few months earlier. I knew, as an objective fact because the staff here had told me, that my sister pulled me—well, sent Sean Joye to pull me—out of the asylum for the service. For weeks I remembered nothing of the day at all, but of late, little wisps of sepia-tinted memory had started to return.

I'm told it was a church service without a body, Taylor already in route to his people in Oxford to join his ancestors' bones in the family vault. I remember Christ Church Cathedral in St. Louis; the place was crowded, and the day hot. And my crimes, I stank of my crimes, and wondered how anyone could even approach me.

To me, Taylor just disappeared. In the train of my memories, one minute he was summoning a magical beast, threatening all our lives, and the next, gone. A very clear recollection hit me just then: One of Taylor's archeology colleagues, standing at the lectern. I watched him from behind my long black veil. He opened his mouth to speak, but I heard nothing, only saw a stream of toads fall from his lips, croaking and hopping across the altar. I must have laughed, as Sean touched my elbow and whispered, "Are you alright?"

"You seem lost in thought, Mrs. Humphrey," Evie said. "I've been trouble enough. You two could go back upstairs."

"Oh, no, I couldn't leave you." I squeezed her hand. "I was just remembering…" I cleared my throat. "I was too ill to…visit… with my husband's body. As things turned out, I never saw him again."

She hugged me and wept in my arms. I can't say that I'd been particularly taken with Evie Elsass—I don't take to many people right away—but we clung together like fast friends as we approached the corpse. Sean maintained a respectful distance.

Without intending to do so, my mind reached out to the man under the sheet. What were you doing out there, in the cold, in the snow?

And you? What were you doing there?

I jumped and turned to Sean. "What did you say?" His mimic abilities were annoying, but I was shocked at the cruelty of making a game of this moment. Yet, even as I did so, I recognized the voice and it wasn't Sean's.

"Me? Nothing." He was all the way across the room, poking his fingers through the wires to stroke a caged rabbit's nose. "Thought I'd give you ladies some space for your keening."

I glanced over at the sheet-covered body. Did the chest move gently up-and-down? Was he alive? We'd made a horrible mistake, relying on Dr. Cole's exam. A psychiatrist. What did he know about traumatic injury?

He's with us now. As are you. That wet and throaty gurgle I knew too well.

I shook my head and blinked. No. I was almost recovered. "Evie? Did you say something?" I asked, hoping I was mistaken about the voice. I refused to be subjected to any further disembodied voices' opinion of me or advice about my future.

Grounding myself, I reached down into the earth with my thoughts and spirit to carve out a calm space. With my intentions and a squeeze of her hand, I invited Evie to share.

"I didn't say anything." She released me and reached out to grasp the sheet. She pulled it back to reveal Elsass's face and chest. His skin was pale and bluish, waxy in the lantern light. *How could I have thought he was breathing?* Then I saw the glimpse of a smile and a flush to his cheeks. I glanced at his wife for a reaction to the change.

"Oh, Henry." Evie's fingers trailed through his hair and across his cheek as tears trickled down hers, shattering like glass on the corpse. She covered the face and looked around. "I wonder where they've put his clothes?"

Odd question. "In a bag for the sheriff, I imagine," I said. "Was there some piece of jewelry or photo—"

"Just a random thought. I feel so jumbled and confused." She took a chair. "I'll say some prayers. Then I'll join you kind folks upstairs in a few minutes." She closed her eyes; obviously she didn't think the dead body was behaving oddly.

"No, no. We wouldn't dream of leaving you alone down here. But I'll give you some privacy." I put as much distance between myself and the corpse as I could, crossing the lab to Sean and his rabbit friends. "Do you think Dr. Cole's legitimate?" I whispered. "I'm not sure that man is dead."

Sean snorted back a laugh, then nodded his head at the framed items over the desk. "Diplomas appear real enough," he said, sotto voce.

I glanced over at Evie. She fingered pink rosary beads. If she heard us, she gave no indication. "Documents can be faked, though."

"Are you being serious now?" He left off petting the rabbit and went over to the body. "Pardon me, ma'am. Just saying a little prayer, I am."

Tears leaked around Evie's closed eyelids. She nodded.

Sean reached under the sheet and lifted Dr. Elsass's right arm. He mouthed, "Quite stiff," then returned to me and the rabbits. Leaning over, he hissed in my ear. "He's very dead. What made you think—"

"Just an odd fancy. It's not like I've seen that many dead bodies." *Just my baby.*

His face softened like he meant to hug me, but didn't. "Sure, don't be thinking on the little one now."

"Are you reading my mind?" I hissed under my breath. "Clairvoyance isn't part of a binding spell."

Sean glanced at the widow, then took my hand and led me out into the dark hall. We stood in a dim pool of lantern light leaking out from the lab. "You're usually pretty easy to read. Which makes it hard to figure how you play me so constantly and well."

I swallowed hard. "I didn't intend to use you. Really. That was the sort of thing Taylor did with his magick, but I…"

See him.

It definitely wasn't Dr. Elsass's speaking, but the voice in my head seemed to be coming from the corpse. Through the open doorway, I could see the sheet quiver, as if breathing in and out. Evie was not in the chair at his side.

"Are you sure you don't you notice anything strange about the body?" I whispered. "Or hear something?"

Sean looked at me, long and hard, his brow furrowed. "I'm guessing you do."

"You know I'm the one who found him last night?"

He nodded. "And you're worried people will think…"

I grabbed his arm. "I'm in a jam here."

"You're just borrowing trouble. Ain't I more concerned about how all this is playing on your frame of mind at the moment?"

"I'm not going crazy again." Although maybe I was. But there were other explanations. I thought I heard a rustling from the lab. Maybe Evie was visiting with the rabbits. Or gathering Dr. Elsass's belongings to take home to their children.

"What's going on? Is this about the voice you hear?"

"It's different."

"Different...how?"

I grabbed his lapels and pulled him close to my face. "I need to explain something to you. About how magic is supposed to work. And what's going on here."

His eyes widened. "You want to talk about magic now? With a widow and her dead man in the next room, and you being accused of his murder?"

"Yes. Because the director is talking to me. Right now. Or, more accurately, something is talking to me through him."

Footsteps rang across the cement floor, tiny silver bells. I looked in the lab to see Evie standing by the corpse again. "I guess I'm ready to leave him for now," she said.

"Would you like to go somewhere...more private to talk?" Sean asked me.

"I suppose."

"You can de-witch me, too. But we should see the widow to the parlor."

I heard footsteps approaching from the far end of the hallway. It was Dr. Cole, hurricane lantern in one hand and a notebook tucked under his arm. When he noticed us, he shouted, "You, Sir. Stop right there." He ran, the storm of his confusion and anger pressing against us. "What are you doing here?"

For once, Sean was speechless.

The doctor held up his lantern to take us in; Sean and I on the threshold of his lab, and Evie bidding the body farewell. "Mrs. Elsass, I presume. The head nurse mentioned that you had arrived, but what are you doing down here? I didn't expect—"

"I can but apologize," Sean said as he stepped forward. "The widow here was keen on seeing her man without any further delay."

Dr. Cole placed the lantern on a table and sat in his battered desk chair. "I suppose as an attorney, you are as close to a court officer as we have here. How did you get in?"

"It was unlocked," I said.

Dr. Cole looked doubtful. "That can't be. I am meticulous in my habits."

"I'm sure you were in a hurry," Sean said. "And we were just on our way to meet you upstairs to hear about your findings."

"I've conducted a preliminary examination," Dr. Cole said. "As Mrs. Humphrey's advocate, you should know there was a note that indicates someone else was with him—"

"Or planned to be with him," I said. "Or wanted him to think they planned to be with him."

"Yes," Dr. Cole nodded. "We can't assume. But certain people interpreted that note as grounds to confine your client last night." To me, he said, "And you *were* with him. You found him."

"But I didn't write him a note," I said. "It doesn't match my writing."

Dr. Cole shrugged. "It's very damaged. I doubt penmanship will be of any help."

"And the body showed—what, that he fell?" Sean asked.

"That's correct."

"Nothing else?"

Dr. Cole shifted in his spot and glanced at the covered body.

"If you don't mind me saying—" Sean had an annoying habit of offering unsolicited advice at the worst possible moments. "You, doctor—might I call you Ibrahim?—are in a bit of a fix here."

Dr. Cole looked puzzled, but only for a moment. "America."

"Yeah, it's not like being an African in France, I imagine." Sean took Evie by the arm, and her pink aura glowed a little brighter.

The doctor nodded.

Sean's familiar tone with Dr. Cole gave me pause, but I saw where he was going with his intrusive advice and had to agree. "Continuing our discussion from earlier this morning, I'd say your position here is even more precarious than mine. Percy is now harping on you as a suspect."

Dr. Cole tilted his head. "That's ridiculous. I'm sure Mr. Emerson is correct that the sheriff will want to close the matter quickly, right or wrong. Death by misadventure would be most convenient..." He ran his hands through his close-cropped hair. "But, to establish an accidental death—"

"Was it accidental?" Sean said.

"Oh, no, Mr. Joye." Dr. Cole stood. "As Mr. Emerson has maintained from the start, our medical director was murdered. His head was held under the water until he drowned."

Violet

CHAPTER THIRTEEN

Clear lividity along trachea, clavicles, and sternocleidomastoid bilaterally, as well as fractures. Copious amounts of water expressed from lungs.

~From postmortem notes re: Heinrich "Henry" Elsass, December 19, 1924. 2200 hours.

I felt myself falling, falling, falling. Icy water swirled about me, and long weeds trailed along my skin, through my hair, and across my face. I felt calm. The water will sustain me if I trust it. More tendrils clutched at my sleeves, pulling me down. Rather than fight, I felt a longing to join them—*show me the way. Show me my baby.* As if accepting my invitation, the weeds grabbed at my face, neck, and shoulders, blocking my nose and mouth as they pulled me below the surface.

"Mrs. Humphrey, can you hear me?" I felt fingers press into my wrist. "Bring that light over here." I found myself flat on my back on the cold brick floor, feet elevated on something hard, with Dr. Cole crouched beside me. A lantern swung close to my face, blinding me in fits and starts.

I'm not prone to swooning and certainly wasn't surprised at Dr. Cole's announcement that Dr. Elsass had been murdered. I somehow knew it, felt it—a lingering taint of blood-red rage about his body when I saw him sprawled near the artesian well. And I knew that a faint green flicker of vitality had clung to him when I first found him. I'd left him alone, as vulnerable as a person could be, and someone had killed him. The attacker, aiming to finish the job? Maybe I'd interrupted them. Maybe they'd hidden among the trees, watching me. Waiting for their chance. I shivered.

"I'm alright." I struggled to my feet with Dr. Cole's help.

Evie hugged me. "You poor dear. Patients really depend on a good doctor. It's a devastating loss."

I pulled away from her motherly impulse. "I need some air." I paced the lab, avoiding the corpse. I turned to Dr. Cole. "Please go on. He was murdered? I'm sure his wife would like to know why you say that."

"I would. Yes, I would." Evie looked warily at me, as if I might start barking at any moment. "But I don't want to upset Mrs. Humphrey."

"Alright, ladies," said Dr. Cole, "But let's join the others. I only want to explain my findings once." He shepherded us out into the hall, then locked up with deliberation and some side-eye at Sean. He offered Evie his arm, but she'd already latched onto her chosen champion.

The doctor led the way through the basement and up the stairs, followed by Sean and Evie. I brought up the rear, thinking about what Percy Emerson would do with the news that all his alarmist suppositions about Dr. Elsass were true. No, I corrected myself, that Dr. Cole agrees with him about murder. I wasn't convinced Dr. Cole knew much about forensic medicine.

I could hear Percy in the parlor, pontificating as the group waited. His words, though muffled, whizzed around me like bright, sharp daggers, each dripping with blood. "…a young orderly. A mental deficient, resentful over wages owed. Certainly big and strong enough to have pushed over an old man. Comes and goes all over the place, and no alibi for the time of death. Motive, means, and opportunity, right there."

Was he now accusing Teddy? Someone's got to find proof of what really happened. I dawdled in the hallway, willing away that horrible man, Percy, and the even worse situation. The rear exit beckoned, a few steps away, through the kitchen and mudroom, and I'd be free. I'd just be postponing the inevitable. Avoiding what I was starting to feel was my responsibility.

I hurried to catch up with Dr. Cole, Evie, and Sean; they'd already gone into the parlor. When I arrived, Sean was assisting Evie to a chair, and Dr. Cole stood near Percy, who was still talking. I grabbed the first available seat and took in the faces as they listened to Percy: Dr. Cole looked annoyed, Blanche alarmed, and the elderly physicians who made up the board were dozing or scanning old, crumpled newspapers. Desperate for something to read, I imagined. "Leave it to the sheriff, man," said the one with the muttonchops—Bertinelli, I was pretty sure. "Not your job. We should go home."

"A word, if you don't mind, Mr. Emerson," Dr. Cole murmured.

"What? Oh, yes, of course you want to clear your report...or confession...with me first." The board president headed to the door. "We can use Elsass's office." They left, and the assembly stirred, impatient.

Carrie's face was set in an angry frown and wrinkled brow, but something else was going on, too. A gray shroud of sadness wrapped her tight; she was sunk in on herself, barely there.

On a positive note, while we waited for the important men to come back and tell us all what to think and do, the electric lights flickered on, and the radio popped and hissed, beginning to warm up. Finn had gotten the electric generator working again. Ironic that he labored away on our behalf while these men cooked up a ridiculous plot to blame the orderly, Teddy—his friend's son—for the director's murder.

Sean fiddled with the radio knobs until he got a clear signal from WLS in Chicago. "This just in. Travelers' advisory. All roads between Chicago and St. Louis are impassable due to snow accumulation, and more snow is on the way, according to reports out of Minneapolis."

"Now, gentleman, listen to that." Carrie gestured at the radio. "That's us. Between Chicago and St. Louis." She went to the window and drew the drapes, gesturing at the circular front driveway. She had summoned the will, or perhaps the courage, to dispel the gray film enveloping her.

Despite the chiding tone of her words, they smelled jasmine sweet. Cloying. Too sweet for the crowded room, which was suddenly too hot. You will not faint again, I told myself. *Control yourself.*

"Mr. Joye's car is stuck in the snow, up to the wheel wells." Carrie approached Dr. Bertinelli and crouched beside his chair to look him full in the face. "There's no way you'll get out on anything besides a tractor."

"So, have your man drive us to town on his tractor," he said.

Carrie sighed and took the chair next to him. "My man will be setting out on the tractor to get the sheriff soon." Her voice dropped. "We have a serious situation here."

"Yes, yes, Emerson talks of nothing else."

"Listen to me," she whispered. Everyone leaned in to hear. Everyone but Sean, who chose a chair near me and seemed more interested in the radio broadcast—some orchestra playing holiday classics.

"None of us saw Ibrahim all afternoon yesterday. He didn't appear for the reception or before dinner with everyone else. Not until after the body was found. And now he's leading the death investigation?"

The parrot, quite neglected in the overnight upheaval, tutted under its breath, "Death…Death…Death."

We all tried to ignore the morbid bird as the very deaf doctor shouted at Carrie, "But Emerson says it's that criminal woman you got here."

"Criminal," the parrot agreed.

Carrie glanced over at me and blushed. "Now, now—allow me to be the judge of the psychiatric diagnoses, shall we?"

Strangely, I didn't feel insulted; the old doctor's words twittered in the trees, an innocuous background noise to my own inner dialogue of regrets.

"That was before the cook was attacked. Keep up, Leiberman," Dr. Bertinelli said into his colleague's tinhorn. "Now Emerson accuses the Black man." He paused, creasing his brow. "Or is it the orderly?"

"Ah, ha," Leiberman cackled. "You can't keep up, either."

"Speaking of Percy," said Blanche, as she crossed the room to refill her teacup. "He went out last night, right after Dr. Elsass left us."

Carrie looked shocked, but quickly recovered. "I'm sure there's a perfectly logical explanation. But," she whispered, "he takes his position as board president too far. He has no clinical expertise to be in charge of the Institute."

"As you do," said Dr. Bertinelli.

"As does Dr. Cole," Blanche observed.

The board members had a range of reactions to Blanche's idea, from insulted to amused. Percy Emerson strode into the dining room with Dr. Cole trailing behind. "Hey, everyone, I'm convinced. And Cole's in the clear; he's found convincing evidence of murder. To Carrie he said, "Any luck with the phone? To call the sheriff?" He turned to Dr. Cole, "Pretty convenient, the lines being down."

Dr. Cole had no reply, but Dr. Bertinelli said, "The farmer will go to town on his tractor as soon as it stops snowing."

"I believe..." Carrie sniffed. "That cause of death is a decision made by the coroner."

"True," said Dr. Cole. "But if you all will allow me to explain. I found clear bruises on Dr. Elsass's neck and both clavicles fractured, in addition to lungs full of water. He was held down until he was drowned in the well."

"Oh, dear," Evie said. "I feel..."

She started to gag and cough. Sean grabbed the ice bucket off the bar trolley and leaped to her side.

I didn't feel so well myself, but had to wonder why it had taken her so long to have a physical reaction to the murder news; Dr. Cole had told us as much while we were together in the lab.

"Now, what I must ask all of you," Percy said, "Is who has denied this death was suspicious all along? That would be you, Nurse Bartowski, wouldn't it?"

Sean

CHAPTER FOURTEEN

Hometown Hero Lies in Coma

St. Louis' own Great War Flying Ace, Kyffin Bernard, was found unconscious on the floor of the Civil Courts Building Library around six AM today. Witnesses on the scene report severe bleeding from a head wound. A police spokesman, Detective Milo Draper, states Bernard is under surgical care at Barnes Hospital. SLPD appeals to the public for information.

~From *St. Louis Post-Dispatch*,
October 2, 1924. Four-star edition.

I watched Violet set the table for lunch in the patient dining room, carrying stoneware plates and sturdy cutlery from a cart to several solid wooden tables. Apparently, the patients all had jobs here. Part of their therapy. She wouldn't let me help, so I stayed out of the way, minding my own business and having a good, long think with my pipe.

I didn't even notice when Violet sneaked up on me—perhaps I'd nodded off—until I heard her voice in my ear. "Want to get our little talk out of the way?"

"What?" I nearly dropped the pipe. "You mean me?"

Violet had guided the cart to the final table, the one where I'd grabbed a seat.

"Yes, I mean you." She arranged four plates, then reached for the cutlery. "I need to clarify a few things I said earlier." Violet focused on her task as she precisely arranged a spoon next to a plate, but said, "I am truly sorry. I know sometimes I might strike you as—"

"Entitled? Defensive? Scornful?"

Violet turned to glower at me. "Don't interrupt; I'm trying to apologize. I swear I had no idea that spell would… my workings never last so long." She frowned at a spoon and polished it with a napkin before laying it to the right of the plate. "Maybe you *want* to stay connected to me. Ever think of that?"

"Did you remove the binding?" Even me, learning magic out of books, knew that much. A spell must be formally dispelled. Hence the term, "di-spell." Else, it just flops about doing who knows what mischief. Violet had studied her craft with actual teachers; surely, she knew that much.

She glared. "I was busy—" She turned back to her work, "having a nervous breakdown."

"OK. Then cut the cords on me. My only concern here is you." *And Carrie. And maybe Ibrahim.* But I saw no need to bring them up. "And you seem to be off the hook. Sad that someone else had to get hurt to prove it, but…"

Violet arranged the last place setting, fluffed up some leaves and flowers in a stoneware mug as a centerpiece, and then wheeled the cart in the kitchen's direction. She said over her shoulder, "Come with me. I'll break the energy between us. If that's what you want."

Was it what I wanted? I wasn't entirely sure anymore, but I followed her into the kitchen. She crouched to warm her hands by a large stone hearth, blazing away on the far side of the room. "How is he?" she said.

She didn't have to explain who she meant. Kyffin Bernard. Her best friend. A tall, handsome Great War flying ace I'd fallen for. Hard. But Violet's sister had damn near murdered him in September. His fate had been touch-and-go for a long time. Skull cracked and brain scrambled, he didn't remember much at first. Certainly not me. Or what we'd meant to each other.

"Much better, I suppose." He did remember me, eventually. Or a version of me. A version he'd decided to blame for every bad thing that had happened to him. "I... tried a small cantrip."

"You what?" Violet leaped to her feet and whirled around. "Sean, what in the world possessed—"

"I was desperate. You don't know what it's like—" I stopped myself, but it was too late. Jesus, Mary, and Joseph— She knew exactly what sort of daft plan could sound like a good idea when you're desperate. She'd lost a child. And decided a supernatural solution was the cure for her pain. I marched to a window and stared out at the snow-covered car park.

Violet laughed, a low, rich purr. "Magic's not so easy as all that. And if I should have asked you before my little binding spell—and yes, I was wrong not to get permission— you should have asked Kyffin."

131

"Yeah, I guess." *Damn logic.* "The book didn't mention that." A brilliant retort sprang to mind, and I turned around. "And besides, I was trying to help him heal, not use him to do my chores."

"Really?"

Honest to God, I used magic because I missed my friend. Missed the chance at love I worried would never come again. "I'll examine my conscience later, if you don't mind."

She dropped the act and ran over to me. "For once and for all, I did know better, but...I should have asked you." Solemn-faced, Violet took my hand, "Like I'm asking now."

"What do you mean?"

"I need your help. A crime has happened here. And people are being falsely accused." Wind whistled about the house, shaking the windows and moaning through the eaves. I thought I heard thunder rumbling in the distance.

Of course, Emerson's taunts at Carrie, Violet's best friend in the whole place, concerned me. She'd been nothing but kind to me. Very friendly, even. Extremely.

Violet nodded. I guess she could read me pretty easily. "I'm very worried about Carrie."

"If anyone's gonna get railroaded, my money's on the Black man." I went over to the fireplace and tapped the tobacco ash into the flames. *Yeah, Ibrahim's fate concerned me, alright.*

"Possible." Violet headed to the dish trolley. "But that horrid Percy—now he has it in for our head nurse. Or even my favorite orderly, Teddy."

I'd heard Emerson's shite, and I'd also heard Carrie tear him a new one. She wasn't going to meekly be made the patsy, no matter what the board president flung at her. "She's doing a good job of defending herself. No one in that room took Emerson seriously. You think he aims to pin it on the kid?"

Violet shrugged. "I don't know. Just something I overheard." She pushed the trolley against the far wall, apparently its home when not in use. "He's a bully—a very persistent bully— who wants this situation wrapped up and settled. He doesn't care if it's wrong or right."

"You'd think he'd want to catch the actual killer."

Violet shrugged. "Maybe he knows who it is. Doesn't see that person as a danger to the public."

"Like, he did it himself?" That was interesting. Emerson was just the sort of blowhard I'd enjoy seeing go to jail. Very, very unlikely thing to happened, guilty or not, but one could always hope. "Mrs. Humphrey, are you proposing to investigate this murder yourself?"

I liked this idea. I'd always thought she was the smartest one in the room. High time for her to prove it. If she took to snooping, it could mean a way forward for me, too, in my currently unsuccessful investigation business.

She frowned. "I…I think I am. I don't want to, but…I need to. I think." She grabbed my arm, "and I need someone I can trust to help me."

"Flattered," I said. "And a bit surprised."

"Why should you be surprised? You've cared, when everyone else—my so-called friends, my family—all abandoned me."

"Ah, but I'm enchanted."

She laughed. "The only way that a cantrip cast in September could still be intact would be that you want it to be intact. You've been tending it, feeding it."

"Me? I wouldn't even know how to." I stared her straight in the eyes. "You're really worried about Carrie?"

"Yes. And there's something else." Violet took a deep breath. "When I think of everything that happened—and then me coming to this place, it's obvious I've hit rock bottom." A smile played across her face. "At least, I hope it can't get any worse. I think by solving this problem I'll be…working through the hard parts, not just dreaming up ways to avoid them."

"You need a win," I said. I'm not one to make hasty decisions, but…when Violet called—"OK, I'll help you. But you must help me—"

"Understand the magic?"

"Yeah." That, too, of course. But what I really wanted from her was a partner in my magical investigation business. I was in over my head and knew it. I couldn't propose she join my investigation agency at this point; she'd turn me down flat. Instead, I could bide my time, soften her up a bit. "I…I may have already messed things up beyond repair with Kyffin, but…"

"I'll try to help you do better. We'll start with that binding cantrip."

"Oh, that. Might as well leave it. Works better than the telephone."

Violet

CHAPTER FIFTEEN

Did Deadly Deb Do in Dad?

Our town's favorite flapper and currently reigning Piasa Lodge Queen, Lillian De Noilles Arwald, was arrested in Alton the night of October 31 for the murder of her father, local financier Joseph B. Arwald. Arwald was found shot to death in his office on October 3rd.

From *The West End Bugle,*
November 1, 1924, Page 1, three-star edition.

Sean and I decided we could sleuth more efficiently separately and chose Percy Emerson as the logical starting point—he had so many opinions. We flipped a coin for the honor of sounding him out, and I lost. Sean offered to talk to the staff.

I stopped by my bedroom to brush my hair, then set out to hunt down Percy. I ran into Carrie outside the female patients' lounge. "Violet, would you make a quick pass through the public areas and invite any visitors you see to come and eat lunch?"

"Of course. And—" I touch her arm in what I hoped was a comforting gesture, just like she had done for me dozens of times over the past few months, "—I don't believe anything Percy said about you."

Her face softened. "You're very kind. His defense mechanisms can be unpleasant for those around him, but they are just that…ways to make himself feel safe. I give it leave to blow right over me and advise you to do the same."

Surprised that she wasn't particularly worried about Percy's accusations, I nodded, then set out to round up luncheon stragglers. The task would give me a chance to corner Percy.

The snow and ice had started up again, and everyone was huddled indoors against the weather, their travel plans abandoned for the moment. The asylum had never been so un-asylum-like: noisy and crowded with extra people around every corner. Yet I was a little surprised to find the institutional routine grinding on as per usual. The orderlies had roused, dressed, and fed the patients according to schedule, snowbound or not. It was apparent that Carrie and her nurses enforced chores, activities, and therapy sessions despite the visitors underfoot at every turn.

I ended up searching the whole building for the board president. Percy wasn't critiquing his wife in the art therapy area or pontificating at the elderly doctors in the library. He wasn't in his bedroom. At last, behind the closed door of Dr. Elsass's office, I heard someone moving about. Papers rustled.

Unfortunately, I knew far too much about suspicious death investigations. That room should have been sealed for the sheriff as soon as Dr. Cole ruled the death a murder. I tapped but didn't wait for a reply before entering. "Are you in here, Mr. Emerson? It's lunchtime."

Percy, sitting at Dr. Elsass's desk, glanced up, his expression surprised, furtive, and as guilty as hell. A folder lay open before him on the desk. He quickly pulled some other folders on top of it. He grinned. "Oh, it's you. Mrs. High-and-Mighty Humphrey."

I ignored his words, his stench, and the guilty purple aura surrounding his head, a perverse nimbus. Guilty and… something else. Some other secret. I filed that thought away for the moment. "Nurse Carrie sent me—" I assessed his reaction to her name. He seemed annoyed, which pleased me. "—to say that lunch is about to be served."

He nodded and leaned back in the chair. "I knew your dad, girl. Handled my investments. Pillar of the community. He built a legacy for his family and his company. What would he say about his business's ruin—between your sister and you—"

I stepped in and slammed the door behind me, a loud thud, unnoticed, I was sure, in the infernal din of the luncheon preparations. He jumped, then appeared increasingly alarmed as I walked across the room to the desk. "Let's cut the crap, shall we? My sister's crimes are completely irrelevant to our situation. And you've already admitted that even if I'm crazy enough to hurt Elsass,

I likely didn't do it, because of the attack on poor Mrs. Holmes."

"Who?"

"The cook."

He grinned, lit two cigarettes on one match, and offered me one.

"I don't like you well enough to smoke with you."

Percy nodded. "Suit yourself." He inhaled, tapped ash, then said, "You're right. You appeared guilty at first, but I guess—"

I leaned over the desk, upsetting a stack of file folders, which slithered across the blotter. "And now you're accusing the director of nursing. I've overheard your speculation about an orderly. Do you just pick random people or what?"

"Now, now, I'm not that bad." He indicated the files. "And I'm checking the records here."

"For clues?" He wouldn't recognize a clue if it bit him. Which reminded me; my task was to interrogate, not berate. I resolved to do better.

"Yes, for clues. Someone's got to do it, us all stuck here for days, snowed in with a bunch of maniacs."

I immediately forgot to confine myself to information gathering. "Maniacs? You love the hyperbole, don't you? Is Blanche a maniac?" His wife didn't seem the least bit unusual in mood or behavior to me. Likely, she'd dared express opinions contradictory to Percy's own. "People come here with illness. Hopefully, for curative treatment."

He rolled his eyes. "Yes, nurse."

I wondered if he was deliberately distracting me. He certainly knew the buttons to push. I pointed to the documents on the desk. "Find anything?"

He looked a little nonplussed as he restacked the folders I'd knocked over. "I dunno, I just started to search."

He'd been reading what appeared to be a medical chart and had covered it with a random stack of letters.

I'd known so many Percy Emerson types—my father and his friends, for instance. My husband, Taylor, who was so different from anyone I'd ever known, had eventually turned into one. I reminded myself that I was there to investigate a crime and tried a different tactic; a familiar, female one, sure to work. "So," I said. "You're the board president. You know what's really going on."

He visibly relaxed, just a fraction, but enough to show I'd hit the right tone. Well, maybe the right tone to get some information. Not the right tone to make me feel good about myself. But my feelings weren't so important at the moment. This man would scapegoat someone, anyone, just to make his life more convenient. "That's true. I've been on the board since the beginning, three years ago, and president since January."

"So," I took a seat, "who wanted Dr. Elsass dead?"

"I'd thought Dr. Cole was jealous, wanted advancement, but now—"

"He supported you, got on your good side somehow. Please, examine the facts. Murders are about sex or money, generally."

He grinned. "You should know, girlie."

"Don't be an ass, Emerson. And I'll take one of those cigarettes."

He offered the pack. "I think you'll like this blend."

I helped myself and accepted the light, then settled into the chair. "So, which is it, really?"

"Not being privy to his love life—isn't that a hoot, the wife showing up like that?"

"Focus, Percy. You know something about the money."

"Yeah, I do. I imagine you've guessed that he was pressing you for a reason beyond, 'you don't get better if you don't pay your bill.'"

I blew a smoke ring. "At the time, I didn't, but the more I think about it…"

"This place has turned out to be a money pit. Debt up to his eyeballs. He was taking on more investors." He wiggled his eyebrows, trying to be funny, I suppose.

I ignored him. Flirting with Percy Emerson wasn't on my agenda for the day. "Say he was in financial trouble. How does that lead to him getting murdered?"

He shrugged. "People in debt make a lot of bad decisions."

"And what have you got here?" I tapped the stack of letters and charts. None of it appeared to be financial records.

"Not that it's any of your business, I have official obligations. I need the succession documents—who's supposed to be in charge of the day-to-day operations and the plan to turn over the administration to the next director."

"Surely Nurse Carrie?"

"Not Doctor Paris France?"

I shrugged. "Maybe so, but he…"

Emerson laughed. "See, even you can't imagine a colored man in charge."

"I was going to say he doesn't appear to be privy to the practical, business side of all this."

"He's strictly a clinician." Emerson nodded. "And not a bad one at that. He's a credit to his race, at least in the academic department. And either Carrie or Cole could have killed Elsass, timing wise, if motivated."

I blew smoke in Emerson's general direction, my fingers frantically drumming on the desk. This man was certifiable. A certifiable ass. And I was sure he'd hidden a patient chart under the pile of letters, not Institute bylaws or governance documents. "So, besides the Institute being low on money, what else do you think was going on?"

Percy put on a serious expression and pretended to consider my question for a moment, then smirked. Leaving the mess he'd strewn across the desk, he stood and offered me his arm. "Luncheon, Mrs. Humphrey?" Just to keep the peace, I took it and let him lead me toward the exit. As we passed the queer stones Dr. Elsass kept in a bowl behind the door, I had an overwhelming, puzzling urge to grab one. *What's that all about?* I resolved to talk it over with Carrie; she always had something wise and insightful to say.

The parlor and hallway were quiet, the only sound a low hum of hungry anticipation from the dining room. As we walked down the hall, he patted my hand. "Don't worry your pretty little head over the murder. You're off the hook."

"Hmm." I didn't want to give him the satisfaction of ever agreeing with him on any topic.

Sean

CHAPTER SIXTEEN

In an island of the ocean is a sacred grove, and within it a consecrated chariot…Only one priest is allowed to touch it. He can perceive the presence of the goddess in this sacred recess and walks by her side with utmost reverence as she is drawn along by heifers…it is a season of rejoicing.

~From *Germany and Its Tribes,*
Cornelius Tacitus, circa 98 AD.

"Now I can talk to you, Mr. Joye."

Lunch was served to the patients and guests, and Lottie settled into a chair at a large oak table and pulled a cigarette out of a packet in her apron pocket. A thin Black woman, quite young, perhaps not even twenty-one, with braided hair tucked under a white, frilly cap, her eyelids drooped over bloodshot eyes, and her shoulders sagged.

I hastened to strike a match and light her smoke, then took a seat myself. "Perhaps a nap is more in order than jawing with me."

She grimaced. "No time. The maids will be in here any minute wanting their own lunch."

"Don't they have the inmates waiting table? Sure, and wasn't Mrs. Humphrey setting out the crockery earlier?"

Lottie made a dismissive grunt and shook her head. "That's part of their 'therapy.' Mrs. Humphrey is pretty good at it now; she could get a job at any restaurant in St. Louis. You should have seen her when she first came in—"

I *had* seen her then, that early October day when she'd slipped into her trance or whatever it's called. But I didn't share that with Lottie. I hoped she'd have something else interesting to say about Violet's progress in this place.

"But most of them, well, let's just say they need help with their chores." Lottie turned her head so as not to blow smoke in my face. Her neck muscles were stretched tight. It looked painful.

"Supervision?"

"Yeah, they need real maids to 'supervise' them."

"You did a great job getting meals out today, without the head cook and all." I commenced to pack tobacco into my pipe.

Her tired eyes shone. "Kind of you to notice. Not that it will do me any good around here. More work for still no pay." The wind howled around the house and rattled the kitchen windows. She startled and glanced around, then relaxed. She laughed. "Now didn't I take that noise as someone coming in here? Don't need certain people hearing me complain."

"Did you mean Dr. Elsass ain't been paying you?" I guess she could hear the irritation in my voice because she held out her hand to stop me.

"Whoa, easy there, sir. You're more riled than I am, and that's saying a lot. He gives—gave—us script and wrote it all down in a book. Things are a little rough right now for the Institute. Patients not paying their bills. The high price of coal and such."

"That's not your problem," I pointed out, rolling a match over the bowl of tobacco and puffing quickly.

"Mmm, that smells nice," Lottie said, standing. "I'm gonna make some coffee. You're right, it's not my problem—our problem—that he don't got the money to pay us. But he talked real polite to everyone, even apologized, and asked us to just have faith in the place a little while longer."

"What else is he gonna say?"

She gave me some side-eye. "You're mighty young to be so cynical. Where's your faith in human nature?"

I laughed out loud. "You're kidding, right?"

Lottie laughed, too. "You're right, you're right—my faith is in Jesus Christ's nature, not humans. My God will take care of me."

"Did you ever think God wants you to find a new job, where the boss ain't a deadbeat?"

"Now, that's just what Mr. Finn says." She put a coffeepot on the stove. "But I don't see him leaving, neither. Best be getting lunch on the table for the staff. You gonna join us?"

I was curious if everyone else took such a Christian attitude to the pay situation; Lottie was single and apparently content to work for room and board for some reason.

I caught wise to that reason when a burly young man showed up for lunch. He wasn't Teddy, the orderly Violet was worrying over; he was called Robert. Lottie served him an extra-large helping of chicken and dumplings and left the breadbasket right in front of him. He grinned his thanks, and she looked away, suddenly shy. So that's how it is, I thought. Lottie's living on love for the time being.

Several more people drifted into the room, served themselves from the cook pot, and took a seat, including a teenage boy.

"This here is Teddy, Finn's…boy," Lottie said to me, then making a few hand gestures as she continued, "Teddy, Mr. Joye. Mrs. Humphrey's friend."

"Hello." He shook my hand. "Mrs. H, she's a nice lady." The boy spoke each word with care, shaping the consonants with effort.

"Pleasure," I said as I turned to help a blonde maid take the seat beside me. "Hearing good things about you, I've been."

"What was that?" he asked. "I don't hear so good. Measles." He pointed to my face, then his own. "Helps if you turn your face right toward me."

Feeling like an idiot, I did just that. "Mrs. Humphrey likes you a lot."

He blushed and nodded. "She's a nice lady."

When everyone gathered, our lunch crew consisted of Lottie, Teddy, two housemaids named Gretel and Martha, and Lottie's sweetheart, Robert. Despite the food in front of them, no one started eating. I soon learned why as Lottie closed her eyes and grabbed Robert's and Teddy's hands for grace. I linked hands with Gretel and Martha. They both grinned, Martha blushing and Gretel giving me a frank once-over.

"Lord, thank you for this food. Bless it to the nourishment of our bodies. Thank you that we is all warm and dry, safe and together this stormy day."

The party mumbled their amens and dropped hands, but Lottie was just getting started. "And bless and keep our poor old Dr. Elsass. Take his soul in your loving arms to his place in heaven among the faithful departed. Amen."

"Amen," they all said. But no one started in on their lunch. They looked me up and down without saying a word, obviously puzzled why a visitor was eating with them.

"Thanks for letting me join you," I said. And what was I doing here, nosing around? I pondered what to say about that and went with a reasonably accurate version of the truth. "I work for Mrs. Humphrey in St. Louis. I'm talking to everyone I can about what's been going on around here since yesterday. I know you're all busy, especially with the storm and the visitors, but I was wondering if I could ask you a few questions while we eat."

"You're right there. We're all meeting ourselves coming and going," said Gretel, a sturdy blonde whose hand was now resting on my knee. "But *I* got time." She batted her eyelashes at me. "All afternoon. I just told Nurse Carrie that I quit."

"You didn't," said Lottie. "Why?" She glanced at Teddy, who was watching Gretel with deep concentration. Lottie touched his shoulder, then made some more of those hand gestures. "Gretel quit," she said.

Gretel nodded. "Sorry, Ted." She made few hand movements of her own.

"How?" he said, a questioning expression on his face as he rolled cupped hands forward.

"I just up and told her. As soon as the snow stops, I'm gone. I'll ride to town with Finn on the tractor if I need to. Or call my dad, when they fix the phone, to come get me."

Martha, a tiny redhead, barely more than a child, shook her head. "That sure leaves me in the lurch."

Gretel shrugged, then turned to Lottie. "As to why, I'm not gonna hang around here and be murdered in my bed by ghosts."

"Now, girl," said Robert. "You sound foolish. And in front of a visitor, too."

I laid down my spoon and, under the table, gave Gretel's hand a little squeeze. "You don't sound foolish at all," I said to her. "There are plenty of things in this world we don't understand."

"There's no such thing as ghosts," said Lottie, although her voice was uncertain. "The dead go to their judgment. End of story. And, anyway, our Lord protects his people from the works of the Devil. Just have faith."

"Oh, I have faith. Faith in getting away from this place. They're taking advantage of you, Lottie. All of us. But you don't realize it."

"What do you think, mister?" Lottie said. "Am I some kind of chump?"

I wouldn't get caught up in these two women's dispute for all the tea in China.

Robert broke the awkward silence with a laugh. "Lottie, honey." He got up to refill his bowl. "You're making things awkward for our visitor. He's got obligations to his employer."

"A boss who pays him," Gretel chimed in. She'd somehow scooted her chair closer to mine, and her arm brushed up against my shoulder. "I'm sure Mrs. Humphrey is on time with her bills."

Teddy had been watching Gretel intently and nodded. "Dr. Elsass hasn't paid any of us in months."

Money owed wasn't a great motive, but it was a motive. "Did you ever talk to him about needing your pay?"

His expression was blank, and I wondered if he resented my question. Or maybe I needed to learn some of those hand signals the staff all had down pat. Then he pushed a small notebook across the table. "Sir, write that?"

He watched me as I wrote, then said, "I asked my fathers for help, but Uncle Finn said to talk to the doctor myself."

Lottie had introduced Teddy as Finn's son, but he'd just called him "uncle" and spoke of "fathers." I was pretty sure

I'd heard mention of Finn's "boarder," someone named Tomás.

These men had a complicated, if not all that uncommon, situation. I wondered if living on an isolated prairie helped or hurt their unconventional little family.

But Teddy was still telling us his story. "Part of growing up, Uncle Finn said. We practiced." He winced. "It didn't go very good."

Robert tapped Teddy's shoulder to get his attention. "Elsass refused?" he said, scowling as he flung his fist, thumb extended, over his shoulder.

Teddy's hands were busy with a reply, but he said, likely for my benefit, "Same old 'Soon, soon.' 'I'll give you extra later.' 'Think of the poor patients.'" Robert and Teddy both shook their heads.

"Ain't right to make you feel bad about wanting what's yours," Robert said.

When was this? I wrote.

"Yesterday morning."

And were you angry? He was young, tall, and strong. It wouldn't take much for him to overpower Dr. Elsass.

"Right then? No, I felt guilty. And I could give him some time; but I mean to go to St. Louis in the spring."

He agreed?

"Yes, he did. I went back to work." Teddy looked a little sheepish. "Then I got to talking to Gretel."

She blushed and dropped my hand. "We kinda worked ourselves up. Teddy got all mad again, and I decided enough is enough myself." She got up, went to Teddy, and hugged him. "I can't wait around here until spring to go with you to St. Louis." She made some hand signs. "I'm going home. Now."

The boy watched her carefully, both crestfallen and relieved. Interesting, I thought. I wasn't sure of all this backstairs romance's relevance, but it *was* entertaining. You talked to Dr. Elsass again? I wrote.

He read my note and said, "No, I was busy. Wanted to talk to Uncle Finn. Maybe try again later."

And between six and seven? See anything suspicious?

"The coal stoker—broke down. I was helping to fix it." He gave us all a wry smile. "Mr. Emerson keeps harping on where we were: We were working. Uncle Finn left to rig up a new part. He had me shift out a bunch of coal that was in our way."

Time?

"No idea." He bit his lower lip. "I was hungry; must've have worked right through mealtime."

"So, Gretel," I said; Teddy had been in the spotlight long enough, and he looked grateful at my shift in attention. Robert had yielded his seat so she could sit by Teddy. Now she hung on him like they'd never see each other again. "You're from the area? You knew this place before Dr. Elsass came?"

"That I did, sir, that I did." Gretel liked to dish the dirt, and apparently, I'd just invited her to a fine mud puddle.

"This is Finn's family homestead." She turned to Teddy and signed her words. "I didn't know Finn then, of course. He's my pa's age. Anyway, he went away and stayed away." Her voice dropped. "But his old man was barmy as they come. No offense, Teddy."

The boy appeared puzzled.

"You know," she said as she signed, "we've talked about it—Finn's crazy father."

The young man laughed. "Uncle Finn didn't get on with his dad."

"I remember him from when I was a little girl, traipsing about the fields," Gretel said, "a couple of times a year, having a procession, all by himself. Didn't care who saw him.

"And the crazy goes back even further—my pa says Finn's grandfather, old Jürgen, had some sort of Holy Roller church, back in the day. And —" she whispered dramatically, "—they say people went missing from the services, ever so often."

The little redhead, Martha, had been silently nibbling a scone through all this. She sniffled. "Please, Gretel, don't go on about none of them ghost stories."

"Yes, Gretel," said a voice from the doorway. Carrie stood on the threshold, surveying the scene. "I believe you just resigned, so go pack your things. The rest of you, break's over."

Sean

CHAPTER SEVENTEEN

> **Section 2.03. Number of Directors and Term of Office.** *The Elsass Institute Board of Directors shall consist of not less than three (3) and not more than nine (9) members. The Board may establish other categories of membership available to Institute donors.*
>
> **Section 2.04. Powers.** *The Board shall have full power to conduct, manage, and direct the business and affairs of the Institute and, except as otherwise provided by the laws of Illinois, delegate to the Institute's Medical Director or other officers of the corporation such powers as it may see fit.*
>
> ~From *The Elsass Institute bylaws*,
> McLean County, Illinois. January 31, 1921.

I scattered with the help, following Robert outside before Carrie could challenge me on why I was so interested in the staff's gossip. I hoped to learn a little more from the orderly, but he was immediately dragged into service by Percy Emerson, who called out, "You, boy. Come here. Help these fellas dig out my car."

The stuffed shirt was standing over a young man in chauffeur's liveries and a middle-aged man in overalls, barn jacket, and cap with flaps; they were digging snow away from a fancy Duesenberg Straight Eight.

"What will Nurse Carrie say to guests heading out, do you think, Mr. Finn?" Robert asked Overalls.

"'Look at the sky,' that's what she'd say, same as I did," Overalls replied. "Another snowstorm will be starting up soon. You won't get as far as the state highway."

"I don't care," Emerson said. "I'm getting out of this nuthouse this very day."

"Don't you want to go inside?" I clapped him on the back like swells do. "Maybe have a drink while they work on your car?"

The chauffeur had shoveled out enough snow to wriggle into the car, but, in the cold, the engine didn't care to cooperate. He kept coaxing it, and finally it sputtered to life. "Sir," he said out the window, "I'm gonna see if I can get any traction." He gestured to me. "This gentleman is right. You could wait inside where it's warm. I'll come for you the moment we can leave."

Emerson sighed and headed across the icy parking lot toward the house. I followed.

"I'm not going anywhere this afternoon, am I?" he said.

I held out my palm, catching a drifting snowflake. "I think that fella's right about the weather. Snow's starting up again." I held open the back door, ever the humble servant. "If you don't mind me asking, what's the hurry?"

"What, apart from two people being killed—"

"I hadn't heard that the cook died—"

"Alright. One person killed, another attacked." We stood in the mudroom, and he stomped the snow and ice

155

off his wellies, then took a seat on a low, rough bench to pull them off.

I wiped my feet on the mat and dried off my shoes as best I could with a handkerchief. "You have a particular reason to think you'd be a target?"

"Who, me? No, no." Then he seemed to really think it over, maybe for the first time, despite his knee-jerk reaction that everyone in the place was in danger from a crazed killer. "I don't think so. Although…"

His voice dropped in volume and lost much of its constant bravado. "I just want to take my wife home." He sounded tired.

"Let's go to the parlor and see if they have brandy."

"I like the way you think."

In the deserted parlor, a coffee urn was set up near the Christmas tree. I poured brandy into a cup and added a splash of coffee. "We could do with a frank talk about this situation, man to man."

"Alright, councilor," he said, taking a chair. "I've nothing to hide."

He accepted the drink, and I allowed some time for lubrication as I chatted a bit with the parrot, offering it an apple slice I'd swiped off Violet's breakfast tray. It eyed me a good long while before accepting it, and swear to God, an intelligence lurked behind its beady eyes that I'd never noticed before.

After a bit of polite conversation with the bird, I took a seat near Emerson. "I concluded yesterday," he said, then took a stiff belt of the brandy-coffee, "that this place is about to go belly up. Elsass was just stringing everyone along. Some sort of scam."

"What makes you think that?"

He leaned forward in the chair, glancing through the open door and down the hall. Sounds drifted in—the scraping of snow shovels on the porch, a piano tinkling a tune, and someone, deep in the house, exclaiming over the snow. I could see the snow from the parlor windows, falling again in buckets. Emerson turned to me, his voice a throaty whisper. "Elsass told me. Not in so many words, but...I followed him when he left the cocktail reception yesterday—"

"What time was that?" Finally, someone was talking about the critical hour, when whatever it was that had happened to Elsass—happened.

"Shortly after six, I think. The hall clock chimed. He suddenly announced he had some work to do and would see us all at dinner. He left, and I followed."

"Why?" An urn of hot water and a box of those American tea bag things also sat on the sideboard, and I decided to give one a try. And give the man some space. You'd think, especially if you've ever been arrested, that pounding away with the questions is the way to get information. But no. Let it be for a bit. Leave them some uncomfortable silences to fill in.

By the time I got my cuppa brewing, or at least the tea bag soaking in warmish water, he began to speak. His voice resumed its standard lord-of-the-manor cadence. "Not relevant, Mr. Attorney." He held out his cup for a refill. "And I will be checking on you with the state bar association when we return to town. We only have your word for it as to when you and Evelyn Elsass—if that's really her name—actually arrived in the area. It could've been yesterday."

I took his cup but ignored the bait. "Suit yourself. Do you mind saying where Elsass went? Or don't you know? And you're just pretending to have inside information?"

Emerson didn't answer; he just stared at the brandy decanter. I made him another drink and handed it over.

"Elsass left the parlor and went toward the servants' area. Now we know he intended to go outside, but at the time, I didn't know or care. I caught up with him—I did have a private matter to discuss—and he said he had to check on the man working on the furnace."

I started packing a pipe while my tea took on a pale brown color. "I wonder if he just did that to throw you off his plans." I was smoking too much, but it was all for a good cause.

"Possibly. And I don't see how watching the man work would help get it fixed any quicker. I doubt Elsass knew anything about heating equipment. But, whatever the reason, we had a conversation on the basement steps. He said, as you may suspect by now, that finances were an unexpected challenge for him. But he had some cockamamie plan to expand the board in exchange for—"

"Big donations." Now, what was I supposed to do with the wet tea bag? I decided to dump it in one of the clean cups.

"Exactly. Now, why would I allow that? Packing the board with his supporters. And is anyone truly getting well here? Blanche sure isn't improved."

I puffed my pipe and sipped some tea. It wasn't terrible. Not hot, but not bad. And quite tidy, once you settle on a home for the used tea bag. "I'd be pretty angry."

Emerson shrugged. "I told him that he ought to just give the crazies a jolt of electricity to reset the brain, like Cole talks about."

"What'd he say to you quoting his junior colleague?"

Emerson laughed. "Not pleased. What did Elsass call it? Oh, yes, 'somatics.' 'Somatics have their place,' he said in a nasal, egghead accent that I had to admit was pretty funny. 'Some derangements are electrical. But do we counter a barbaric manifestation with an equally barbaric remedy?'"

"That don't sound unreasonable." I finished the tea and thought about making another cup.

"I guess so, not when I repeat it. But you should have heard the way he said it! Like I was brain damaged or an idiot, just to bring up the idea." Emerson's fingers curled into a fist. "I was furious. And told him I was going to take Blanche and leave for home immediately. He started to at least pretend to give up on the expanded board idea. He said, if worse came to worse, he had a benefactor in the wings."

"Who?"

"Imaginary, I'm quite sure. Just more of his con job. I wouldn't even discuss it with him. I left him there and went to hunt up my driver. But got lost trying to locate the servants' quarters."

"You finally found your man?" I said, careful to keep my voice neutral. Emerson was about to admit that he had no alibi for the crucial hour of Elsass's death.

"Finally, but too late to do me any good. It turns out they keep the male help out in a carriage house, and he was napping out there."

"Think hard—you were wandering around at the same time the killer was stalking the doctor. Did you see or hear anything strange?"

He settled back in the chair and drained his cup. "We stood on the basement steps, and I heard the custodian, Finn, I think he's called, talking to someone, or maybe he was just cursing out the furnace. Then I went trying to find my driver. I walked through a day room—half a dozen or so patients, completely gaga. I found the female staff area, although no one was around. In the kitchen, the cook and her helper were busy, but one of them said the driver would have been quartered for the night in the carriage house. So, I put on my galoshes and went outside."

"About when was that?"

"Perhaps 6:30. It was past dark. Oh, yes, 6:30, I remember I checked my watch."

"Anyone about outside? We now know the doctor had gone to the well."

Thoughtfully, Percy said, "I heard someone moving through those trees near the house—they call it 'the Grove'—but then I was distracted by the headlights of a car pulling up."

"Did you see who was driving?"

"No. I was in no mood to be sociable. I took the car's arrival as evidence that the roads were passable and continued over to the men's dormitory."

"Your driver can confirm?"

Emerson smiled. To hide his annoyance, I thought. "Why, Mr. Joye. I'd think you're some sort of policeman, not a lawyer at all."

I shrugged. This gent was on to me, but I didn't much care. "Officer of the court and all that jazz."

"I found him, but I'm not sure how much he'll remember. He'd been imbibing in a bit of Christmas cheer with the other men."

"So, maybe you weren't so eager to go anywhere last night."

"I could have driven myself," he said. "But, no, I gave him a piece of my mind and told him to be ready first thing in the morning. Then I thought they were surely serving the food, so I went inside."

His empty coffee-brandy cup rattled against a side table as he put it down and stood. "But I never saw Elsass again after that talk on the basement stairs. By the time I'd cleaned up and changed for dinner, he was dead."

Violet

CHAPTER EIGHTEEN

My Dear Miss Arwald,

Of course, I remember your mother, may her gentle spirit live on in the Light, and would love to meet you and introduce you to our little community. Our home is quite near New Forest. From what you have shared in your letter, I think a visit will do you good. When do you mean to make the crossing?

~From letter to Violet Arwald from Susie Mason,
South Hampton, February 15, 1913.

My routine as an institutionalized patient ground along as per usual under the watchful eye of the head nurse. As soon as I appeared in the patient dining room after fetching Percy, Carrie set me to my regular task of feeding Berta. I nibbled at a sandwich, anxious to get on with our investigation, or perhaps merely to get our investigation over with. As soon as we finished lunch, I dashed to Dr. Cole's office for my daily session. I enjoyed the thought of interrogating him for a change.

This room was the Talking Cure sanctum sanctorum, a space for the mental healing method on which Dr. Elsass had staked his professional reputation. And possibly his life, I thought, although I wasn't quite sure where that notion had come from. Did his death have something to do with the Talking Cure? Had someone regretted a confidence?

"Enter," said Dr. Cole in response to my rapping.

My stomach full of knots and butterflies, I turned the handle. "Nurse Carrie says we are to continue with all our regular activities. I guess that means therapy?"

He stood when I entered and gestured to the fainting couch. "I, too, have been so instructed." He made a face like he'd just swallowed a bug. "Not that I don't concur; obviously we must keep everyone safe and busy. Order is important to the disordered mind."

"So why the long face?" I deliberately settled into a wingback chair, avoiding even a glance at the upholstered couch where I was usually required to recline during the sessions.

He touched his cheeks. "My face? I don't understand."

"Just an expression. You look sad. Maybe angry. Or something."

Dr. Cole pursed his lips.

Ah, now he's regretting our little talk earlier. Let his hair down too much. I giggled at that—another confusing American idiom to tease him with. Maybe later.

I realized I felt…strange. And that strange feeling was something like happiness. How sick I must be, I thought, that murder makes me happy.

"…oversteps her authority." I realized he'd been venting for a while. "Although Nurse Carrie is correct to direct day-to-day patient care and supervise the staff, in other matters—"

"She's not your boss?" I relaxed into the chair, willing him to relax, too. "I'd say Percy Emerson is more of a threat to your authority, even freedom." *And life.*

"He is playing at policeman, but seems fixed on Nurse Bartowski as his culprit, at least at this moment." Dr. Cole shook his head and muttered in French as he settled into the other wingback chair. I wasn't familiar with the words. He consulted his notepad. "Now, yesterday morning we talked about your habit of digging about in the dirt."

I didn't remember any such discussion or any such behavior. "I agree Percy is being ridiculous in his accusation." A little bluffing was in order and might lead the discussion away from my boring neuroses. "And Percy will realize it, too, or at least the sheriff will, when he eventually gets here. Then their attention will turn to anyone who was alone—without an alibi, as they say, between the time Dr. Elsass left the cocktail party and when I found him around seven."

Any pretense of conducting a Talking Cure therapy session had flown away. His eyes grew as round as his spectacles, and a bead of sweat appeared on his brow, despite the chill seeping in through the window glass. "Are you referencing me?"

"I hear you were out of pocket."

"Pocket?" He patted the breast pocket of his suit coat, his expression quizzical.

"Ah, not where you should have been. Where were you between six and seven?"

Challenged and confused by American idioms, he seemed to forget for a moment that I had no real authority to question him about his movements. "At six o'clock, I was returning from Chicago."

"How did that take you all afternoon? The snow didn't start until around six."

"I attend mosque at noon each Friday. Chicago is the closest place for congregational prayer—salat al-jama'ah." He looked at me square in the face, inviting a challenge. "It is my responsibility."

I held up my hands in a calming gesture. "I don't care. Good for you if you like it."

"When the service was over, I had mint tea with the imam and some other friends." He smiled. "It was good to talk for a while. To receive counsel from people who understand. I left Chicago after two."

I nodded. "You're all alone here. I don't know that I've ever met a Mohammedan before. Even in St. Louis."

"We are there. And prefer you say 'Muslim.' But to explain my delay. As I said, I enjoyed some social time after the service. As the weather from the west appeared more threatening, I began my journey home to the Institute. I stopped along the road at sunset for evening prayer."

Now it was my turn to be confused. "You'd just gone to church. Didn't that count for the whole day?"

He laughed at me, but it wasn't mean. I think maybe he enjoyed talking to me like a normal person rather than a patient. "No, it did not." He placed the pen and notepad he'd been holding on the small table at his side. "We pause throughout the day to thank Allah for his goodness and ask for his guidance."

I nodded. "That sounds very comforting. A scheduled reset as things get to be—"

"—too much? But I want to return to you and your problems. I'm here to listen." By way of illustration, he relaxed into the chair. "This is your therapy session, you know."

And I was there to listen, too. But I had to give him something. "I'm concerned about people being falsely accused over this death." I scooted to the edge of my seat and leaned toward him. "Like you, for instance. Are you sure Dr. Elsass was murdered? And what about the cook, Mrs. Holmes? Could...her injury be an accident?"

"I thank you for your worry on my behalf." He made a half-bow, still seated. "And yes, I am sure about the director. As his body warmed, clear lividity—bruising—appeared around his neck and shoulders, inconsistent with a fall. As for Mrs. Holmes, the coal cellar was locked from the outside. If I were the criminal, I would use my position to hide this evidence."

"That makes sense, but you don't know these people like I do. Please indulge me and answer a few questions about yesterday. I'm trying to understand all this, to piece it together in my mind."

"Mrs. Humphrey." He nodded. Perhaps he was trying to take me seriously, but I doubted it. "So engaged with reality. Remarkable."

His condescension was irritating, but I put that aside for the moment. "I've told you lots of personal stuff over the past few weeks," I said. "I think you owe me a little."

He picked up his pen and opened the notepad. "That's not the way it works. But I will aid your 'investigation,' as I deem it to be therapeutic." He jotted down a few sentences. "I could submit a paper on this for publication. At least a case study." He settled back in his chair. "Please, continue."

"So, you stopped along the road to pray. About where? And did anyone see you?" I wished I had a notepad of my own. Of course, I wouldn't be allowed possession of a pen.

"I wouldn't think so. Perhaps a farmer, gathering his livestock against the coming storm. I went to a peaceful, secluded location that I enjoy, in the woodlands, not far off Route 4. It was about 5:30."

"And you arrived here, after dark, obviously. Most everyone was inside, either at the cocktail party or dealing with the patients' dinner. As you were parking the car, did you see anyone?"

He at least pretended to think on that, long and hard, as if reviewing the events of the previous day one by one. "As I pulled into the car park, someone went in the back way. The kitchen door. Almost immediately, they exited and moved into the shadows."

"Did you know who it was?"

"No, although my impression was of someone... familiar. But..." He closed his eyes in concentration. "As I walked through the ice and snow to the kitchen entrance, I thought—"

"Someone else was out there?"

Dr. Cole opened his eyes. "It's the strangest thing. I remember noting... something... at the time. Something out of place. But it is like a blank in my memory." He scribbled some notes. "This is most interesting. I can't imagine why I wouldn't be able to remember." He went on writing, murmuring, "Transient ischemic attack? Surely not. Transient global amnesia?"

I left Dr. Cole in the therapy office as the hall clock chimed two. Walking past the parlor, I heard quiet voices and peeped in to see Sean and Percy Emerson, deep in conversation over coffee. My colleague was on the job. Although not particularly bright or insightful, I'd always found Sean reliable and persistent. Of course, that binding spell last September didn't hurt. I smiled a little, both ashamed of my ethical lapse and unreasonably proud of myself for such a successful working.

I do regret treating him that way. It hadn't been right. I wondered how many other people I'd used as means to my own goals. Maybe not with magic, but in other ways; the ways my position in society allowed. Or using the loyalty of my friends. A sobering thought, which wiped the grin off my face.

So, this is where I berate myself about Kyffin, I thought. My sister had nearly killed my oldest friend in September.

The whole situation felt like my fault. I'd manipulated them together, determined to fix everyone's social problems with a convenient lavender marriage. I gave little thought to the downside or the dangers.

I needed air. I was supposed to go talk to Blanche next, but I made my way to the side porch exit instead and slipped on someone's jacket left hanging on a peg near the door. Sean would find me when he had something to say, of that, I was sure.

I'd noticed the snow had started up again when I'd walked to my "therapy session" not even an hour ago, but, once more, it had stopped. A chill ran up my spine, but not from being cold. In fact, the air felt warm, unnaturally warm, after the morning's icy start.

Melt dripped off icicles festooning the holly and pine boughs that Finn and Teddy had hung over the porch eaves. The air was still, and the snow was mushy, melting on the porch chairs. To the west, green-black clouds rolled across the prairie. It would snow yet again before very long. Yet lightning flashed as the clouds mumbled and rumbled at each other. Maybe they brought rain.

From here, I could see the grove of ash trees—Nerthus's Grove, Finn called it. And hear it, much more clearly than indoors, with all the hustle and bustle of people.

The Grove seemed to have its own climate, with wind rubbing the branches against each other and fog enveloping the trees. I turned away from it to stare at a wind turbine over on Finn's farmstead portion of the property. The day was quiet, but for the Grove whispering to me, as it had since I arrived here, words I couldn't quite make out. At least that annoying voice in my head was silent. For the moment.

"You look a little worried there, Mrs. Humphrey."

Startled, I just about bolted into the house, only to see Comfrey rounding the corner of the mansion. I took a deep breath of relief at her friendly face. "Oh, I was wondering if more snow is on the way. That would further delay the sheriff. You know," I waved back at the house, "about all this."

Comfrey carried a gathering basket, full of plant snippets and a small pair of shears. She climbed the shoveled-and-cindered steps to join me on the porch.

I generally enjoyed talking with Comfrey, unusual in that I don't enjoy talking to anyone. I assumed she was the gardener, although she paid little attention to the deliberate landscaping in favor of encouraging the wildflowers and digging about among the fence rows and wooded areas. Comfrey was almost always around when I took a walk or even just stepped out for a breath of air on the porch.

She wore a thin jacket, and her red curls were tucked under a woolen shawl. "You should have something on your head and neck," she said, handing me a headscarf.

"I'm only out here for a minute." But I wrapped it over my head and tied it under my chin. "What are you doing today?"

"That snow yesterday came up all of a sudden. I missed the last of my fall collecting. Trying to salvage what I can."

The trees rustled and whispered, vying for my attention. Concerned she might hear a message meant for me alone, I glanced at Comfrey.

"My oh my," she said. "They are in a state, aren't they? That's something else I didn't get to before the snow."

I felt a twinge of hope—someone else could hear the strange things that I heard—but wasn't sure I could trust her. "Who's in a state?"

Her expression held a little pity and a lot of impatience. "The Grove, of course. Don't act like you don't have any idea what's going on around here."

"Me? The trees?"

"Mrs. Humphrey—"

"Please call me Violet."

"I might just do that. It's time, I think. Things are moving fast, Violet. And that old one, he's talking to you, ain't he? Wanting you to do things?"

I stared out at the western horizon. The clouds were closing in on us, preternaturally fast, as if summoned. I wondered by whom.

"Who are you, Comfrey?" I said, watching the storm front. "Why are you here? I have my doubts you even work for the Institute."

"Fair enough, fair enough," she chuckled. "My story doesn't matter much. I'm here for the land. And for you. And, no, they don't pay me, which don't make me much different than the rest of them."

I turned to her. "I don't understand."

"You're mostly connected with the stars, ain't you? But you feel the land, too, Mrs.—Violet. Its taint. And you can hear him, the source of it all." She tsk-tsked and gestured vaguely at the mansion. "Of all the places on earth to put a home for folks with diseases of the mind, this is the worse."

"Because of...'a taint' on the land? Who are you talking about?"

"An old power. With its own ways."

I felt quite nervous, thinking on the voice I'd been hearing in my head, but laughed to cover up my worry. "Oh, ghosts, is it? Is the mansion built on an old burial mound?"

Comfrey glanced down at her feet, sighed, then glared at me. "Now, what's that supposed to mean? You of all people—you have Osage kin. By all that's sacred, you know better. Or should know better." She glanced at the house. "We don't have a lot of time. I'm here to help you."

The screen door slammed, and I heard footsteps creak across the porch. "Violet." Sean tipped his hat to Comfrey. "Ma'am."

Grateful for an escape from the bizarre conversation, I seized his arm. "Miss Comfrey—this is my friend, Sean Joye. Over here to visit from St. Louis."

"Pleased to meet you," he said.

"I'm Comfrey Rouse—was a Calhoun, but I left him long ago. You the one that brought the director's secret wife along?"

"That was me. But she was a secret?"

She chuckled. "Oh, to some, to some. I weren't all that surprised. The director liked to walk with me about the property and chatter away."

"So, you were the doctor's doctor," he said.

"In a way."

"That sky is a fright," Sean said, filling the awkward silence. The dark green clouds had taken on a purplish tinge as they reflected the lightning. "And the wind's picking up. Don't you ladies want to come inside?"

"Yes," I seized on the escape strategy. "Let's go in by the fire."

Comfrey shot me a freezing glance. "You're gonna want to listen to me."

I ripped the headscarf off my head and returned it to Comfrey, dragging Sean into the house. "I will. Soon. We'll have a coffee. I've got to talk to Mr. Joye right now."

Violet

CHAPTER NINETEEN

...a subtle link subsisted between the natural beauty of the spot and the dark crimes which under the mask of religion were often perpetrated there...

~From *The Golden Bough* (1917), James George Frazer.

I slammed my bedroom door behind us. "You don't have a drink on you by any chance?"

He shrugged out of his topcoat and dropped it along with his hat on my bed. "No. I don't work for the Judge anymore, so no need to lug poteen around in my pockets. I could go get you some tea, which is likely more in order in this situation, if you don't mind my advice."

"Forget it." I kicked off my shoes, tossed aside his things, and flung myself on the bed.

"What's got your back up?"

"Comfrey. She was saying strange things."

"About the deaths?"

"More about..." I couldn't seem to form the words to describe the voice in my head, and exactly what it had said. "The land here. Curses or something."

"Hey, I heard about that today, too." He thumbed through the pages of a small notebook as he sat next to me. "Here we go—"

I buried my head under the pillow. "Don't tell me the house is haunted."

"Well, not exactly—"

"What did Percy say to you? Surely, he's not imaginative enough to be spooked."

"No, Emerson had no complaints in that department. He thinks there's something hinky going on with the finances. And that the Talking Cure is a bunch of hooey."

I sat up on the bed, crossed my legs under me, and hugged the pillow. "That makes sense. Dr. Elsass's money troubles."

Sean tapped his notebook with a pencil stub he'd fished out of his pocket. "I'd say we can't eliminate Emerson from suspicion: He had a blow-up with Elsass between six and half past. Emerson claims to have stormed off, intent on leaving right then and there. Went out to find his driver."

"Did anyone see him?"

"He talked to the kitchen staff; Lottie confirms it. But that's not really an alibi. It puts him wandering around the Institute grounds at the critical time."

"Did he find the chauffeur?"

"Not right away. Says the driver was drunk in the men's dorm. Need to check on that."

"So, no one saw him?"

"He saw a car pull up, so if that person also saw him—"

"Oh, that must have been Dr. Cole." I plumped the pillow as I cast my mind back to our discussion. "At least that confirms he did return just when he said he did. I suppose he could have gone out to the well, bashed Dr. Elsass, and come back to the house in half an hour."

"We could check his wellies, if they haven't been cleaned yet."

"He went out to supervise the men bringing in the body, so muddy boots wouldn't mean much."

Sean consulted his notes. "Now, this is interesting. Emerson thinks someone else was out there, too. He only heard a noise."

"Creepy. But maybe it was me."

He nodded without cracking a smile. "As you say. Creepy."

If there was anyone I could talk to about uncanny events, it was Sean. We'd seen the worst together. "You said someone told you about a curse?"

"Yeah, the maids are local. Apparently, when Finn's father owned the place, there were a lot of strange goings on."

"Strange how?"

He hesitated, as if he couldn't find the words. I'd never seen him without something to say. That alone told me the situation was serious. And real, no delusion of my damaged mind.

"Ain't I wondering if the Good Folks might be involved. Or your New World fae that the old Osage and Shawnee believed in." He scratched his head. "But maybe not."

I had spent enough time among witches in Great Britain to know what he meant by "Good Folks"—faeries. And, it was true, our region's natives had some similar lore. "Hmm, I've never connected the old world fae with Grandfather's Osage stories. An interesting thought. But you have doubts?"

"I took a stroll through that grove earlier. It feels different than a fae-touched spot. And that well. I'm used to watery places of power; Ireland is lousy with holy wells. But this one feels just the opposite.

"Whether old man Osteen—Finn's father—was aiming to summon an entity or just control a force he couldn't get rid of, it's hard to say." He bit his lower lip, lost, once again, in my problems.

"Summon an entity? Like my husband did?" *Like I tried to do.* I knew that's what he was thinking.

Sean just shrugged, as if such things weren't all that remarkable. He spends a lot of energy, I realized, projecting himself as someone older, smarter, and taller. Trying to be a much harder case than a twenty-four-year-old had any right to be.

A few months ago, I watched him coolly shoot a man— my husband, Taylor Humphrey. I still couldn't completely believe Taylor had utterly dissembled the entire time we were together. *Was every understanding word and kind gesture a lie?* I blinked away a few annoying tears and focused instead on the person in front of me. Taylor threatened us with lethal force, both magical and mundane. Most likely, Sean's quick action had saved the lives of everyone in that room. But at what cost to him? How does a person go on after killing someone? Someone they knew and, perhaps, liked, at least a little?

There was so much I didn't know about this strange young Irishman who, as things had worked out, might be my only friend. I wondered if I should try, yet again, to talk to him about the voice. *Would the voice allow it?* It hadn't, up until now. "So, an evil entity attached to the land, no alibi, is clearly a suspect. As is a wealthy St. Louis businessman. Anyone else?"

Sean laughed. "The director hasn't paid his staff, maybe his other bills, in months. So, anyone could have gotten sore over that."

I thought about that, rubbing my temples. "This attack, or whatever it was, likely wasn't planned. A heated argument, a bit of shoving, and he fell on the ice."

"Don't forget the bruises on the throat. Those don't happen by accident."

I scooted to the edge of the bed and picked up a shoe. "We need to see the financial records for ourselves. And Dr. Cole's notes about the postmortem exam."

"You're the boss." He handed me my other shoe.

"And we're needing exactly what now?" Sean asked me. He was once again bent over the doorknob to Dr.

Cole's basement lab, manipulating lockpicks, and I held a lantern aloft.

Upstairs, the board members were gathered at dueling late-afternoon events: cocktails hosted by head nurse Carrie and mint tea and cookies served by Dr. Cole. The two of them had spent their snowed-in Saturday politicking for control of the Institute. Dr. Cole centered his strategy on cultivating the widow Elsass's favor, while Carrie lobbied for the Board's ultimate responsibility and their obligation to name her administrator. It was the perfect time for a more thorough search of Dr. Cole's lab, if there was a perfect time.

My visit with Dr. Elsass's body earlier in the day had upset me more than I cared to admit. More than anything, I'd wanted to send Sean down here alone. But I guess I didn't trust him to see everything that I could see.

"Clues of any sort," I said, "but mainly notes about Dr. Cole's exam of the body." A chill ran up my spine, and I shivered. "We—could examine the body, I guess." That, I'd rather not do. But sometimes the only way forward is through the hard thing.

"There, got it." The hinges squeaked open. "I was thinking when we were here earlier, it's a bit of a sturdy lock for an old barn like this place. Shiny and new."

I held up the lantern so I could find the light switch. "I don't trust Percy Emerson. He'll get tired of accusing Carrie and move on to someone else. Or accuse me again. I only have an alibi for the time that Mrs. Holmes was attacked."

He laughed. "They're too cowed by your family name and money—"

"I don't have any family money," I said. "Gone with father's—unwise—investments, apparently." After father's death, the true financial status of his brokerage firm was discovered.

I'd been thinking long and hard about why our family man of business hadn't paid my bills from the trust. He'd obviously thought the funds were there when he had me admitted to the Institute. Then wisps of memory, facts that seemed inconsequential at the time, started to come back. Father's late-night phone calls, his tone hushed, but the whispers alternately angry and cajoling. And his trips to Havana for reasons he'd never explained.

"Ah, your sister must have paid her lawyer by selling her exclusive, made-up story to the rags."

"Of course; I wondered how she could afford Jimmy Peel. OK, find some proof of what happened here."

Although we'd visited the lab earlier in the day, I hadn't really taken in the space properly in my agitated state and with Evie distracting me. It was as tidy and cold as Dr. Cole himself. And it was *his* lab, reflecting his true interest—somatic psychiatry, the equipment a cobbled-together array of salvaged bits and pieces. I took a moment to ground myself, to relax, and to open my senses. His workspace, especially the desk, glowed deep blue.

A noise distracted me; rabbits rustling in their straw-lined cages, and I lost my sense of Dr. Cole's aura permeating his work area.

To my more mundane visual inspection, the desktop was clear. "I imagine the notes are filed somewhere. Maybe locked in the desk." Sean rattled each drawer, then went to work with his lockpicks. I drifted over to the sheet-covered corpse on the battered, old table, compelled to check yet again for the gently up-and-down chest movement I'd seen earlier. He appeared to be thoroughly dead, and no disturbing voices claimed otherwise. I sense no psychic evidence—color, odor, or proprioception.

Sean had the desk unlocked in short order, and we searched it without success. Then I moved on to the cupboards while he rifled through a file cabinet. We found nothing useful.

"Dr. Cole must have written *something* down about the examination." Vexed, I approach the animal cages, five of them stacked on rough planks supported by sawhorses. The rabbits twitched their pink noses in the air and ambled over to the cage doors.

"Well, hi, there." I offered my hand to a small white rabbit for sniff inspection from what I hoped was a safe distance. When it didn't make a move to bite, I hazarded to stroke its side with my index finger through an opening in the wires. "Oh, no." I turned to Sean. "Their water bottles are empty."

He closed the desk drawer. "Don't see nothing about the stiff. Dr. Cole must be carrying his notes around with him."

I unscrewed the bottle from the first cage and went to the sink. "I guess with all the excitement and confusion, he forgot the animals." A hose connected to a water tap was lying in the sink. "Here's the water."

"I doubt very much Dr. Cole feeds his own lab animals." Sean began removing the other bottles. "Appears he's had an escapee."

"What do you mean?" I replaced the now full bottle, and the cage's occupant immediately commenced to lick the spout. "Oh, poor things! Go get them some carrots or something—"

Sean was focused on the empty cage. "See this here, how it's open?"

"Maybe that was the leader. Went to get help."

We filled the rest of the water bottles, then Sean pointed at the dissection area. "I'm thinking the escape theory ain't gonna hold up."

The electric lamp was so dim I turned up the wick on the still-lit lantern I'd brought. I was afraid he was showing me a dead rabbit, but all I saw was a stainless steel tray soiled with a brown, crusty residue and small bits of fur. "Is that blood?"

"I'd say so." He watched my face.

Does he think I'm going to faint? Go catatonic at the sight of rabbit blood? Although I had to admit I didn't feel well. I staggered to a swivel stool near a microscope desk.

"I'll find someone to feed these bunnies," Sean said. "You might need to have a bit of a lie down, as soon as you feel like walking upstairs."

I nodded, examining each detail of the microscope to keep my eyes from straying over to the blood-tinged tray. A slide was on the microscope's stage. "What's this?"

"I'm sure I don't know. Some tiny bit of the stiff?"

I switched on the small electric bulb fixed to illuminate the microscope's stage and looked through the eyepiece, turning it to focus. I saw light pink blobs arrayed in a darker pink, granular matrix. It was quite interesting, and I once again regretted my lack of a real education. My finishing school's curriculum certainly didn't cover cell biology. But beyond that, I also felt it was significant to the death. Why, I couldn't say.

I switched off the lamp, removed the glass slide, and stood. "Have you a handkerchief?"

"Why don't you women ever have your own?" But he gave me one. "I didn't pack a whole valise of these things, you know. What did you find?"

"I don't know, but…it feels important." I wrapped it in the cloth. "We'll have to ask —"

I heard the hinges creak again and saw Finn Osteen standing in the doorway. He held a hurricane lantern and a pail brimming with vegetable scraps in one hand, a small bundle of hay tucked under his other arm. Our eyes met. "Mrs. Humphrey, what—"

"I can but apologize for being the nosy parker," Sean stepped between us. "All the accusing and counter-accusing around here got my back up over my client's prospects and, well—"

"You thought you'd snoop around a bit, your own self." Finn placed the lantern on the table and sat his burdens down on the lab bench. "You city folk, think you own the place."

"Now, Finn," I said, suddenly so frightened at his tone that I forgot the differences in our station and to demand the respect due to me.

"Now nothing, Mrs. Humphrey. I've about had it." His hands clench and unclench as he strode across the space to Sean. I wondered which man was in more danger. Finn must be dead tired and weary to the bones, but he towered over Sean. *Did my friend still carry a gun?* That alarmed me even more. Sean shooting the handyman would not help the situation at all.

Sean raised his hands as he inched away. "Didn't mean to intrude. But let's send Mrs. Humphrey upstairs. I didn't want to leave her alone with those board members, but perhaps she don't need to be seeing you and me sort things out."

Finn looked ready to fight, but he glanced at the rabbits in their cages, lapping up water from their bottles. He sighed and plopped down in the desk chair.

"You're as close to a court officer as we have at the moment, I expect. But how did you get in?"

"Lab was open," I said.

"Dr. Cole is pretty particular."

I didn't think Finn was buying my silly story.

"I'm sure he was in a hurry," Sean said. "Mrs. Humphrey was concerned about these animals."

"Me, too," Finn said. "We've all been meeting ourselves coming and going. Teddy normally cares for them, but with one thing and another…" He walked over to the cages with the food pail, and the rabbits rushed to their cage doors.

"So, we'll be on our way," I said, moving toward the exit, but noticed a worried expression on Finn's face. "What's wrong?"

He was staring at the empty cage. "I was afraid of this," He bit his lip. "Didn't want to believe it."

"Oh, the escapee?" said Sean. "Animals get hungry enough…"

"No, no," the caretaker said. "Like I say, it's been a blur. But when I was working on the furnace and stoker yesterday, I found—" His face twisted in distaste. "A dead rabbit. Sort of butchered, but poorly."

"Oh, no. How upsetting." I sank back to the stool.

Finn went from cage to cage, opening each and offering a handful of food. "Someone had thrown it in the furnace, not realizing it was on the fritz, I reckon."

He watched the animals eat for a moment, then turned to us. "It was one of Doc Cole's animals, though he never done nothing like that before—sneaking the body into the furnace and just leaving it." He removed one of the rabbits from its cage. "You want to hold her, Mrs. Humphrey? Tending the bunnies always puts me in a calmer frame of mind."

I wasn't so sure about that, but accepted the rabbit, tentatively stroking it.

"When you get tired of her, just set her down to stretch her legs." I thought that was a much better idea, and gently lowered the bunny to the ground.

"Just gotta keep that lab door closed," Sean said.

"Yeah," Finn laughed, scooping out the soiled litter into a trash can. "Doc is strict about that, which is why you gave me such a turn. Mind now, these ain't pets; they're scientific animals."

Finn certainly wasn't treating them like anything but pets as he removed the next one from its cage, stroked it, and set it down to hop about the lab. I bet Teddy pampered and played with them also.

"Sure he 'sacrificed'—that's the scientific word—one every now and then." Finn cleared out the soiled bedding. "Needed to do things to its brain and whatnot. But if he wants a carcass destroyed, he asks me to do it. Makes it respectful, somehow. Anyway, it slipped my mind to ask Doc about that bunny in the furnace. I'll tell him, straightaway."

Sean

CHAPTER TWENTY

Section 20. *Be it further enacted. That any person committing sodomy or the infamous crime against nature, with mankind or beast, shall on the conviction thereof be fined…imprisoned… whipped…*

~From *An Act Respecting Crimes and Punishments.*
Approved March 23, 1819, Laws of the State of Illinois
Enacted by the General Assembly.

Violet glanced at the wall clock, which showed it was almost five PM. "I imagine that I'm still expected to set the table for the evening meal."

Finn Osteen nodded. "They may all be arguing about who's in charge, but the people that really run the place are sticking to good order."

She caught my eye, gave me a curt little nod, and moved to leave. About back to her old self, I thought. Lady of the manor. "I'll just stay here for a bit," I said, "and give Mr. Osteen a hand. Keep the bunnies in line."

Her hand on the doorknob, she turned back, looking a mite surprised. Was it my sudden interest in rabbits or that I weren't jumping at her every command? We could discuss that later.

Three rabbits were hopping about the lab. "Mind the coneys don't get out," I said to her as she left us.

"I don't really need help." Osteen handed me the final rabbit and began pulling the soiled litter out of its cage. "But thanks."

"Nice to meet you, rabbit," I said, scratching behind its ears. "You might want to stretch your legs a bit." I sat the animal on the rough cement floor. "Lived here all your life?"

Osteen went on working.

"Mr. Osteen?"

He looked up. "Oh, you're talking to me, not the rabbit. And you can call me Finn. Everyone does. Short for Finley; nobody but Doc Cole ever calls me that. No, I grew up here but got out as soon as I could. After the army, I lived in Springfield."

"And now you're here?"

"Well," Finn continued his work, "My father passed. I had to settle his affairs." He spread clean litter on the cage floor.

"So, wouldn't this house have come to you?"

Finn didn't answer. I suspected he might actually be a talker if you got him wound up, but he was cautious. Trying to decide how much he wanted me to know. "My own da passed real sudden," I said. Murdered by the police auxiliary in Belfast, but I didn't see any good in bringing that up. "But I had older brothers to deal with the property and such." My mam being out of the picture.

Finn grabbed a rabbit to return it to the cage. "There isn't anyone but me. And I found Dad had settled the property himself—sold most everything to Dr. Elsass." The bunny squirmed in his arms. He held it maybe a bit too tight.

"Here now, I can take that coney off your hands."

Finn surrendered the rabbit. "The thing is, the land's been in my family since my grandfather, old Jürgen, came over from Germany."

I nodded. "Must be hard to work here, as an employee, I mean. Didn't I see a little farmstead across the road? People keep running over there to try the phone. That your place?"

He wiped his brow with a bandana and shoved the rag in the back pocket of his overalls. "So, that's the thing. Dad left me a letter, saying that the cottage and attached grounds was mine if I wanted them. But Elsass claims—claimed—that he'd bought the whole place and that him and dad had a rental agreement for the cottage—work for lodging there. He'd let my father stay on since he didn't currently need the space."

"And you took the job over?" I returned the rabbit to its clean cage and gave it a handful of chopped veg.

"It's a long story." Finn changed over the litter in the next dirty cage as I leaned against the lab bench and watched the rabbits nose about the room.

At last, he spoke. To me or the bunnies, it was hard to say. "I made a good friend when I lived in Springfield.

189

Tomás—" Finn's tone turned flat, words measured and neutral. "I rented a room from Tomás for years—he's a widower—got to know him and his son, Teddy. Like family, almost."

He turned and jutted his chin, a sudden chip on his shoulder. "Like a...brother. And Tomás was interested in living on a farm. His family are greengrocers, you see? He knows his vegetables, but growing them was his dream. I wanted to return the favor and make a place for him in my home."

I captured a rabbit chewing on my trouser leg and handed it to Finn, who put it in a clean cage. "You ready for the others?"

"A few more minutes of freedom won't hurt."

"You know," I said, again relaxing against the bench as if I hadn't a care in the world, "if 'like family' means 'this is my family—my mate in this life and our child,' that would be OK."

Finn blanched, then turned red. "No, no, no. Nothing like that." He strode across the room to trap a rabbit under the autopsy table, grabbing it by the scruff of its neck. "Why would you say that?"

"I mean you and yours no harm. It's a fine thing to find love and a family."

Finn just glared. "I ain't no fairy."

"Never said you were." I needed this fella to trust me and didn't have a lot of time to devote to the task. "I thought I found real love a couple of times. Odd that I could court a lying, traitorous lass at home in Belfast freely enough, but loving the most honorable, generous man in the city of St. Louis needs be a secret."

Finn returned his captive to its home. "Alright. You know, then. Can't be too careful. People will get hurt."

I thought of Kyffin and nodded. Hurt in all sorts of unexpected ways.

"I pegged you as sweet on Mrs. Humphrey." Finn binned the final cage's old litter. "Following her around like a puppy dog."

"Ouch." I'd caught the final rabbit, and it promptly bit me. "Mrs. Humphrey is a dazzling dame; I can't deny that. Not sure things would ever work out for us. Most likely, she wouldn't want them to."

I handed the animal to Finn and resolved to leave future rabbit wrangling to the professionals. "I remind her of bad memories." Not to mention I'm the fella that shot her husband. He was a raving homicidal lunatic at the time, but still. "Now that we've tended the rabbits and put all our cards on the table, what exactly did Elsass have on you?" I returned to my pipe.

Finn gave the last rabbit a bowl of veg and shut up the hutch. "At first, he was…nice, I guess, in a hoity-toity sort of way. I just wanted to bury my father. Elsass made it clear he didn't think he owed me nothing, but I was welcome to take over the caretaker job from Dad and live in the cottage. He didn't act like he realized, or maybe he just didn't care, that Tomás and I love each other." He watched me for a reaction, I guess. I simply nodded and gave him room to talk.

"I want to get the property back, a legacy for Teddy, although I don't see how I'll ever afford it. But Elsass wouldn't even discuss it."

"I see." Actually, I didn't see. But I suspected Elsass had blackmailed Finn into working for free.

"But here lately, this past summer, things changed. He decided I needed to be paying him rent. How could I do that? He don't pay me hardly anything, and Tomás's truck patch is the only other source of cash we got. Then the director started not paying anyone at all. Not Teddy or the other kids." His voice rose, working up a good head of steam. "I told him he was welcome to this cursed land. We're out of here—I'd take me and mine to Springfield or St. Louis—maybe Teddy would rather be there, anyway, with all his old school friends."

Finn appeared ready to hit something. Or someone. I retreated a bit.

"Then he started in with the hints and threats about me and Tomás. He had connections to the county sheriff, he said. Even the state police. We might move, but the cops, they talk to each other." He grabbed my coat sleeve. "You won't say nothing, will you, mister? For the boy's sake?"

Violet

CHAPTER TWENTY-ONE

You are hereby commanded to appear at the Piasa Lodge Thirty-Fifth Annual Ball given in honor of our revered visitor Chief Ouatoga, ruler of Cahokia and all its environs, and his Beautiful Court of the Confluence. St Louis, Saturday, February 1, 1913, eight o'clock in the evening. Civil Courts Building.

~From invitation, Piasa Lodge 1913 Debutante Ball.

"Not tonight, Violet. I'm giving you the evening off," said Carrie as I sat down with the most impaired patients at their feeding table. I shivered from the cold draft through the partially opened window—the radiators were on full blast, and I was both too hot and cold at the same time.

"You always help so much with the old dears." She pried the spoon from my hand and shooed me away. "Sit down and eat properly yourself. I'm helping with the meal service tonight." One of the female patients trundled by with a cart, and the maid overseeing her work began distributing plates of food.

"Are you sure?" The head nurse seldom appeared at mealtime. Although with the cook injured, I supposed everyone was pressed into service. "And how is Mrs. Holmes?"

Carrie grimaced, then set her expression in a bright, fake smile. "As well as can be expected, I suppose." She took my place at the feeding table and offered a spoonful of applesauce to a gentleman staring out the window. As sleet struck the windowpanes, his toothless mouth smacked, and his tongue licked his lips in anticipation.

"Off you go," she said to me. I buttoned my cardigan up to the neck and glanced around the room. I didn't have a usual place here; either someone had fed me, which I didn't remember, or I'd been helping the others. Then I spied Blanche. She must be having a bad day; Teddy was bringing her to dinner in her wheelchair. Her face was pale and drawn, and her shoulders slumped. I wasn't sure if that made it a good time to question her about Dr. Elsass's murder, or not, but I decided to try.

"Mind if I join you?" I said, pulling out a chair opposite her at a small corner table. It was clearly intended for the most functional of the patients, set for two with a tablecloth, a late autumn flower arrangement in a bud vase, and heavy molded-glass goblets. Just spoons, though, for utensils. The Institute trusted the patients only so far.

Blanche looked up, surprised, and nodded. "Of course." She grimaced. "I guess we're both sent back down."

I didn't understand. "'Down?' From where?"

"Oh, the real dining room. With the real people." She took a sip of her water. "I don't mind, though. All those old doctors. So boring. Ibrahim—I mean—Dr. Cole—is the only lively one of the lot. He'll be a much better director than Elsass was."

Blanche's open disrespect for the dearly departed director surprised me, but I nodded. "Dr. Cole is quite smart, I think, but perhaps the Board will find him too... young for the job." I sat down, draping the napkin in my lap. "Dr. Elsass allowed you to eat with your husband in the 'real dining room.' That's something in his favor."

Blanche made a face just as the patient on meal-service duty, a pale, thin middle-aged woman, arrived with a basket of rolls. "Sorry," the server muttered.

"You don't need to apologize, Ruth," said the young maid supervising her. "You're here to give them their supper. They're happy to see you."

"Of course we are," I said, accepting the butter dish.

"Sorry," she repeated, steadily watching her own wringing hands.

"That's all she says," the maid told us as she set the plates of food on the table. "Doesn't actually matter who she's with or what she's done or hasn't done."

"Thank you, Martha," Blanche said to the maid, then to me, "Oh, Percy didn't come here to see me."

"Board business, you mean?"

Blanche shrugged. "Our late director was interested in all sorts of illnesses. Especially if a good fee was involved."

I thought Percy Emerson a total ass, but it was interesting that perhaps his wife agreed. And here was yet another person pointing out how strapped for cash Dr. Elsass was. I diverted the conversation in a new direction, aiming to come around to Percy and money later from a different angle. "You seem a little tired, if you don't mind me saying so."

Blanche stared at me. "What do you mean by that?"

"I…I…I'm just concerned. It's not a criticism."

Blanche's face relaxed. "Sorry. I am…a little weak today." She slapped her right leg. "Polio is such a bore. Ibrahim keeps telling me how blessed I am to have recovered so well, but…"

I made a vague but, I hoped, sympathetic sound and struggled to scoop up a bite of Waldorf salad with my spoon. "How old were you?" I remembered Blanche, vaguely, from our debut year, the whirl of parties, balls, tableaus, and "civic service" events each spring that the eighteen-year-old girls—no, women—underwent. Although our families treated us like children—children being put on the marriage market. I wasn't aware of any of the debs wearing a leg brace, but I had to admit I wasn't paying particular attention, either.

"Right after the Piasa Lodge ball," Blanche said. "I might have caught it there. Several of us got sick. Although I think you were off to England shortly thereafter." Blanche started eating, tearing off bits of bread to pop them into her mouth.

She really doesn't like me, I realized. Someone else I've wronged? "I do remember you among the debs, but did I snub…"

Blanche laughed. "I *am* being a bitch, aren't I? Your set was so high above me, perhaps I just imagined you were looking down. But you probably weren't looking at all."

I shrugged. "I don't know about 'high' and all. I don't think I snubbed anyone. I was so uncomfortable all the time. Miserable, really. Just thinking about how to get away."

"And you did. Went to England and—" Blanche's voice dropped, "and became a witch."

I laughed. "And you became an artist. Sounds just as disreputable."

Blanche laughed out loud, her eyes merry and cheeks flushed. "No, no—I'm a watercolorist. Of flowers and domestic scenes. Dr. Elsass told Percy that sort of art is alright. Anything more—stimulating—would exacerbate my 'hysterical condition.' But I always wanted to study in Paris. Figure drawing. Oil painting—I have tried my hand at it here, a little. Ibrahim says I need to see the masterpieces in the museums. And learn at the great schools of art."

"I agree." I turned my attention to the slivers of fried ham and potatoes. "You do need to go to Paris. Surely Percy can get over himself long enough to arrange that."

Blanche's face glowed as she laughed.

"And Italy would be so good for you," I continued. "Warm weather, art everywhere. Good food. Good wine. My grandfather is—was," my heart skipped a beat, his recent death another loss I hadn't mourned properly, "an old boring doctor, too. But he recommended wine for everything."

Blanche looked a little alarmed. "I don't know that I could manage all those steps and cobblestones."

I had a wild thought. We hadn't even considered Blanche as a suspect. "So, your walking...will it ever get better?"

Blanche didn't act offended at the personal question. "Sometimes it's better. Ibrahim is a great believer in physical training, like the Turner Society programs in St. Louis. To build up the muscles, retrain them. He's devised a regimen, which I think helps." Her face fell. "But, likely as not, I get very weak, right out of the blue."

"Can you ever walk any distance?"

She thought about that. "On a good day—a strong day—I can walk outside, around the property. I must take my time and wear the leg brace, but I've walked into the Grove before, as far as the creek." She shivered. "Spooky place."

I agreed. And Blanche had just verified she could walk almost as far as the artesian well. Who's to say she couldn't walk a little farther, if angry or excited? We need to check where Blanche was during that critical hour around Elsass's death, I thought.

Ruth returned and slid a serving of cake for each of us across the table. Her hair hung over her downcast eyes; I suspected she had been crying. I scanned the room for Carrie—someone needed to put a stop to this charade—but saw no staff members at all. "Thank you. You're doing great."

She shuffled off without reaction.

Blanche picked up her spoon. "Percy would never take me to Europe, though. He hates my art; I know it." She gulped, and her hand reached out to squeeze mine. "Maybe if you talk to him for me?"

"Do you feel safe?"

With misty eyes, she said, "My paintings will tell you everything you want to know about me. It's all there."

"Well, darling, I'll be sure to do that," a voice boomed from behind us. "Your paintings tell the whole story, eh?" Percy Emerson stood in the doorway just a few steps from our table.

Sean

CHAPTER TWENTY-TWO

The tradition of cunning folk, individuals blessed (or cursed, as seen in the sporadic uprising of witchcraft hysteria) with special knowledge and abilities in divination, influence, and healing is a common, if secret, feature of rural village life. Some practitioners confide that their ability is derived from fae realm assistance.

~From *The Heritage of the Wise Ones: Cunning Folk in Ireland, Scotland, North England, and the Isle of Man* by Vincent X. Chumbley, Herald Press, Carlisle, Scotland, 1899.

I left Finn with assurances that his secrets were safe with me and aimed to wash up for dinner. As I headed to the jacks, something I'd been putting off stirred in the back of my mind, and it was time to have at it. I lifted a mac and someone's wellies from the mudroom just off the kitchen and stepped outside, then paused on the kitchen stoop.

The sleet had ended, and the sky was clear enough for the setting sun to light up the snow-covered world before me. The air felt warm, though the cars, trees, and fields beyond glowed with ice crystals. And something else. It was all fae-touched. I crunched across the car park, trying to clear my head, crowded as it was with thoughts and memories.

I'd been at the craft only a few months, cobbling together a hodgepodge of hedge witchery tales from my youth and ceremonial magic from books. I'd managed a few possibly effective charms and a disastrous enchantment on my amnesiac lover, Kyffin. At least I had begun to develop an approach to the work, a system, if you will.

Much like a military assignment, the first step was to look around. To find the source of the energy shaping events. Because every parcel of land, street corner, and building held its secrets, its life force, as it were. "Aura" was the word, at least in Taylor Humphrey's grimoire.

I took a turn around the car park, settling myself down as much as I could manage. Then I opened myself up to the energy of the place. Most obvious were glowing smudges scattered here and there around the house's perimeter, hidden under the snow. If a regular pattern to them was intended, I sure wasn't seeing it. There'd be two or three a few feet apart, then a great gap, before a few more right on top of each other.

"If thee declare what thou seeketh, gladly assist, would I." A voice I knew all too well echoed through my mind—Éire was her name, and messing with my head and heart was her game.

She hadn't decided to physically manifest—yet—but 'twas only a matter of time. "You can't be here," I said. Aloud, 'cause I'm daft like that.

"I can and I will go whence you go. Thine familiar spirit I be."

"I don't need no familiar spirit."

"Thou doeth. To work the magical craft, as, by my troth, thou wisheth—all renown mages do employ a fairie servant." Then she dropped the Shakespearean cant and affected a twentieth-century American accent. "That's the straight lowdown, buddy."

I'd been slogging down the lane from the manor toward the farm cottage—Finn's place. Ignoring Éire as best I could, I concentrated on the snow-covered fields. My eyes were open, but I didn't see the countryside. I saw its magical energy. And, oh boy, was there a lot of it. Deep and rich, a place of primal, ancient power. Yet something else, layers of new, alien magic. And a dark purple stain.

"Interesting place, this," she said. Since I was paying her no mind in my head, Éire decided to show herself, a tall, auburn-haired beauty in a flowing green dress. "Old gods have been honored here with full rites."

"But now it's cursed," I said. "What would cause that?"

"I could help you, if our troth were plaited and bound." She smiled a glorious smile.

"Or you could help me without all the mumbo-jumbo if you really wanted to."

Éire gave a pretty pout and leaned over to kiss me, lips warm as any human and breath sweeter. My head swam for a moment as her nearness transported me to faraway green hills. I found I'd wrapped her in an embrace, pulling her close. "Oh, you do like me a wee bit, I think," she said into my ear.

"I like…" I cleared my throat, "you fine. It's just that," I put some distance between us, "you're a lying, conniving, baby-stealing faerie who I can't trust any further than I can throw you."

She tried to appear angry. "Suit yourself. And, to show my good will, here's a hint. Ask the humans about Dagon."

"Who's Dagon? Did they stop honoring…her? Him?"

"Them," Éire said. "Dagon and Hydra. Old gods; their followers praise them as Father Dagon and Mother Hydra."

"So, two old gods murdered a man?"

She shook her head. "Unlikely they'd take such direct action. And as for the two, humans often discern the dual nature of the gods and so name them as such. The Father, Son, and Holy Spirit, whom you're so fond of. Or the three Morrígna. Even Nerthus and Njord."

"The Osteens named that ash grove Nerthus. What is that—German or something?"

She shrugged, then wandered off to pack a handful of snow into a ball and throw it at my fedora. With some effort, I didn't react, much. As I retrieved my hat, I thought about other encounters I'd had in the woodlands and prairies of North America. "Before any people came from Europe with their beliefs and worship, powers were already here."

"Oh, yes." Éire, suddenly at my side, whispered in my ear. "The actual spirit of the place—the genius loci. But I don't think they care to get involved in all this. No, you'd best seek out something…else."

"Does the doctor's murder have something to do with the worship of old gods?"

"I've helped you one kiss's worth," she said. "If I were your familiar, you could command all sorts of magical help, but since you claim I am not—" Éire said with a grin, "—keep your eyes peeled."

Inside the mansion, wet and muddy despite my borrowed rain gear, I realized I'd been in such a hurry to get on the road to Illinois that I hadn't even brought a change of clothes. I gave my suit a once-over with a lint brush I found in the jacks and called it a day.

I could easily chalk up my vision of Éire and the magical landscape to a light head from missing yet another meal. That's what I told myself. Food was in order before I thought about any of the lore she'd hinted at. My grub options were to either join Violet with the patients or eat with the kitchen staff if they were in a hospitable mood.

I stood in the vacant back hall, weighing my choices. I'd about decided to go eat with Violet, when Carrie staggered into me as she stepped out of the kitchen. She was pale and a little shaky, with beads of sweat along her brow. "Oh, Mr. Joye. You startled me."

Her formality surprised me. At my last visit here, we'd gotten along like a house afire. But my immediate concern was that she seemed likely to fall. I grabbed her arm and guided her down the hall to one of the chairs in the foyer. "You don't look so good. Need a drink of water?"

"I'm just…busy. Thank you." Her gaze narrowed. "I've a lot on my mind. You, for instance. Do you have a moment to talk in private?" I didn't think she meant for another petting session.

Without waiting for a reply, she set her jaw in a determined pose, rose from the chair, and headed up the stairs. I followed her to the second floor. She stopped at a counter, much like you'd see in a store, then walked around it to an open area. Several desks, racks filled with patient charts, and storage cupboards lined the wall.

A young nurse sat at one of the desks, writing in a hospital chart. "Grace, leave us for a moment, please," Carrie said to her. "The patients should be about finished eating. You can check on them."

Grace looked flustered. "Mr. Belvedere just claimed to be Jesus. Again. I need to document—"

"Goodness, child! You'll remember his delusions for a few minutes if they were all that significant." Carrie chuckled. "Now, scoot."

The nurse returned the chart to the rack and left, her steps clicking down the hall. Carrie pointed to the now-empty chair. "Sit, 'Mr. Attorney'."

I sat, thinking maybe the jig was up. "How can I help?"

"That's just it. What *are* you doing here? *Is* it helpful?"

"I try."

"Like encouraging my staff to repeat superstitious nonsense and gossip?"

I laughed to kill some time while I thought up a good story. I suspected she didn't really object to me chatting up the kitchen staff. "We was just talking. I've never been to this part of Illinois before. Well, before October."

Carrie rocked a little and swiveled in her chair. She leaned forward. "Why'd you bring that woman here? What do you want?"

I wasn't expecting that. But maybe I should have. Carrie was the lady of the house, in a way, even if the house was an insane asylum. I'd shown up, on her most stressful day ever, with a potential rival, since Mrs. Elsass stood to inherit the place. But nobody loved their job that much. If Evie took over, surely Carrie could handle her as easily as she handled the doctor. Maybe more so.

I pulled my pipe and tobacco out of my pocket and glanced at her. "Do you mind?" I didn't really want a smoke, but felt the need to kill some time while I thought up a better cover story.

If you can't think of a good lie, you can always give the truth a try. "I was coming to see Violet anyway, and gave Mrs. Elsass a ride. The bus she was on got stuck in the snow and ice."

Carrie made a sort of harrumphing sound, her hands trailing across the fabric of her dress stretched tight across her abdomen. "And you're Violet's lawyer, so you say? You've never mentioned that before. If you're here to pay her bills, you're just a little too late. You could have saved him, you know, by paying her bills on time." She pulled a hankie out of her sleeve and dabbed a tear. "He was so, so worried, so distressed about operational funds."

I packed the pipe with tobacco and lit a match. That rang true enough. It sounded like the place was about to go under. Maybe the director had done himself in. "I'm hearing he ain't paid anyone in months."

Her snuffled turned into a quiet wailing. She nodded her head. "This type of care is very expensive to provide. Requires something like Mrs. Humphrey's resources. It's just not fair. And of course, I understand she's not well, not responsible, so you businessmen and family members, you shouldn't have abused the director's good heart." She blew her nose and glared at me.

Ah, she's gonna really tell me off, I thought. But I preferred that to the tears, truth be told.

"You're really devoted to this place." I tried for a smoke ring without success. "And Dr. Elsass." I was suddenly sure there was more to it, not that I was any expert on the ways of ladies. I hazarded to pat her hand, aiming for a neutral, comforting presence. Platonic, I believe it's called. Which was a little difficult, given she'd been pretty darn "friendly" the last time I was here. But I sensed we were pretending that little flirtation hadn't happened.

"He's—was—so brilliant. Innovative. His model of mental hygiene could have become the standard. It's both humane and effective. And I was right by his side. We were building it together." The tears stopped, and she spoke with calm authority. Her words were gospel, and she believed them, unquestioningly, her face lit up by a holy fire of devotion.

I nodded and made a vague, encouraging sound. I'd seen women in love before, and Carrie had it bad. And if she wasn't already in the family way, I was Rockefeller. "Now, it sounds like that other doctor—Cole, is it? He has a completely different take on things."

Carrie sniffed. "When did you hear that?"

"Oh, I dunno. Around. He does a lot of real scientific stuff. Animal experiments and microscopes and such."

If looks could kill, Carrie would have skewered me to the wall. "Social sciences are also real."

I could play along if she was gonna keep on pretending that Dr. Cole's brain experiments were the most interesting thing about a hutch full of bunnies. "But don't it seem more—I dunno—official, using equipment and measurements? I happened to be in his lab just now, helping Finn out with the rabbits. Dr. Cole had something under that microscope. Maybe brain cells, or whatever, dabbed onto a bit of glass. It would be great to just be able to check on something like that and see what's wrong with a sick person."

The more I talked, the more Carrie sweated. "Well…" she swallowed, "there are problems with that. People aren't rabbits. And how to get the brain cells?"

"That's true enough," I said, though in my opinion, people were very like rabbits, and among those that traffic with the fae—cunning folk, witches, faerie doctors, whatever you want to call them—rabbits were a favorite disguise. "It appears that maybe one was killed to get to its innards. Finn found a dead one in the furnace. He thinks whoever put it there didn't know the stoker was on the fritz at the moment."

She gripped the chair arms. "He...what?"

"Found a dead rabbit."

Carrie nodded, then blew her nose on a hankie and grabbed a chart, seemingly at random. She picked up a pen. "So brutal. The callousness toward animals is another problem I have with traditional medicine. They call the killing a 'sacrifice.'" She squared herself at the desk. Ready to work. "And now I need to review all the nurses' notes from the day shift. Good evening." She was giving me the bum's rush after cornering me in the first place.

I didn't think she'd really achieved much beyond chewing me out about Violet's asylum bill. Maybe that was all she wanted to say.

I thought again about my last visit here. We'd flirted a long while in a private corner of the front porch. The conversation had ended with one hell of a kiss. It was all a bit of a blur as to who started it. I would've said me, but I now pictured us in that secluded nook, right outside Elsass's office window. *Played again.* I'd bet the car I'd borrowed from Malcolm Yates that she and the late doctor were a secret item, and I'd been recruited to make him jealous. I wondered if it worked.

"You act like you've got something on your mind," I said. "You've no reason to confide in me; you don't know me at all," I arched one eyebrow, and she had the decency to blush, "but sometimes that's better. I always go to a parish on the other side of town for confession."

A hint of a smile played across her face. "I used to do that, too. Of course, living here I'm some miles from the nearest Catholic church."

I stood. "I can't offer you the sacrament, but sometimes talking is good for the soul."

Carrie bit her lips into a tight line. "That's what we do here, the Talking Cure." She lay down her pen. "Oh, is that slide—that's what you call it, the bit of glass one puts under a microscope—still there? Dr. Cole is very particular about his things."

Was he really? I took one parting shot, maybe totally off kilter. "Just between you and me, we thought the microscope slide might have something to do with Dr. Elsass's murder. We saved it for the sheriff. Dr. Cole can have it later, if it's not relevant."

She jumped to her feet. "You have it? You should give it to me. I'll lock it up in the medication cart."

"No, I don't have it." I tapped the pipe ash out into an ashtray on the counter.

"Finn has it, then? And what did he do with the dead rabbit?"

"You'd have to ask him about the bunny. Violet was there, too. She kept the slide. She's very particular about things as well." I stood. "If you don't mind, I'm gonna go see about some grub."

Violet

CHAPTER TWENTY-THREE

If a physician of high standing, and one's own husband, assures friends and relatives that there is really nothing the matter with one but temporary nervous depression—a slight hysterical tendency—what is one to do?

~From "The Yellow Wallpaper" by Charlotte Perkins Stetson, *The New England Magazine*, January 1892.

Percy grabbed one of the handles of Blanche's wheelchair. "I thought you'd like to join us in the parlor, darling. Have a brandy with me."

We'd been talking about Blanche's art. Innocuous, surely. Her eyes darted around the room, all the world like a trapped animal. They met mine. She obviously had the same question as I did—how much had he heard?

"But we were having such a nice talk," I said. "To think we've known each other for many years but never took the time to become friends." I stood and grabbed the other wheelchair handle. "The patients' evening sharing time starts in a few minutes."

"It's alright." Blanche's voice was low and meek. "Nurse Carrie won't mind if I miss it to visit with Percy. I am rather exhausted. It will be an early night for me."

"Quite right, my dear," he boomed. The room fell silent, everyone enjoying the floor show. "If you don't mind." He nudged me away from the wheelchair. "Darling, I have some new evidence about the murder. I think I've been barking up the wrong tree." Percy rolled Blanche out of the room and set out in the parlor's direction. "I suspect one of the hired help as our culprit. The director had a lot of enemies."

"Oh, really?" Blanche's voice drifted back, sounding both bored and disheartened.

"Oh, yes. We can gossip all about my latest investigations. I've got some juicy tidbits of information to share."

I gathered our plates and spoons and walked them into the kitchen, where I found Sean, eating supper and mesmerizing the assistant cook and an orderly with some fairy tale or other. He stood when I came in, and the young people looked up, their eyes dreamy.

"I don't mean to interrupt. Go on with your meal." I had an idea, but needed to ensure Percy really intended to spend the evening curled up by the fire with his wife. I doubted that very much.

"Not needing me just yet, then, are you?" He was laying the brogue on thick for some reason. I knew him well enough to suspect an ulterior motive: His goal might be as simple as securing a second serving of pie or as complex as starting up a romance with one—or both—of them.

As best I could see, Sean found just about everyone he met attractive in some way or other. If he wasn't interested in their bodies, he was compelled to get into their minds. Or hearts.

I truly didn't feel jealous of his attention to others; he simply didn't interest me in a romantic way. And despite our magical entanglement, we hadn't put any time or effort into really getting to know each other. Sean acted like the twenty-four-year-old that he was despite the maturation inherent in wartime experiences. On any given day, or within an hour even, he could shift from overconfident, naive trust to bewilderment at some betrayal, real or imagined.

Way too young for me. But I'll admit I did envy his ease at making connections.

I intended to search Dr. Elsass's office and wanted Sean to act as a lookout. But I said, "No, I'm fine. Enjoy a meal in peace." Percy and Carrie were the only people likely to visit the director's office; I'd grab my first opportunity as soon as I knew they were both busy.

He took my words at face value and turned back to the young people. "Sure, I was telling you what now?"

"A fairy warned you about an English attack, during the war," Lottie said.

"Ah, yes. And they're easily offended. The fae, I mean, although the English can be a mite prickly, too. So, we always say, 'the Good People,'" he glanced over his shoulder, too dramatically, I thought. "Even here in the good old U.S. of A."

That was about all the guff I could take for the moment, and I headed to Dr. Elsass's office. Walking by the parlor, I glanced in to see Percy and Blanche sitting by the fireplace. Nurse Carrie was with them. Cigar smoke and faint mumbling wafted out of the dining room on the opposite side of the hall. I stepped into a shadowy corner and listened.

"My understanding has always been—" said Dr. Bertinelli.

"The incorporation articles included a written plan." I didn't recognize the voice. One of the other board members, I supposed.

"I'm his heir, me and the children," Mrs. Elsass was almost whining for attention.

A better chance wasn't likely to arrive anytime soon. I scooted down the hall toward the director's office. My search had to be quick and focused. What I most needed to find was tangible evidence of the Institute's financial situation, not just rumors about salaries unpaid. As Father used to say, bad luck and bad choices were always about money.

My hand was on the doorknob when I heard a voice. "Good evening, Mrs. Humphrey." It was Dr. Cole. His usual bright and eager persona was evident. "Evening sharing time starts soon. Will you attend?"

"You know I don't like it," I said, walking back toward the parlor to lure him away from the office. I had an inspiration. "I've found something peculiar." I produced the microscope slide from my pocket. "Can you tell me about it?"

Dr. Cole took the small glass rectangle. "How odd. I believe I'm the only one here who ever performs microscopy, but I haven't prepared tissue samples in weeks. And I always file them away. This one isn't even labeled properly Where did you find it?"

While I tried to come up with a reasonable alternative to "I found it in your lab, right where it belongs," his curiosity got the better of him. "I need to magnify the specimen in order to identify it."

He dashed toward the basement stairs, and I followed. In his lab, Dr. Cole quickly examined the slide, then turned to me, a thoughtful look on his face.

"Well?" I said. "What is it?"

He didn't reply, just strode over to his desk and shuffled through some medical journals. He held one up. It had been folded open to an article accompanied by several photographs of gray blobs, the best I could tell. "Curious. I know I did not leave my journal in this condition. Nevertheless—"

"What does your medical journal have to do with this microscope slide?"

"I believe the stained specimen to be rabbit ovary—and Finn tells me he found the carcass of one of my lab animals. This article describes a new test for pregnancy."

"Who would care if a rabbit were pregnant?"

"No," he laughed. "The test is for pregnant humans. A woman's urine or serum is injected into a female rabbit. If the biological fluid contains certain hormonal markers of pregnancy, they induced a change in the rabbit's ovaries. A change we can see on microscopic examination."

I was stunned. Some woman at the Institute might be pregnant. "And what does the slide tell you?"

"I've only learned this from a journal article, but the test appears positive to me." Dr. Cole made a few squiggles on the edge of the slide, then filed it in a case filled with other prepared slides. "Perhaps Dr. Elsass performed this test—I can't think of anyone else with the expertise." As he sorted his journals back into their proper order, he said, "I have much to think about, Mrs. Humphrey. Please go on to the group session."

I had a lot to think about, as well, but put speculation about who might be pregnant aside for the moment. Evening sharing time was optional for the patients, yet would occupy most of the staff, and my best opportunity to search Dr. Elsass's office. Maybe I'd find clues about a pregnancy in addition to financial evidence.

The closed door was a heavy oak slab and effectively blocked the drone of conversation from the parlor. While no one was likely to hear me stumbling about, I wouldn't hear anyone approaching the office, either. It was only shortly after sundown, but the winter sky was dark as midnight, with thick snow once again blowing up against the windows as inexplicable peals of thunder shook the house.

The room might be shrouded in shadows, but I knew its layout by heart. Designed, in my opinion, to unnerve and intimidate patients and visitors alike, it featured a sitting area with a throne of a chair for the doctor and a fainting couch for the patient to recline. For sane visitors, a small ladder-backed chair sat facing an eminence expanse of desk.

I hadn't thought to bring a flashlight or candle. Good thing I don't sleuth for a living, I thought. So, I switched on a small desk lamp. It likely wasn't a good idea, but I needed to be able to read any documents I might find.

Percy had been searching the desk earlier in the day. *For something about the pregnancy?* I let that tantalizing prospect go for the moment; financial records were more likely to be in a ledger. I knew that much from helping at Father's stock brokerage firm. Dr. Elsass was a methodical, tidy individual, and I expected no less from his recordkeeping.

I examined the shelves, but they held mainly decorative books or various texts on medicine and psychology. I remembered one corner of the room being shielded by a chinois screen and groped around in the near-dark to find it. Folding it back, I found a stout wooden file cabinet. One drawer hung open, and half the files were gone. Probably that pile on the desk. "Ah ha!" I whispered. Would Percy really need to review patient files? I had no doubt that Dr. Elsass told him everything about Blanche's case, but perhaps someone else held his interest. Me, for example.

However, I was on a mission: financial records. I tried the lower drawer and was rewarded with a blue ledger book, which I took to the desk.

I started with the latest page and aimed to work my way backwards. I'd always had a knack for mental math, so I checked the calculations every few entries. After a good hour of review, I hadn't found anything wrong. I shut the book and frowned. Dr. Elsass's accounts showed adequate income to cover monthly expenses and all the normal bills, including wages, being paid each month. Directly in conflict with what people had told both me and Sean. I needed to find the actual bills from vendors, cancelled paychecks, and receipts.

I checked the folders on the desk for such papers. But, as I'd assume, they were all patient files. It was the first half of the alphabet, as if Percy intended to read all the charts and had grabbed an armload.

I sighed. Percy Emerson was the most irritating man I'd ever met, and that was saying something. The nerve. I couldn't figure out what he'd read and hadn't read. Rather than neat piles, the files were in a disarrayed heap.

When I'd talked with Percy earlier, he'd hidden a chart at the bottom of the pile. He might have returned for it, but if so, wouldn't he put away all this evidence of snooping?

Sliding my hand under the pile, I found a patient record without a name on the outside of the chart, simply XXXX. A note with yesterday's date read: Patient is a forty-year old railway executive from St. Louis. Married about three years. No children. I flipped to the intake page: the patient was Percival Emerson.

Not believing what I'd just read, I skimmed ahead.

Chapter Twenty-Three

C/O: Frequent headaches, light sensitivity, and hallucinations.

Social Hx: Overseas military service, 1917-1918, frequent travel to Cuba, as well as domestic business trips.

Medical Hx: Unremarkable, except for transitory genital chancre some years ago, now healed. With some questioning, also admits to episodes of confusion and others around him complaining of his irritability and erratic behavior.

Physical exam: Well-nourished White male. Diminished reflexes.

Mental exam: The Institute's standard instruments administered. Indications of paranoia and manic tendencies.

Presumptive Dx: Neurosyphilis psychosis.

Tx plan: Options include arsenic therapy, for which I would refer him to the university medical center due to the unstable nature of the medication and complex administration regimen, and malaria-induced fever, a therapy we could provide here at the Institute. Patient agreeable to fever therapy and wishes to begin right away.

Dr. Ibrahim Cole had signed the note. I didn't see a co-signing by Dr. Elsass. Although that didn't mean he hadn't seen the chart or talked about the case with Dr. Cole.

I took a long moment to ponder the significance of Percy Emerson with a venereal disease—syphilis. That was a big secret, certainly a potential bargaining chip for Dr. Elsass. And Percy would hate the director having that sort of power over him. The only reason I could imagine he'd sought treatment here was that the scandal possibilities back in the city with his own doctor were worse.

Even if Dr. Elsass hadn't played the blackmail card, Percy might have gotten violent with the doctor. His mind was affected by the terrible disease—it said as much, right in the report.

I stood, too excited by my discovery to bother with coal bills and grocery receipts. I noticed my own chart just as the door swung open.

Violet

CHAPTER TWENTY-FOUR

Deaf Children Can Listen and Talk! Give your deaf child the best education possible—Dr. Max Goldstein's innovative curriculum and medical care. Schedule a school visit today to see for yourself.

~From Central Institute for the Deaf brochure, 1918.

Momentarily blinded by the glare, all I could see was a man's shape, backlit by the corridor's ambient light.

"Who's in here?" Teddy said, and I breathed a sigh of relief. "All the bosses are in the parlor, so you better not be..." His voice trailed off as he stepped into the room and peered at me in the dim glow of the single lamp.

"It's just me, Mrs. Humphrey." I began to gather the charts strewn across the desk into a pile, and with a burst of inspiration, decided to alphabetize them. "I glanced in here and saw this mess. It...made me so anxious. Here's an A—" I grabbed another folder. "This one's a B; it goes after."

Teddy shut the door behind him and flipped the wall switch to turn on the overhead light. "Mrs. Humphrey, you know I need to see your face when you talk. Nurse sent me to find you. She's not gonna like—"

"Oh, you won't turn me in, will you?" My ruse of suddenly developing a neatness compulsion was lost on this teenager. I tried another tactic. "Teddy, I'm concerned. Percy Emerson may be aiming to blame someone from the staff."

The young man plopped down in the chair opposite the desk and stared at me a moment. "Did you say, 'Blame the staff'?' For the murder?"

I nodded.

"Does he really think one of us would hurt the director?" He patted his breast pocket, then all his other pockets. "What did I do with it?"

"Did you have your notebook at dinner?" I asked.

Teddy shrugged and grabbed a legal pad off the shelf. "Could you write what he said about us?"

Mr. Emerson wants this situation settled and needs a scapegoat, I wrote. Or Percy needs to deflect attention from himself.

Teddy was a bit teary. "What can I do? My dad and Uncle Finn will be worried. And...angry."

I could easily picture Finn punching Percy Emerson, quite soon and thoroughly. I need evidence of what's really going on, I wrote, then made a little shooing motion.

He shook his head. "I want to help."

"I'm just a crazy lady." I pointed at my head, circling my finger and crossing my eyes. "Doing something crazy."

He laughed. "What do you need me to do?"

But you could be fired. I wrote *FIRED* in big letters. I wanted no misunderstanding.

"I don't care. I'm going to St. Louis come spring."

I glanced at my chart on the desk. Did I even want to know what the director and Dr. Cole had written about me—and what I might have told them in my weak moments, beyond remembering? Whatever I'd said to the therapists, Percy Emerson might have read it when he was in here earlier. Would it suit him at some point to switch out who he intended to sacrifice; back to me instead of Teddy or some other staff member?

I pointed to the locked file cabinet.

"Sure thing," Teddy walked around the desk, opened the center drawer, and removed a small key. He unlocked the cabinet, and I crouched to thumb through the files. In the rear of the cabinet was a thin, unlabeled folder. I shivered, suddenly chilled.

"These appear to be…" I remembered to look up so he could see my face. "These are the property transfer records." I showed him what I'd found. "I'll go through them." *Find the household bills and receipts in the other cabinet*, I wrote on the pad.

He nodded, and we set to work.

Sitting on the floor to read the file, I saw it was the property's sales contract and deed. I startled at a sudden sensation of being watched, but Teddy was intent on the records in the open file drawer; whatever I felt, it wasn't him. I tapped his shoulder. "Do you know much about old

Mr. Osteen. Finn's father, Noble?" I pointed to the name on the contract. "Why did he sell the farm to Dr. Elsass?"

Teddy shivered, bit his lip, and glanced around. Perhaps he felt the gaze, too. "Uncle Finn won't talk about his father." He glanced into a dark corner of the room. "Or his grandpa, Jürgen, either. None of his people."

"Family can be complicated." Mine certainly was. "Not so loving and supportive, like yours." I wrote it as well.

He nodded. "Sometimes I feel—but we shouldn't talk about them here. I could show you some strange stuff I found. Maybe you could make sense of it."

I nodded. "I can try."

"Meet me in the morning. You know the log cabin?"

"The ruin at the edge of the woods?"

"It was Jürgen Osteen's first homestead."

"This place..." I thought of my grandfather's house in Lafayette Square, built by his own father in the boom times. My sister has probably sold it by now, I thought, to pay her lawyer. "It must mean a great deal to Finn."

Teddy shook his head. "Sorry. Write it, please."

How does Finn feel about losing the house? I wrote.

"He says he hates this house; that it's an evil place, but..."

"But what?"

"Uncle Finn wanted to get the property back. Maybe because my dad loves to grow things—the whole farm life."

"But you?" I pointed at him. "Where do you want to be?"

"St. Louis. I went to school there, Central Institute for the Deaf. It's a good school; they teach talking for the deaf. I have lots of friends in the city."

I had to agree Teddy would find St. Louis much more interesting than this place. *What would you do?* I wrote.

"I want my own company." His face lit up with excitement. "People are rich all of a sudden. Buying up big homes with big yards. I'll take care of lawns and flowerbeds for all those nice houses. On a contract basis."

Impressive. Teddy seemed to have a good head for business, especially for a teenager. "You'll do great."

"Thanks. But my job now is to get all the patients to bed. So—" He pointed to the exit.

"I will. But we shouldn't leave together in case anyone sees us. You go, and I'll follow in a minute." I also wrote it, just to be sure he understood the plan.

He paused, assessing my motives, I thought. "Alright. I'll check on you upstairs in fifteen minutes."

"Agreed."

He cracked open the office door, glanced both directions, then slipped out.

I stared at my record on the desk across the room. But then my eyes lit on a pile of colorful, oversized paintings stacked on a long, narrow table in front of the windows. A tendril of invitation beckoned me, a whiff of tropical flowers and warm seawater. It arose from deep in my mind, but also from the art. Without any conscious decision, I found myself thumbing through the stack.

225

They mainly were watercolor paintings in a familiar style. The well-trained lady, finishing-school style. Workmanlike attention to drafting skills, an eye for pleasant color juxtaposition, and studied avoidance of any image too challenging for the artist's abilities. Landscapes and still-life compositions. Blanche had done them all, I was almost sure.

But as I progressed through the pile, the images progressed as well. The medium shifted to tempera on canvas, and even a few oils. The palette grew in intensity and the familiar countryside morphed into a place of shadow and abstraction, at once more interesting and yet, off-putting.

The voice in my head sniggered at the veiled sexual innuendo of one particularly vibrant scene. It was an open-air market, lush, ripe, verge-of-decay fruits and vegetables rioting across the page, barely contained by stalls with no fixed perspective. Smears of color and movement suggested shoppers and vendors in an elaborate and sensual dance of commerce and celebration.

And the fountain. Central to the whole scene was a stone structure, water spouting from a fantastical fish-frog creature. It lifted stony claws to embrace the bright plaza, and water poured over it to splash into a deep basin beneath.

The more I stared, the more immersive the image became. The painting invited me in. "Join me," the voice murmured. "Why do you struggle so? Your child is here, your mother, your father…"

My fingers trailed along the image of falling water, the paint rough against my hand. I sensed moisture, too, as if I'd dipped my fingers into a cool fountain. I felt far, far away from the cold, snowy house.

I was strolling through Plaza Vieja in Havana, a place I'd visited once with Father. The warm breeze caressed my face and stirred my hair. The air was a mélange of ripe fruit and sweet, sweet flowers. So sweet, I could curl up in the scent and sleep, long and peacefully. The vendors and the shoppers, their Spanish words soft and melodious in my ear, flowing over and around me, paying me no mind at all.

Just then, the sky darkened as a flock of bright plumed birds flew overhead, squawking. Planets twirled across the sky at impossible speeds, while stars flared and winked out. The wind picked up and whipped palm fronds to-and-fro. I felt a cold, wet slap on my hand, and then another on my opposite wrist. The fountain's sculpture had caught me. It pulled me toward the water, urging me all the while to join it. I struggled, but half-heartedly. I was sick from the sweet floral aroma and the stench of rotting fruit. Tired, too, of the struggle. I wished, once again, that I'd died when my little Tony did. Buried together, him in my arms. I'd have avoided so much pain.

I surrendered to the struggle and slipped under the water.

At first warm and welcoming, it grew chilly, and a yammering in my ear drowned out the pleasant buzz of the marketplace. A familiar voice, but it didn't belong here, at my death by drowning in a Cuban fountain.

I was cold—gods—the water was freezing. I struggled, aiming for the surface, but found myself trapped under ice. The voice's accent—Yorkshire? Lowlands?—No, Irish. One of my teachers of the craft? Those old people were surely all dead by now. Perhaps I am, also, I thought.

"Violet, Violet." The water was not only cold but turbulent, battering me back and forth in its current. "Wake the fuck up!" It certainly wasn't the voice that had intruded in my mind since I arrived at the Institute. "You don't have time for this. Violet, damn you." I pounded against the ice, desperate for air. The voice was just beyond the frozen surface. Someone was chopping at the ice. "Die on your own time."

Whoever it was, I felt pretty sure it was someone I knew. I shivered in the cold and, with a burst of energy, broke through the ice.

I opened my eyes to Sean Joye's face—as angry as I'd ever seen him. The air crackled with ozone and faint sparks, all the world as if he had worked a spell on me. I was on my back, lying in the snow piled up on the front porch. Snow had covered my legs and feet, and hard, brown needles from a shriveled evergreen garland poked my face.

I struggled to rise. He made a few quick gestures—dispelling gathered energy?—I lost the thought as a wave of queasiness overtook me. "Not so fast there. Feeling dizzy?" He helped me sit up.

"Yes. And freezing. Why are we out here?"

"Freshest air I could think of. Take some deep breaths. That office reeked of ether."

"Saving me from magical drowning will be of no use if I catch pneumonia." I struggled to stand, leaning on Sean.

"Drowning? You were out for the count on the floor." He put his arm around my waist. "But 'tis true. Cold out here. Can you walk?"

I demonstrated that I could, and we moved inside to the now-empty parlor. He wrapped me in a knitted Afghan and stoked up the dying fire. My icy fingers itched in the sudden onslaught of heat pouncing on me like some great beast. The flames cast the corners of the room in shadows that whispered threats. I stared at the fire, my mind blank and head pounding, until I felt my hands being wrapped around a hot mug. The scent of strong tea dispelled the sweet ether smell lingering in my nose.

"Back in a jiff," Sean said. He returned in a moment from Dr. Elsass's office with a wad of white fabric captured in a small, lidded jar meant for paper clips.

Just looking at it made my head hurt worse. "I take it that's the weapon. What happened, exactly?"

"Well, you tell me. I came by your bedroom to gossip about what'd I'd found out this evening. Ran into Teddy—who's pretty sore at you, by the way."

I shrugged. "I did promise him I'd go right to bed."

"And you didn't. I offered to find you, and since he had two other patients yelling for something, he let me.

Although I'm pretty sure he fully expected me to mess it up."

I smiled. "And I'm not yet in bed for the night, so his low opinion of us is confirmed."

"Right. I went straight to the office and found you, out for the count. I thought I heard a noise somewhere in the office, but I was distracted by whatever was wrong with you."

I stared at the fire again for a while, trying to remember. "I was looking at Blanche's paintings. I thought I'd...fallen into one of them, but maybe it was just the gas."

"So, who'd do that to you? And why?"

"*Who* could be almost anyone here. *Why*—I think we must be getting close to an answer about the director's death. This attack pretty much confirms he was murdered." I grinned and grabbed Sean's hand. "I'm so glad this happened. You say you heard the ether-person leaving the room?" I was downright giddy.

"I think so. I guess we need to locate how they got in—"

"And you had just left Teddy upstairs in the patient dorm." I reminded myself not to jump to conclusions.

"Yes, he had two of the male patients with him. I saw him heading upstairs. And—"

"Don't you see? It couldn't have been him. Whoever is behind all this isn't Teddy."

"You feel sorry for the kid, eh?"

"Not at all. But he didn't do it, for one thing."

Chapter Twenty-Four

"And he appeals to your motherly instincts."

"Don't be an ass," I snapped. "Do you think that's the only thing that can motivate a woman?"

"Far from it," Sean crouched before the fire, preparing it to burn low for the night. "But it's not an insult to observe that you have natural feelings."

"As I believe I've told you before, you're really not all that smart."

He grinned. "That you have, and you'd be right."

"What are you smirking at?"

"You. All piss and vinegar again. You're surely on the mend."

I stood, wrapping the blanket around me. "I'm going to bed. I need to be up early. Teddy has some important evidence to show me."

"Show us, you mean." He stood, replacing the tongs on their rack.

"Your presence is not required. We've just determined he isn't the murderer."

Sean sighed. "Even so, I might notice something you don't. What's he got to show you?"

"I don't know, exactly. It's out at the old log homestead. Something to do with Finn's family." I started to leave. "Good night."

"I should go with you."

I spun around. "Fine. I don't care. Be on the kitchen stoop at six. Good night."

"I don't think you should sleep in your bed tonight."

"What?"

"Less than an hour ago, weren't you attacked? If Teddy didn't do it, someone else did."

I paused, feeling lost. "What should I do?"

"Don't sleep where they expect to find you, for one thing. Is there anyone here you trust?"

Sean

CHAPTER TWENTY-FIVE

> *...the moon shall be full, or near unto it. Mark a mirror with the divine coordinates, then allow a white candle to drip onto the surface. Invoke thine faerie servant or the gods...*
>
> ~From "A Cantrip to Open the Perceptions," grimoire of "Hector" (Taylor Avebury Humphrey), 1904.

Violet decided her safest option for the night was with Finn and Tomás in the small farmhouse they shared with their son, Teddy. I wasn't all that easy about Violet setting off alone into the cold and dark; the sky was dumping great buckets of snow all about, such that you could hardly see. But Teddy was knocking off for the night and offered to walk her over there. Violet trusted him, so I decided to trust him myself.

At the second-floor nurses' station, I found the nurse who Carrie had run off earlier in the evening, when we'd had our private little talk. "Evening, sister. Grace, wasn't it? The head nurse, would she be about?"

She looked puzzled, then smiled. "Ah, you're from the UK. We don't say 'Sister' to mean a nurse here." She extended her right hand. "Yes, I'm Grace Martin. I'm the evening charge nurse."

"Sean Joye." I took her hand. "Aren't you the clever one for sure. From Belfast, being my home now." Grace regarded me blankly, and I realized I was laying the brogue on with a trowel and tried to resume a more neutral tone. "And Nurse Carrie is…?"

"Head Nurse is exhausted. I don't think she's slept a wink since Thursday, before all this trouble began. She just went to lie down for a bit."

"Ah, and ain't she entitled to a good night's sleep now? I thought I should tell someone that Violet Humphrey was just attacked." I brandished my jar of ether-soaked gauze. "By persons unknown."

Grace gasped. "Is she alright?" She had one of those things for listening to hearts at the ready and leaped to her feet. "I must assess her right way."

"I can assure you she's walking and talking and drinking tea fine."

She snorted. "I'll be the judge of that."

"Violet wanted to sleep at Finn and Tomás's cottage instead of her room—she has already gone over there with the help of an orderly. I'll be up the rest of the night, patrolling the premises."

"Where did this happen? What was she doing?"

"I think she was admiring some of Miss Blanche's paintings," I said, and left out the part about her snooping around the director's office at the time.

"Well, I have to get the head nurse." Grace closed the chart before her. "Why did you encourage her to leave the building?" She wasn't smiling at me anymore. "It will be very inconvenient for me to go over to the farmhouse in the snow."

"Sorry. We should've thought of that. Quick question—where is the ether kept? Who has access?"

"I've no idea, really. We don't do surgery at the Institute."

"What about the research lab?"

"I don't know what goes on down there." She hurried out from behind the counter and knocked on a door labeled "Head Nurse." There was no answer. She turned to me and pointed to a chair. "Wait right here," she ordered, then clattered down the hallway.

I decided I'd rather be forgiven later than get permission now and hurried down the stairs, skipping the two treads I'd noted as squeaky earlier in the day.

The house was quiet. Nobody was in the parlor, library, or dining room; it appeared all the guests had turned in early. The parlor, where I'd taken Violet to recover, was not only empty, but someone had snuffed the candles on the Christmas tree, turned off the electric lamps, and draped a cover over the parrot's cage. Dying embers in the hearth and an oil lantern turned down low were the only lights in the room. Through the front windows, I could see it was snowing hard.

The director's office was unlocked but shut. That bothered me; I felt like I'd left it open but couldn't really be sure. I entered, closed the door behind me, and struck a match to at least be able to find my way to an electric switch. The place still smelled faintly of ether.

My match produced a paltry flame, but enough to see a room crowded with bulky furniture and a desk stacked with file folders. That must have been what Violet and Teddy were about; finding financial records. Money is always a good bet for a murder motive, but I had a feeling that other passions were involved in this case. And Éire had tattled on some old gods, although, considering the source, that was likely a load of shite.

I'd squandered whatever chance I had of catching up with Violet's attacker when I'd performed the very necessary first aid to bring her around.

But I had a theory.

Yeah, someone could have come into the room while she looked at those paintings. However, Teddy had told me that everyone was where they were supposed to be when he left Violet alone in the office. The kid could have missed someone or lied, but I had to wonder if the attacker was hidden in the room the entire time the two of them searched it. Or had come in another way.

I turned on the overhead light and started a tour, which bore out my initial impression: a room too crowded with stuff and cramped for comfort. It just wasn't the kind of place to relax and talk about your troubles. The scratchy upholstery managed to be both dusty and smell of mildew. Behind the furniture, the walls were lined with bookshelves.

I needed more light than the dim ceiling bulb for a serious hidey-hole search. Not having thought to bring a torch, I lit a kerosene lantern. Behind the door stood a slender table, which displayed a bowl of dirty stones and odd knick-knacks. There was something off about the lot.

I've been trying to notice the aura—the energy, I guess you'd call it—coming off people and things. Likely, I've always heeded it, all those gut feelings and snap judgments that made no sense but kept me out of jams in wartime. Through my whole life, really.

Now that I studied magic, I could put a name to it and call up the power, when I remembered to, anyway. So, this pile of rocks, bottles, and broken crockery reminded me to consider if magic was part of this story.

But magic is time-consuming, ineffective, and vague. I was impatient—impatient to find a flesh-and-blood bloke who'd, in a mundane yet effective way, just gassed Violet. Likely locked the cook in the coal cellar and coshed the director. I decided to continue my old-fashioned search before trying magic.

Methodically, I felt up the walls and built-in cases for good hiding spots or secret levers. The bookcase behind the director's desk particularly interested me—I didn't see how anyone could have hidden in or behind it, and couldn't locate any sort of latch or push button. But it felt colder than the rest of the room and smelled more mildewy, although its shelves only held some very dried-up skulls and a plaster brain model. I checked the floor around it, and sure enough, I found scratch marks.

Now was maybe the time to try a spell. Given I was the one working it, it would be crude and likely blow up in my face. But I was thinking the lost dog cantrip might be applicable here, with a bit of a tweak. The most important thing was setting a firm and exact intention as to what I was trying to do. No, what I would do. *Think positive.* A lesson, there.

The working was basically a divination spell I'd parsed out from an old grimoire I lifted from a dead man last fall. I'd tried to make it slightly less pagan by swapping out Taylor Humphrey's appeal to Hermes for a time-honored prayer to St. Anthony, patron saint of lost items. I angled a mirror on the desk to show the bookcase's reflection, but I had little of value on me for a sacrifice. Maybe smashing a carved stone from that bowl would do. Some of them looked valuable. When I picked up one with a fancy pattern, it nicked my finger. Which smarted like hell, but I had the presence of mind to let the wound drip over the mirror. Then I heard a voice from far, far in the distance. "Who seeks to bar me from my home?"

Shite.

I crushed the stone under my heel, then sprinkled the pebbles and dust in front of the glass. Not much happened for a moment or two, but I soon felt like time had stopped and I wasn't quite right in my body.

My blood droplet began to glow faintly and run down the mirror's surface. While at first on a course set by gravity, the blood soon made a right-angled turn. The case's reflection in the mirror began to glow, well, at least one corner did, round back and near the floor. I located the corresponding site on the actual case and, sure enough, found a spring-loaded latch, which slid the case over to one side about two feet.

A blast of icy, damp air hit me. The opening was dark as pitch, so I grabbed the kerosene lantern and held it up to see a nook filled with dust and cobweb covered shelves. As I crossed the threshold to have a better look, I must have brushed up against the latch. The case slid shut behind me just as the lantern flame snuffed out.

Sean

CHAPTER TWENTY-SIX

> *Ghosts, or as they are called in Irish, Thevshi or Tash, live in a state intermediary between this life and the next. They are held by some earthly longing or affection, or some duty unfulfilled or anger against the living.*
>
> ~From *Fairy and Folktales of the Irish Peasantry* by W.B. Yeats, 1888, Walter Scott, London.

Was I in a bit of a panic, shut up alone behind a false wall?

I'll just say that it took quite a lot not to start beating on the wall and calling out. I had matches with me and relit the lantern, which gave me enough light to see that it was almost out of fuel. Since burning a lantern in an enclosed space wasn't the best of ideas, anyway, I turned the wick down way low, the faint glow being more a comfort than actual illumination.

I felt rather than looked for a latch to open the hidey-hole from the inside—obviously there must be one, for I was sure this was how Violet's attacker had gotten to her.

I didn't find it, and after a while gave up and sat on the floor for a think and a smoke. Maybe the intruder had been in here the whole time Violet and Teddy searched the office.

But why? Most likely, they'd come here from somewhere else in the house. Whatever route they took would be my way out, too, and the thought cheered me some.

And—hadn't I a glimpse of books? Maybe this closet had some source of light to better enjoy a secret horde of forgotten lore or French postcards. Or whatever it was they'd hidden in here. My vision had gotten used to the dark, enough to be able to figure out that the bit of light in the place was coming from somewhere above. With that, I poked about again.

I found the shelf I'd glimpsed before, and on it a candle stub. We were getting somewhere. The shelf held only a few books, but they were doozies, most of them huge, heavy, and old. The leather binding of at least one of them was—wrong. Creepy in ways I couldn't explain. There was serious magic at work.

The first thing to do with such items was to respectfully greet them and gauge their power. Sense the aura and whatnot. That kind of working required calm, and my state was agitated, to say the least. But maybe some of my seek-and-find working still hung around. In any case, with only a little effort, I was able to see a faint purple glow about the books, and they all hissed and crackled when I tried to touch them, delivering a nasty nip to my fingers. I thought I heard a voice. "Intruder, state your intention."

I'd not heard of talking books before, but what did I know? More likely, it was a person. It sounded like a person. Truth be told, it sounded like the voice I'd heard earlier, when I first started the locator spell. Could it be Violet's attacker?

I snuffed the candle and sat, quiet and ready, I hoped, for them to return. But I heard nothing else, neither a voice nor steps, just the wind creaking through the old house and the occasional thunderclap.

I gave up and relit the candle. I open the least hostile-feeling book. It didn't say anything when I opened it, which was a good sign. I couldn't read a word of it, but the woodcut illustrations were, in turn, horrid, mystifying, and a few times, silly.

I decided to leave the magic books alone for the time being. They were just the sort of thing that might be useful to me, but I didn't want to lug them about. And my instinct told me to keep them away from Violet; they'd do her peace of mind no good at all. They really were the sort of thing her husband, God rest his soul, crazy as a loon he was, would have collected.

I made one last try to find the well-hidden latch with a locator spell, but it sizzled and fizzled out before I could get it invoked. That's the trouble with magic. As hit or miss as mundane solutions can be, magic is even more of a gamble.

Standing there, calmer, I had the sense to take in the place. To feel the air currents and see the flicking tricks of the shadows. A passage downward definitely existed; I couldn't know if it was an actual exit or a hole in the wall, but damp, warmer air hugged the floor. Feeling along the slats, I attempted to follow the air current and ran smack into a staircase going up. Behind it, another flight going down.

I opted for down, and it wasn't long before I found myself wandering about in the basement. It was easy enough to find Ibrahim Cole's lab. It was wide open, the dim electric lights spilling out into the hallway. An open door was all wrong, and I prayed he wasn't the next one coshed.

"Hello?" I said, standing on the threshold. "Dr. Cole? Ibrahim?" I didn't really think he'd be in there at two o'clock in the morning, but it was hard to say; the Institute's routine was pretty topsy-turvy. I got no reply, not from Ibrahim, the rabbits, or the stiff.

Venturing in, it was easy to see where the ether had come from. A container of gauze pads, the same sort as I'd collected at the attack scene, was upturned, and gauze was scattered on the counter. The door to a cabinet of chemicals hung open. They were arranged alphabetically, and a bottle was missing in the "D" section. Which gave me pause, until I noticed the small-print label beneath, "Diethyl Ether."

Feeling rather pleased with myself, I'd about decided to hurry along to the secret steps and see where the upper staircase would take me when a voice spoke up. "And again I bid you, divulge your name, intruder."

I about jumped out of my skin and looked sharp, searching the room. It wasn't the rabbits. Or the man on the slab, although Violet thought the body had behaved oddly earlier in the day.

No one was hiding anywhere in the lab or under the corpse's sheet. The mortal remains of the Institute's director was just as I'd left him earlier in the day.

Checking for auras seemed the thing to do, but I find them tricky. You need to shut down your brain and stare a bit cross-eyed at the thing, then sort of melt into it while it melts into you. Form a connection, or at least that's what I have to do, to make the cantrip work at all.

I made my best attempt to search about me with a magically attuned eye. At first, all I saw was a blurry room. Soon specks of brightness pinpricked around my peripheral vision. Then the headache started. These were all typical reactions to looking at things cross-eyed at two o'clock in the morning on almost forty-eight hours of no sleep.

Then, just as I thought I was going to make myself faint, I saw it. A purple swirl crept out from under the chemical cabinet and started forming up into a vaguely body-shaped cloud of vapor. *Ah, hell.* This was way deeper than I'd intended to venture. "State your name. I cannot linger."

I wasn't telling no haunt my name or anything about me. "Sorry to disturb you. Being Dr. Elsass's spirit are you now? Got something yet to do, this side of the Veil?"

The shape jiggled, all the world like it was laughing. "No, I'm no ephemeral human spirit," it intoned. "I am the true master of this property." The smoke, or whatever it was, loosened, becoming more transparent.

"Grand. Could you be more specific, now?"

The form was losing all pretext of human shape. "Come to me. All will be revealed." Then the vapor dropped to the floor and rolled toward a drain.

"Wait. Where should I go? Who are you?" But it was gone down the grate in the floor.

Sean

CHAPTER TWENTY-SEVEN

Rolling down to old Maui, my boys,
Rolling down to old Maui.
We're homeward bound from the arctic ground.
Rolling home to old Maui.

~From "Homeward Bound" in *Shanties and Other Psalms
of the Deep,* Tenebrous Press, Avebury, Oxfordshire, 1830.

I'd no mind to linger. I grabbed the lantern and hightailed it back the way I came, through the basement, to the hidden staircase, and up. Heart racing, I didn't stop until I reached the little reading nook. My mouth dry as a bone, I was mainly concerned with breathing as the dank crept up on me. Weird shadows played about in the corners and crannies. It was bitter cold; a strong down draft the only thing keeping the distinct smell of mildew and dead mice to the lower level.

I dropped onto the chair, suddenly weak in the knees. What was that in the lab? Elsass's ghost? Some other haunt?

With my hands shaking, I lit a smoke and tried to logic out whatever I'd just seen. In the office, where I first blundered into this sorry mess, I'd heard the same voice say...what was it? That I was trying to bar its way.

Certainly not my intention; I was aiming to find the secret passage, using a mirror. Then I'd accidentally cut myself on a rock. Maybe that blood was some sort of food for it. I'd heard of spells to summon a nasty sort of fae—what some folks call demons. They'd want a bit of blood. Mages who used such spells generally aimed to get a supernatural creature to work for them.

I'd had enough sense to do no such workings and refuse any offers. Yet this—ghost, faerie, demon, whatever it was—styled itself the master of the house. As yet, it had made no offer of service in exchange for my blood or anything else. And it had challenged me to come find it, somehow.

I couldn't make heads nor tails of it. And those books had acted strange, too. I hadn't imagined that. They'd glowed and bit at me. And as I was looking at the books, the same voice had called me an "intruder."

Something supernatural was behind it all, but some type new to me. I stared at the books again. Maybe one of them had the answer.

I examined the shelf carefully and found five in total; I'd overlooked two earlier. I didn't touch the three thick ones that had been so hostile before. Rather, I went for two thinner volumes with more ordinary binding. They appeared to be in English, at least their titles were. *Shanties and Other Psalms to the Deep* and *Prayer Cycle of the Father and Mother: Invocations, Praise, and Promises.*

I'd learned a lesson tonight. Actually, several, but the care and handling of enchanted books was a study in itself.

I ground out the cigarette butt under the toe of my shoe and assumed a respectful attitude. "Excuse me, book named *Shanties and Psalms*. I'm just an ignorant bloke aiming to learn from you. Ain't I asking your permission to open your cover now? Hope it's OK."

With my pocket square—I'd lost or given away my last handkerchief at some point over the past day—I gingerly touched the cover. I'm happy to report it didn't bite me. Opening it, I was glad to see it was in English for the most part. Things were looking up.

The book was old, with yellowing rag pages and published almost a hundred years ago. It was a songbook, like you'd find in a church. I knew the words to many of the songs; I'd heard them before. In pubs. I guess those were the shanties mentioned on the cover.

However, the psalms weren't at all familiar. They weren't the Psalms of David, that's for sure. Many of these weren't in English or any language I could even guess at. Certainly not Irish, Latin, German, or French. From the few that were in English, praise for "Father Dagon," like "God, The Father," and "Mother Hydra," like "Mother Mary." Éire had mentioned the both of them, so I must be on the right track. But there were praises for other gods, with impressive songs, too.

Nothing about this book squared with what people had told me about the Institute director, Dr. Elsass. Didn't sound like his kind of thing at all. Then I found a bookplate glued to the flyleaf. This book was the property of the Congregation of Mother Hydra, Lyme Regis.

How did a hundred-year-old hymnal belonging to a church in England end up behind a wall of a house on the American prairie? I read further. It was checked out to a Jürgen Osteen in 1825. Osteen. Finn's last name. The name over the entrance gate to this place.

Grand. This book might put Finn in the picture, and I'd just sent Violet off to his house for the night.

Maybe neither of these books was warded, but I took no chances. I went through the same permission-getting routine with *Prayer Cycle* and was duly rewarded with access. It was set up like a missal, with the order of community and private worship laid out, with seasonal variations. A sort of library stamp labeled the prayer book as coming from Innsmouth, Massachusetts, Property of the Esoteric Order of Dagon.

I didn't have the time or light for a lot of reading, but the woodcut illustrations told quite a story. A fuzzy, disjointed impression of Finn's people began to take shape between the pictures and the English passages. And that shape wasn't all human—quite a strain of fish and even frog in there, too. But it was a process. They changed, and eventually became so well accustomed to the watery life that they longed for greater immersion, so to speak.

In song and prayer, they begged their gods to take them to the underwater paradise, sooner rather than later. Not an uncommon attitude for religious zealots of all stripes.

What struck me—truth be told, many parts of this story struck me—most forcefully was the change. These hymnal-writing people seem to start off as fairly typical human types, but then changed into a water creature. Not as free and easy as a selkie, but similar. Like a merrow, for instance. As dangerous a faerie as you're likely to meet.

I tried to relax and think, torn as I was between making Finn confess whatever there was to confess to and throwing Violet in the car to head back to St. Louis, even if I had to plow the roads myself.

I liked that idea; just leave. What was I doing here, really? If this homestead was plagued with fae, it sure was none of my concern. Could a merrow murder a human man? I didn't know, but it wasn't unreasonable, given what I'd heard about the size and strength of them. Especially if Elsass had dabbled in summoning him. Violet didn't need to be here. It wasn't her problem.

In the time it took me to examine the false wall one more time for a latch, I cooled off a bit. Whether due to my meddling nature or her magical effects on me, I wanted to save Violet.

And she'd told me what she needed. She needed to figure out this mystery, not turn tail and run. The puzzling, the thinking, the talking to people—she liked it. Whether just a distraction or something more healing, she'd started to find her way back to life.

I had no right to stop her. No one did.

Sean

CHAPTER TWENTY-EIGHT

*Almighty Father, who hast blessed us with the promise of thine
image in life eternal, grant us grace to fearlessly contend against
evil and make no peace with oppression.*

~From *Prayer Cycle of the Father and Mother: Invocations,
Praise, and Promises,* Aeon Press, Boston, 1837.

I decided to explore the steps going up, stumbling a few
times in the dark. They connected to a flight of service
stairs, which led me to a corridor, dimly lit by electric
lamps at either end.

It was the nurses' dormitory, judging by the name tags
on each room. It wasn't a good place for a man to be
found prowling around at three AM. I was plotting my
escape route when I noticed the door at the far end of the
hall, just beyond the stairwell. "Director of Nursing. Carrie
Bartowski."

Each of us for our own reasons, Violet and I both trusted
Carrie. But we'd found no one who would definitely say
they were with her at the time of Elsass's death. Carrie's
story was that she was with the group having cocktails,
but people were in and out. Important evidence might be
amongst her personal belongings.

Most people are asleep at three o'clock in the morning. But these Elsass Institute folks weren't most people. They were hospital people. Someone was always on duty. Maybe I'd hit it lucky, and Carrie would be out and about at this moment. Nurse Grace had mentioned going to find her to talk about the attack on Violet.

I pressed my ear against the door and heard not a stir. Maybe she was a sound sleeper. Then I knocked, quietly, hoping not to wake anyone else. No response. Slowly, I tried the knob. Locked, of course. But it wasn't much of a lock, and I quickly had it open. I listened again but heard nothing from inside the room.

I opened the door, just a tad, and peeked in. The weak light from the hall behind me was enough to see that no one was in the narrow bed. I slipped in, locking up behind me. I was in a hurry, so I risked flipping the electric switch. The bare bulb hanging from an overhead cord revealed a sad cell of a room, sparsely furnished with a thin-mattressed bed, a desk with lamp, and chest of drawers. The room had no closet, and some dresses on hangers hung on wall pegs. This shouldn't take long, I thought.

The thing was, I had no idea what sort of evidence I was looking for. Some secret, I supposed. A secret worth killing a man over. What that might be for a perfectly pleasant nurse, I'd no clue. Even if she *did* have a crush on the late director, that didn't seem like a motive to kill the man. *Jealous?* Evie hadn't shown up until after the death.

The desk was as good a place as any to start a search. It wasn't a desk where she did much work—she had an office near the patients. About all I found were some letters from people in Chicago, pens and paper, and a few romance novels. Tucked in the stack of books was what appeared to be a diary. Just as I sat down on the bed to read it, I noticed a bunch of scraps in a trash can. A letter.

I put the diary down for the moment and pieced together the note, spreading the bits out on the bed's threadbare quilt. It turned out to be a letter on Elsass Institute stationery, and it was a doozy. To Carrie, from Elsass, it said her services were no longer required and gave her until the New Year to move on along.

She'd obviously read it, yet was carrying on with her duties as if nothing were wrong. How often had she mentioned her ongoing work with Dr. Elsass? I slipped the scraps into my pocket as I thought about it.

Just then, the doorknob turned. *Shite.*

"Who's in—" The angry voice of the head nurse. Oh yes, it was Head Nurse Voice, ready to hand me my ass. "—here? Sean…?" Carrie's voice dropped to a whisper. "I mean, Mr. Joye. This is…" She cleared her throat, "highly inappropriate. I…probably have given you a wrong impression."

"So sorry," I grabbed my hat and stood. "I might have drawn a few wrong conclusions from our necking session the last time I was here."

Carrie threw back her shoulders and stood stiff as a board, grasping the knob, quite ready to see me on my way.

The only other play I could think of offhand was that I had some important matter to discuss that just couldn't wait. "If that's the way it is, I'll go. I just wanted to make sure you'd heard about Mrs. Humphrey."

"What about her?"

"She was attacked earlier this evening. I told Nurse Grace."

Carrie sank into a lumpy chair in a dark corner of the room. Her lower lip quivered; the waterworks were about to start. Start again, judging by her already tearstained face.

"Hey now," I crossed the tiny room. "She's fine. Staying the night at Finn's. We thought it would be safer."

Blowing her nose on a hankie, she nodded. "Oh. Good."

"And, may I say, she's acting quite her old self again. You folks have done a great job."

"Thank you. And I'm sorry. I'm not normally so emotional."

"I'm sure. Stressful day."

She paused for a good bit, pondering me with bloodshot eyes. "Don't you think getting her away from here would be best?"

"Oh, yeah, I do. But she's fixed on figuring out what happened to Elsass. Thinks the sleuthing will help her snap out of it."

Carrie frowned and stood. "One doesn't 'snap out of' a serious mental disorder. In fact, validating the fantasy that this accidental death was something more sinister could make things worse in the long run."

I'd always thought Carrie had such an interesting face and her body an appealing softness. "Point taken," I inched in a little closer, enough to catch a whiff of gardenia scent mingled with the smells of a hospital. "But hasn't Dr. Cole ruled it a murder?"

All the crying had somehow erased the cute little crow's feet at the corners of her eyes but made the sprinkle of freckles across the bridge of her nose pop. I felt a smile creep across my face as my stomach made a little backflip.

Carrie tossed her head, deep dimples forming in her cheeks. "He's a psychiatrist, not a pathologist. And not a particularly good one, really. I've my doubts he even finished medical school." She sniffed and smoothed my coat lapel with her right hand. "You should return to St. Louis and take Violet with you. The snow has stopped, and Finn will have the drive cleared by morning."

"What about you?" I grasped her hand. "Have any plans for the night?" Despite the chilly room, her hand was moist.

"Maybe a few," she said, reaching for the knot in my tie. "What I'd give to just forget it all for a little while."

"That can be arranged."

Sean

CHAPTER TWENTY-NINE

I've heard it again, the skittering behind the office walls. I'm sure it IS NOT my imagination, despite Henry's opinion. Must get Finn to set out some rat traps.

~From personal journal,
Carrie Bartowski, December 17, 1924.

I slept like the dead for a few hours, despite Carrie's hard mattress and her fine blonde hair tickling my nose. When I awoke around dawn, she was gone. As was the diary that I hadn't had a chance to read. And the shreds of her dismissal letter I'd found earlier.

At least the snow had stopped. Someone had shoveled a path between the mansion's rear parking lot and Finn's cottage. But when I trudged over to the house, Tomás informed me that Violet and Teddy weren't there. "Violet mentioned a log cabin. Where's that?"

"It's a hike, but you can't miss it. Go around the front of the house, then across the creek and past the well. If you find yourself in an old-growth forest, you *have* missed it somehow."

I didn't want to waste any more time conversing with Tomás, though he was an entertaining fella and making buckwheat pancakes to boot. "Sorry to miss her and Teddy, but I best be going." I also meant to ask Finn to share a bit more about Jürgen Osteen. "Finn around by chance?"

Tomás rattled on with an account of the difficult morning. "Ah, no. Funny story. Not ha-ha funny, just... wrong, the way they treat Finn. Mr. Emerson woke me around five this morning, banging on the door to roust Teddy to shovel snow. I realized then that Finn had never come to bed, working over there all night."

Tomás was winding himself up for a rant, so I said, "I best get moving. Catch up with Violet and Teddy."

"Just Miss Violet, you mean. I tried to get her to wait until Teddy came back from clearing the paths—I'm making my special company pancakes," he gestured with the spatula in his hand, "but she said Teddy would know where to meet her as soon as he got free. And that you'd be along presently, anyway."

So, Violet was wandering around the property alone. "I'd better hurry, then."

The more I thought about it, the less I liked the setup. I'd assumed Teddy would be watching over Violet, and that turned out to be wrong.

As I retraced my steps to the mansion, I noticed fog along the far side of the building. Perhaps the effects of the creek or the little grove of trees adjacent to the house. I was absurdly pleased with that bit of nature observation—wouldn't Granny McGuinn be proud of me now?—when I noticed something else.

The fog was thick, but not too thick to see someone up ahead, doing something magical. Their aura was golden and blue, and the ground shook ever-so-slightly with energy moving about, hither and yon. They were singing. Or praying. The figure was bent down, fiddling with something on the ground.

Perhaps they'd be so intent on their devotions they wouldn't notice me. I tried to be quiet, which was impossible in the snow-wrapped stillness of the Sunday morning, given that I gasped and wheezed like a sixty-year-old as I slogged through the snow.

The person stood and turned to face me. "Yule greetings, friend." She was the woman who'd upset Violet so much yesterday afternoon. Comfrey, she'd called her. A tall ginger woman, her cheeks were pink in the cold. Her voice held the twang of southern Illinois hills and hollows.

"'Morning, Miss Rouse. Nice to see you again." I walked a little closer, curious what she was doing. "You been out awhile? I'm trying to find Violet."

"I haven't seen her, but I just arrived here. Been all over the property this morning." Concern clouded her face. "Was Miss Violet going to the well? I've warned her against it."

"She was going to some cabin. But why would you—"

"I warn everyone. I'm warning you, right now. Stay away from the well. It's dangerous. And the Grove is tricky, too, if you're not prepared for it."

I found the countryside full of peril, but had a feeling this woman was talking about an entirely different level of menace. "Like snakes or sinkholes? Stinging plants?"

She laughed and slapped my back. "Maybe, but I mean real danger."

I felt her power, energy, whatever you want to call it, when she touched me. I hadn't imagined the aura I'd seen around her. Comfrey was some sort of magic user.

She searched my face. "I didn't want to upset Miss Violet earlier, but I can see their mark on you. Perhaps you choose to ignore them."

While her words were cryptic, I understood completely. Yet another person who could see the wounds the fae had left on me.

"What are you doing out here, Miss Rouse?"

She tilted her head. "Gonna play it that way, eh? Alright, I'm checking my wards on this property. Setting up special ones for Yule. We're getting into the season of power for the Deep Ones."

"Faeries?"

She shook her head. "I've no quarrel with them. I don't bother them, and they don't bother me."

"They do bother me, quite a lot."

"That is easy to see. But, no, the aquifer around here is a refuge for something old and…"

"Evil?"

"I don't judge my elders. They have their ways. But they don't mix so good with human activity. We are so willful and irreverent."

"Is Violet in danger?"

Comfrey looked distressed. "Yes, which is why I have to make sure the wards hold. And she's not making it easy."

I felt a small knot of panic twist in my gut. "I need to find her. Right now."

She nodded. "I agree. The cabin is a relatively safe place, but today of all days, she shouldn't be wandering around alone in the fog. Continue along the tree line. But stay out of the Grove. That's most important. It will try to lure you in and distract you. Follow the stone wall, and you'll come to the cabin."

Violet

CHAPTER THIRTY

Fraxinus excelsior (European Ash). *A dioecious species, long-lived (up to 400 years). When fully grown, the European ash can reach a height of thirty-five meters. In a grove, they form a domed canopy. Black, velvety leaf buds are visible in the winter, arranged opposite each other on smooth twigs. The "Tree of Life" in Norse mythology, the ash is thought to have protective properties.*

~From *Trees of Europe: Their Ornamental and Industrial Uses* by E. Jasper Tremony, Jackson and Son Publishers, London, 1790. Handwritten marginalia, *"Be sure to gather a quantity of seed pods before departure."*

As things turned out, I ended up going to the cabin alone, without Teddy as a guide or Sean as a... whatever he was becoming to me. I really can't explain why I went off on my own. Anxiety, I suppose.

My head still pounding and throat sore from the ether, I'd given up on trying to sleep when I heard someone knocking on the house's front door. It was almost five AM and dark, a darkness that stank of frozen rot. *Death is always out there.* Surely the morning would dawn soon.

Once upon a time, the rising and setting of the sun and moon prescribed my activities and signaled the clear and comfortable order of my day. Another lifeline I'd abandoned.

Tomás was rattling about in the kitchen by the time I dressed and readied myself for the day. "Is Teddy up yet?" I asked.

"Oh, you need Teddy this morning?" he said, clearing a breakfast place setting. "Sorry, he got called into work. Supposed to be the boy's day off, but everything is in such a state this weekend." His bright blue words took on a hard gray cast. "Are you alright, miss? You don't look so good."

I didn't feel so good, either. I hoped whatever Teddy had to show me would provide an answer—at least a clue—to who'd attacked me. "Is Finn available?"

"No." Tomás bit his lower lip. "Never even came home. They'll work him to death."

I was no closer to the resolution of who'd killed Dr. Elsass than yesterday morning, sitting on the floor of the observation room and pondering crime and my escape from insanity. I must be close, I reminded myself. Someone attacked me; that means something.

I didn't need Teddy; I knew perfectly well where the cabin was, having walked past it enough times over the last two months. A clue is a clue. I'd surely recognize it.

Tomás bundled me in a mismatch of wraps smelling of mothballs and love. The most important items were sturdy boots, too big, but the extra woolen socks took up some of the space around my narrow heels.

The snow had stopped, and stars twinkled overhead, crisp and minty, although the eastern horizon was a gray blur. The winter solstice, I realized. Yule. A day of importance to me, now almost forgotten.

The perpetual fog that seemed to hang about the Grove was unaffected by the cold. I felt a powerful, no, overwhelming urge to search about the roots of the tree closest to the house. Something important was there. I knew it. I could see a faint glow under the piles of leaves and snow. I tried to ignore it and trudged on toward the creek, struggling to avoid the Grove. I had no time for its whispered opinions about me and my plans.

Yet, I found myself there, right under the tree I'd tried to avoid, scooping away the drifted snow. A frantic anxiety clawed at my chest—*what was I doing?* Under the snow and leaves, I saw a suspicious pile of rocks. I scattered them in my haste and pulled off the thick gloves to dig with my hand. Whatever source of warm air that kept the Grove foggy had also prevented freezing. The earth was cold but yielding. All the while, a corner of my brain observed me, snidely commenting, "You are quite mad, you know? This is a ruse to distract you from solving the murder."

"I know," I shouted. "I can't stop."

And the trees, oh, they had thoughts, too. "𝔏eave it be. Come to us and rest. It doesn't matter. 𝔥e's already won."

In a few moments, my nails clinked against something hard. A small star-shaped stone. It was familiar, somehow. Perhaps I'd seen the design before, although it could just as well be a naturally occurring pattern. *Maybe a fossil?* Its odor, blood and cold iron, assaulted my senses. I needed to rid this place of its stench, but knew I couldn't throw it far enough away. Aiming to drop it deep into the well, I slipped the stone into my pocket, pulled the gloves on over my muddy, cold hands, and resumed my walk.

At least the compulsion to dig had left me. I felt good. In control and clear-headed.

"Cabin" made the place to which I was headed sound comfortable and interesting; in reality, it was little more than a ruin—some tumbledown log walls held together by the remnants of a crossbeam and trusses. The safety of standing too close, let alone going inside, was a compelling question, but I resolved to be quick and careful.

The sky was lightening in the east, and birds in the forest greeted the dawn, the new season, Holly King's reign. But no morning birdcall sounded from the Grove. Or from the shrubs around the artesian well. Perhaps more snow was coming, but I didn't really believe in a natural explanation. Something was very off with the world.

I crossed the cabin's threshold and trailed the beam of the flashlight Tomás had lent me around the room. It was unexpectedly neat given the exterior's ramshackle appearance. Maybe I'd been too quick to condemn the building. In the old days, they really knew how to build things to last. At least that was what grandfather always said.

A table, two chairs, and a narrow bed furnished the room. On the table, a vase of dried wildflowers, holly twigs, and ornamental grass fronds sat on a tablecloth next to a kerosene lantern. A picnic basket yielded plates, wineglasses, and a half-full bottle of Riesling. The quiet song of a faded, but serviceable, quilt covered the bed.

Obviously, someone has a private retreat...no, I touched the glasses and plates...two someones. Or someone and a series of guests. Was this what Teddy had intended to show me? But from our conversation, I'd gotten the impression that whatever was in the cabin had something to do with Finn's father. Or possibly grandfather. Hadn't he said, "I found some of *his* stuff"?

I put thinking about secret trysts on hold for the moment; maybe they'd trusted this building not to fall in on itself, but I certainly didn't. I needed to finish my search and get out.

Exploring further, I found a lean-to attached to the cabin's rear wall. A rusted caldron suspended over a stone fire circle, a rough plank table with a central groove, and meat hooks hanging from a pole comprised a pioneer kitchen. The past clung to me like sticky cobwebs as I opened and slammed shut an outhouse door, peeked in at an abandoned chicken coop, and stomped through the snow to look in a shed. I guessed it might be for wood or farm equipment.

It was the only building out here with a padlock, which, from a distance at least, rang out shiny and new. Not brand new, but modern, certainly. *Now* I wished I had Sean along with me.

Why *had* I gone off alone? As Dr. Cole urged me to do in session, I tried to remember my feelings from earlier, as precisely as possible. In my daily therapy sessions, we were usually talking about things that happened in the distant past. Surely, I could recall emotions from an hour ago. But my sleepless night didn't help my powers of concentration.

In my mind's eye, I retraced my steps from the time I'd gotten up. Giving up on sleep, I'd checked the time and saw it was morning, near enough anyway. Finn's house was wrapped in the aroma of coffee and frying meats, and I was pretty sure these smells were real, not some hunger-generated hallucination.

I was anxious, verging on nameless panic, which sometimes envelopes me. It was a sensation that I might jump out of my skin, right then and there. Earlier, I had struggled into my dress, the fabric as abrasive as sandpaper, rubbing against me with irritating squeaks.

And dread? Perhaps. Coming to this cabin to see some mysterious evidence, or maybe irrelevant farm antiques, did hit a fear of the unknown that I took great pains to control. Getting here, facing it, and knowing whatever it was seemed the quickest way to dispel the anxiety and dread.

I also realized that I'd begun to find Sean annoying. That made little sense, except that maybe I'd been kidding myself about our continued psychic connection being something he'd chosen to maintain.

Well, he's not here. Maybe I came alone because I wanted to figure this out myself. To be in that much control of my fate, at least. I set my mind to the task and examined the shed carefully.

Whoever installed the lock likely has the key, and this shack was way below Dr. Elsass's level of attention. I wasn't even sure the Osteen ancestral home was part of the Institute. If I had to guess who'd placed the lock and had the key, it would be Finn.

The bark-clad shed had a steep-pitched roof designed for the heavy prairie snowfalls. A good twelve inches of white stuff covered it and had also drifted halfway up the entrance and front wall. I cleared away the snow with some pine boughs, still not sure how to get in. Maybe the clasp is rusted, I hoped, but no, it was secure.

I walked around the shed, looking for a loose log or some other crevice I could peek through. It was easily seventy-five years old or more. Not that difficult to burgle, surely. It was then a key on a small hook up under the roofline at the rear of the shed sang out to me.

"Thank goodness." A Yule blessing, indeed. The thought warmed me a little. I hadn't observed the holiday or even noted it since my son drowned. For just a moment, I allowed myself to feel the promise, the joy of winter's short rule.

I grabbed the key and found it turned in the lock easily, and the door swung open.

Deep, bitter cold rolled out in a blue wave, along with dust and an energy decidedly alien. Dawn crept over my shoulder into the gloom ahead of me, and I clung to its light as I advanced into the shed. Glowing eyes blinked from the shadows, and something hissed. I heard a rustle and a bang as whatever animal denned in here escaped.

I sensed something like magic, too. Not my dead husband's ponderously boring ritual "Magick," as he insisted on calling it. Something very old, gray, and beyond the human mind. Fishy and damp.

The rising sun's beams spread further across the plank floor, warming the shadows. I could make out the interior now; it wasn't a woodshed but rather a place for the storage of a small cart and the crumbling remains of a straw person.

The wagon's colorful paint was faded and peeling. Carvings on the wooden slats picked up the illumination of the rising sun. The crudely cut letters wriggled like worms under my fingers as I traced them. "Mutter Hydra" "Vater Dagon." I knew a tiny bit of German: "Mother Hydra, Father Dagon."

That sounded familiar—perhaps Berta's delirious mutterings on Friday? I felt like it had been an eternity since then. Had her strange fit really happened not even two days ago?

When I stayed at the New Forest Colony in Southampton, some strange people had visited. We were all pretty strange, I guess, but these guests were even odder. They were quite set on reviving the Germanic traditions of the north. They didn't last long at the Colony, and neither their superior attitude nor devotion to blood magic won them any friends in the coven.

I hadn't paid an enormous amount of attention to their attempts to proselytize. At that time, anyway, I felt any deities that wanted to guide me would make themselves known. They didn't need to be sought out.

But Hydra and Dagon did not sound familiar. Wasn't it…Nerthus, who those German witches were so fond of? Or Njord? Both names, I recalled, two aspects, male and female, of one god. And the Romans invaders had seen and recorded their rituals. Blood sacrifices in a sacred grove. Hangings, but also drownings. In a well.

Along with the German words, a few familiar runes were also carved into the cart, covered in years of dust and bird droppings. I couldn't interpret them, but I was sure I'd seen them recently. I wished I'd thought to bring a pencil and paper. *Some sleuth.*

Finally, I remembered. The well. These same runes were also a faint but recognizable etching on the stonework around the now infamous artesian well.

Violet

CHAPTER THIRTY-ONE

> *The Underwater Spirit motif, often some variation of a flying snake-like chimeric beast, is common at archeological excavations across eastern North America and seems capable of inhabiting both the upper and lower worlds.*
>
> ~From *Ancient Iconography of the Mississippi River Valley* by Francis La Flesche, University of Nebraska Press, 1915.

I decided to double-check the symbols on the well against what I had just seen on the cart. Intellectually, I knew it wasn't important—of course, an old cart belonging to Finn's father or grandfather could have similar markings to the well they'd built. Why not?

But something bothered me. A nurse had pointed them out as we once walked around the grounds, saying they were made by the ancient indigenous tribes of the area. At the time, her words didn't register. It had been early days for me at the Institute, although I at least knew where I was. But I had lost all capacity to think or speak.

In retrospect, the iconography was all wrong. My grandfather collected and studied Mississippian artifacts his whole life, trying to make sense of his own French-Osage heritage. I was no expert, but those images on the well were clearly from some other tradition entirely. One that might be important to whatever troubled this place.

A shadow blocked the light behind me. Teddy must have gotten off work and caught up with me. "Is this what you meant to show me?" I had just begun to turn so that he could see my face when I found myself flat on the floor, my cheek scraping against the frozen earth as I struggled to at least see my attacker.

"Don't," a voice growled as a rag was pressed against my mouth and nose. I fought the sweet fumes to stay conscious, to not slip away. A knee in my back firmly held me down as the person pulled at my coat and patted the sides of my dress. *What do they want?* But I could resist the gas no longer. All went dark as I fell through ice, through water, through the earth itself.

"Welcome, child of land. Welcome home." I understood the message, although the words weren't English.

I tried to breathe, but just gasped into the void. Was I drowning? Finally? Joining my son. Joining my mother. Show me my Tony, show me my child, I shouted without audible words. I sensed a hesitation, a pause. Perhaps whatever entity invited me to death didn't understand what I meant.

"Violet?" In the space of that moment's hesitation, I heard a familiar human voice shouting nearby. "Violet, are you here?" My heart wrenched itself away from the depths as my mind popped above the surface of consciousness. Whoever had been holding me down bound away, the door slamming behind them.

"Teddy? Where are you, mate?" It was Sean. I felt I'd lost some time—minutes? Hours?—and in the interval my mind had continued to work on the puzzle. Just as I struggled to find my voice and answer him, the significance of the old gods to this place and to the Osteen family shifted into a new configuration.

By the light seeping through the chinks between the logs I crawled toward the exit, then struggled to my feet.

"Sean," I wrenched the door open. "I'm here."

He was several yards away, peeking in the door of an abandoned chicken coop. He looked up and nodded, apparently unaware of my distress. "Find anything?" He poked his head into the shed. "Dark as pitch in here. Don't you have a torch?"

I staggered out and, suddenly ill, began gagging and retching.

"Hey, now," he held back my coat and hair. "Get it out, then." I vomited in the snow. "I've given away my last handkerchief. Sorry."

"I—I—" I wiped my tears and mouth on the hem of my dress.

"Deep breaths. In and out. And sit." He guided me to the cart inside the shed. "Jesus-Mary-and-Joseph, this is quite a daft shay," he said, taking in the faded, crumbling flowers and ribbons, the straw effigy, and the peeling paint on the wheel spokes. "You've travelers in these parts?"

"No, I think it's something else entirely. Old world magic."

"And that smell—not ether again?"

I nodded. "Must be the same attacker. But I think I understand now." My head throbbed, and my throat burned. I wanted nothing more than to stretch out in the cart and sleep away into oblivion. But I forced myself to think through my conclusion.

I had to clear Teddy with solid proof of the real criminal, as painful as it might be for him. I couldn't help that. "I'm not sure exactly what happened. But I know who attacked Dr. Elsass and why."

Violet

CHAPTER THIRTY-TWO

> *This agreement for the purchase and sale of Property (the "Agreement"), is made and entered into as of the 27th day of September 1920 (the "Effective Date"), by and between Noble G. Osteen of McLean County, Illinois (hereinafter referred to as "Seller") and Heinrich Ludwig Elsass, MD of St. Louis, Missouri (hereinafter referred to as "Purchaser").*
>
> ~From Real Estate Purchase Agreement, McLean
> County Recorder of Deeds.

I ran to the house, slipping and stumbling through the Grove as its branches tangled in my hair and roots grabbed at my galoshes. Sean ran behind me. "Wait," he panted. "Can't ya just take a moment and tell me who—"

"No time," I called over my shoulder. Thunder rumbled in the distance. "He may be finishing off the cook—" I gasped in a lungful of frozen air, "—as we speak."

"So, it's a man then?" Sean muttered, plodding along behind me. "Then my money's on that Emerson fella."

As we approached the house, we heard car engines and the scrape of metal against frozen gravel. Dashing past a stand of evergreens at the edge of the Grove, we burst upon the parking area behind the kitchen.

Robert, the orderly, steered a car pushed by a couple of the younger male patients out of a snowdrift onto a cleared section of the parking lot. A tractor fitted with a snowplow idled, its driver apparently awaiting the car to be moved. Clouds obscured the rising sun and thrust warm breezes across the prairie. We'd soon have rain rather than snow, I thought as everyone looked up at the sky in response to a thunderclap.

I spotted Carrie in a hat, coat, and boots on the kitchen's small stoop. "Ah, Violet, there you are." Her face was streaked with tears.

We rushed over to her. "What's happened?" I said.

Sean tipped his hat to Carrie, who turned away without acknowledging him. "Mrs. Holmes has died, and Percy has 'arrested' Teddy," she said to me.

"What?" Sean said. "I'll just have a word—" he reached for the doorknob, but I grabbed his arm. I might need some reinforcement very soon.

"I was afraid this would happen." My mind was on the murder and how best to explain the solution, but my feelings were all of sympathy for Carrie. If our places were reversed, if I was the one crying in the cold, my friend wouldn't hesitate to hug me.

I wrapped my arm around her shoulders, tuned to any signal that my touch wasn't helpful, but she melted into my embrace. "That's all wrong," I said. "Teddy is innocent. I know who really did it."

"You do?" Carrie pulled away and stared at me, her eyes wide.

"Finn," I spit out. "It's Finn. I hate to say it, but it's true. Did he attack the cook again?" *And what does attacking the cook have to do with sacrificing Dr. Elsass to his old gods?* A lingering loose end for which I had no explanation. She must have seen or heard something incriminating; I told myself. *Must have.*

"No, she died of her injuries. Should have been in the hospital," Carrie said. "Let's go in. It's going to rain." She opened the kitchen door.

"Wait," I said. "We need to…arrest…" I realized I didn't know the procedure, "or….restrain Finn until the sheriff comes. He could be getting away, right now."

Carrie pointed to the tractor. "He's there."

I whirled around. The men had moved the stuck car, and the tractor's snowplow had commenced clearing another section of the parking lot. I started to run on the ice to the tractor, then thought better of it and stopped. I turn to Sean. "Come with me. We need to get him."

Carrie followed us. "Why Finn?"

"He was angry over Dr. Elsass cheating his father— I've seen the property sales contract—and wanted the land back. He'd even offered to work out a deal to buy it, but the director wouldn't budge. Finn had plenty of opportunity that night as he worked on the furnace and stoker, dealt with the snow, and so forth."

I paused, thinking of the real reason I suspected Finn. The old gods still expected blood sacrifice from the keepers of this place. Finn's father and grandfather had followed the old ways. It must be time for Finn to take up the mantle.

And what better sacrifice than this enemy, this man who stood in the way of his hopes and dreams? Although how I'd explain this motive to Carrie, I'd no idea. She was so sensible and scientific.

"Finn, eh?" Sean said as we slid across the ice. "The whole place was busy from six to seven that night. From what folks have told me, at any rate."

The chugging tractor went silent, Finn climbed down from the cab, and the only sound to be heard was muted conversation from the men. Cigarette smoke drifted through the air.

I stopped and turned to Carrie. "I've been attacked with ether, twice. Just now, as a matter of fact."

Sean's eyes held questions, but he addressed them to Carrie. "Ah, excuse me, Nurse Carrie. How long has Finn been out here, clearing the car park?"

For whatever reason, she wouldn't talk to him. "I haven't been watching the workers the entire time," she said to me. "I couldn't really say."

I was struck with a sense of doubt, a panic deep inside me. Being wrong would destroy me. It would be the end. Worse thing ever. The trees in the Grove whispered amongst themselves, then laughed.

Sean was oblivious to Carrie's snub and my growing dis-ease. He shouted across the parking lot, "Finn. Hey, Finn. Could you be coming over here for a moment?"

Finn looked up, dropped his cigarette, and ground it out before walking slowly toward us.

I could feel my face flush. Doubts were taking hold, firmly. I tried to remember the feel of the attacker as they held me down. The voice muttering in my ear. Had it been Finn?

"Whadda ya need, Mr. Joye?" he said. His demeanor was total innocence. Just a very tired man.

"I don't suppose you've heard," a voice boomed behind us. All heads turned to see Percy Emerson, who stood in the kitchen doorway. "Wow, look at that sky." As he skidded over to us, he said, "I was just about to explain the situation, Finn. I've detained that kid, your friend's son. Pains me to say it—I like him—but I'm convinced he killed old Elsass. Probably an accident, but—"

Finn hauled back to take a swing at Emerson, and Sean tried to restrain him. "That's a lie," the big man said.

"Yes, it is," I blurted. "Because you did it yourself."

"What?" Finn stopped his struggle.

"We've—" I glanced at Sean, "been to the little shed behind the cabin. I'm sure it's what Teddy meant to show me before he was—detained."

"And what does that mean?" asked Carrie. "What's in the shed?"

Finn reddened. "Some nonsense of my father's. He… followed some of the traditions from the old country, after a fashion—Grandfather Jürgen's Dagon-cult foolishness."

"I know exactly what those traditions involved. Did you mean to carry them on?" I asked. "To please the gods and retrieve your property?"

Finn half-smiled. "Don't think old Father Dagon is a real estate attorney." He shook his head as he took a wide stance and crossed his arms. "I didn't hurt Dr. Elsass, and Teddy didn't either. We was both fixing the furnace and stoker Friday evening."

"Someone has attacked Mrs. Humphrey here, twice. About an hour ago, as a matter of fact," Sean said. "How long have you been out here with these fellas?"

"Since before dawn," Finn said. He turned to the smokers. "Ain't that right, boys? All of us been at it since six AM, at least." The men all agreed.

"And I found Teddy about half an hour ago, trying to run off somewhere," Percy said. "We're all safe now. I'll stay until you get the sheriff, Finn. Then I'm taking my wife out of this madhouse, as soon as she's had her lunch."

I stared at the dark clouds, stalled over the eastern horizon. My vision narrowed and grayed. Everything seemed to slow down as I replayed the scene in my head—my accusation, Sean asking the obvious question, Finn speaking the truth. And I knew his version was true, even before his coworkers confirmed it. I'd known all along that whatever logic I applied, in the end, would be wrong. I always make a mess of things. *I'm a stupid, useless woman.*

As I marched away, toward the Grove, someone grabbed my arm to stop me, but I shook them off. A voice, somehow muffled as if I were underwater, cautioned the others, "Leave her be." The rest of them twittered like birds, their murmurs growing faint as I walked deeper into the woodland. *Nothing of importance should ever be in my care.*

I thought the trees would laugh at me, but they were the soul of sympathy. "𝔇𝔬𝔫'𝔱 𝔴𝔬𝔯𝔯𝔶. 𝔖𝔱𝔞𝔶 𝔥𝔢𝔯𝔢. 𝔥𝔬𝔫𝔬𝔯 𝔲𝔰 𝔥𝔢𝔯𝔢," they whispered.

I hated these trees; I'd endured their mockery ever since I'd come to this place, despite all the claims of friendship. I wondered what they knew of the latest voice in my head; the one demanding I join it. Perhaps it was time to follow that voice. I knew in my heart where it would lead.

Yet to avoid its call, I rambled the entire property, heedless of time passing, the damp chill, and the threat of rain. The day grew cold again, freezing, I was sure, but still I wandered.

Eventually, I found myself at the spring which fed the Grove, the water trickling under a paper-thin sheet of ice. The spring had a voice, too, much older and deeper than the trees. I bent down to listen to it, my face touching the ice. Here, the water flowed out of a rock crevice to feed the creek, frozen into a block of futility and regret. The water planted a thought—my troubles could all end here.

Finn had once told me that this spring had a deeper branch, the source of the artesian well. The place where Dr.

Chapter Thirty-Two

Elsass had died. "𝔑𝔬, 𝔫𝔬, 𝔫𝔬," the trees whispered. "𝔖𝔱𝔞𝔶 𝔴𝔦𝔱𝔥 𝔲𝔰."

"Be still," I ordered them, my voice weak, then I hurried to the well, misty in the afternoon light, its flow from deep within the earth warmer than the frozen air. A sulfuric rotten egg odor crept along the frozen mud.

I sat, exhausted, on the stone-flagged path for a long, long time. I could die here. Follow my son, follow my mother, under the water. Make it all stop. I lay my head on the pavers, the cold providing a pleasant numbing of body and mind. It was an odd angle from which to view the world, and I found myself examining the minutiae of the ground's debris poking up through the snow: weed stems, fallen branches, and dead leaves.

A curled leaf sheltered something, something white. Not snow; a roll of gauze. How very odd. I pocketed it, and overcome with exhausted remorse, lay down again.

I dreamed of falling on ice, cracks slowly snaking out from under my weight until I fell into the frigid water.

When I awoke I was confused for a moment, but remembering what had happened and how I came to be there, I scrambled away from the hideous well.

Yet I couldn't look away from the water, for I saw a face, obscure, distance, and all too real, under the ice.

Maybe face wasn't the right word. A visage, in repose. A scaled form with bulging, closed eyes. As I stared, it opened them and grimaced, revealing rows of pointed teeth in its wide mouth. Powerful claws reached out for a moment to scratch the ice but then it dove deep and was gone.

Dr. Elsass's body had marks around his neck. Had this thing in the water attacked him?

That makes the situation as clear as mud, I thought. No human murderer to discover at all, just a monster in the water. *The sheriff will like that solution.*

But this could be more evidence against Finn—he lured Dr. Elsass here as a sacrifice to this genius loci. Everyone will think I'm crazy if I say there's a monster in the well. Yet, I've seen such things before. Awful, awe-full things.

Maybe the monster had a hand in it, but no monster lured Dr. Elsass with a note. No monster met with him in the cabin. No monster had attacked me with ether, searched me for...I didn't know what.

The attacker had felt in my pockets. *Was something that I carried now missing?*

I examined myself and my memory again, and then recalled the microscope slide we'd found in the lab. I'd given it to Dr. Cole, but only the two of us knew that.

The sun, low in the sky, peeked out from behind the clouds, and the mist off the well was thicker. The pieces of the puzzle began to slide together in a new configuration. Then I smelled smoke.

Sean

CHAPTER THIRTY-THREE

The peasantry say they are sometimes what they call 'púca led,' that is, that they are occasionally waylaid in the night by a mischievous sprite who leads then into ditches, bogs, pools, and other such scrapes.

~From *Fairy Mythology: Illustrative of the Romance and Superstition of Various Countries* by Thomas Knightley. Rev. Ed, 1892, George Bell and Sons, London.

Honestly, I was all at sixes and sevens—my impulse was to go after Violet, but she'd probably want me to watch Finn. Not that I believed her theory about him for a minute. If anyone had helped the director along to the other side, my money was on Percy Emerson.

Knowing Violet, she'd likely prefer to pull herself together in private. Our investigation would be best served by me having a word or two with Emerson. I couldn't help but smile; I was treating Violet like her old, bossy self rather than a fragile mental patient.

The trouble with this case was that every witness was also a suspect. I would have loved to think it all over, calmly with a cup of tea and a pipe, but an elderly gent had appeared on the kitchen stoop to hector me. "And what are you grinning at, young man? We're not paying you to stand around. Hop to it."

Finn left off his explanation to Carrie and said to me, "I know you're a guest, but..." he glanced at the growing group of elderly board members who had come outside to supervise the car park clearing. "Could you give us a hand? We need to get these cars dug out and the driveway cleared. Then I'm going for the sheriff. This should have been his problem from the start, and the sooner he takes charge, the better."

I tried to be logical for a change. What trouble could Emerson cause between now and when the road becomes passable? He's got a scapegoat for the moment, anyway. It made no difference to me if he took his wife to St. Louis or not, although I imagined Violet would have an opinion about that.

Something wasn't sitting easy in the back of my brain. It told me Violet would need me before very long. I trusted her abilities, but had seen enough uncanny things around the place to still worry.

Yet I asked Finn, "What do you need?" and we worked steadily all morning. It never did rain—just thunder and lightning to the east—and by afternoon, the car park started to look passable. Carrie stepped outside to check on us as we took a smoke break.

Me, her, and Finn gathered on the stoop, and he said, "I'm going to head into town now. Robert can keep on plowing with the truck. Will you watch over Teddy while I'm gone?"

"Of course," Carrie said. "Percy is being ridiculous."

"Should I go get his dad?" I asked.

"Best not. No point in getting Tomás all riled up over a misunderstanding that will be cleared up in a few hours. Once I explain things to the sheriff."

"Anything else?"

"Wish me luck, I guess." Finn glanced at the sky, then collected all the wraps he'd shed while plowing the car park. He bundled himself up against the cold and chugged off down the driveway on the tractor.

"The sheriff will see reason; it was an accident," Carrie said, scanning the car park. "Violet's not out here with you, Sean?"

A wave of worry seized me. "I thought she wanted to be alone, but…it's been a while. She didn't go inside, eh?"

"No. I've just made rounds and didn't see her."

And Violet had run off into that púca-filled grove. Cursing my stupidity, I said, "I'll have a look around the property."

Carrie loosened up a bit now that we had some privacy. She bestowed a lovely smile and a peck on the cheek. "Thank you. For everything."

"I live to serve, ma'am."

I spent the rest of the afternoon searching that deceptive copse of trees—much bigger on the inside than it appeared, then moved on to a small family burial plot and the frozen creek. It was almost dark when I found my way back to the woods near the artesian well. Maybe I'd unconsciously avoided it. And then I heard familiar voices. Violet was deep in conversation with…someone.

Violet

CHAPTER THIRTY-FOUR

Dear Diary (or whoever reads my journal when I'm out of the room),

I've heard a voice since I first came here. It calls on me more and more frequently. I know I should have told you, but it won't let me. The trees still chatter away whenever I'm outside, but this voice is different. It feels dangerous.

~From patient's journal, Violet Humphrey.
Entry dated December 1, 1924.

I suppose I'd grown accustomed to the rotten egg smell of the artesian well, but the smoke on the air revived the stench. I felt nauseated again and began to breathe through my mouth.

The smell of smoke wasn't unusual, especially out in the country. But something about it—a scent of chemicals and hopes destroyed—triggered a deep sadness. And although the actual smoke reaching me was negligible, I felt smothered. Crouching low on the icy pavers, I stared once again into the water.

It offered peace and escape from the mistakes I continually made; I was so often wrong about so much. Teddy would be better off without my paltry efforts to help him. So many others would do a better job in his defense.

Some bit of information tugged at me, striving for attention. By now, I was fully convinced a monster lurked in the well. A monster that had attacked and killed Dr. Elsass. But why?

I didn't know much about nonhuman entities, but I would think such a kill would be for food or self-defense. Dr. Cole hadn't mentioned any wounds or puncture marks, just bruising. I suppose I should have examined the body more closely. Or was there another purpose altogether to the altercation with Dr. Elsass? I thought of the Underwater Spirit, both feared and revered by the ancient Mississippians, gently carrying off my dying grandfather, and his ecstatic expression as they took to the air.

Though I didn't understand how or why, the well was a dangerous influence. I started to stand up, blinking and shaking my head to break the mesmerizing effect of the water's ebb and flow.

But I felt the presence of the well's inhabitant before I saw their webbed appendage hovered over me, as if hesitant to stroke my hair; a gentle, courteous posture. Their skin was beautiful in the gathering gloom, an iridescent sheen of green-purple-silver.

An offer of comfort hung in the air, a pause for consent. I acquiesced, not quite sure why, but I had to know what they wanted to share with me. What they had to show me. I felt very alone. Alone and worthless.

The touch was firm and warm against my cheek, and recognition hit me immediately. We were linked, somehow. They did want something, that was clear, quite a lot, actually—devotion, worship, my very life—but they wanted me to freely give my allegiance.

Who are you? What are you? I formed the question in my mind, in my heart. The answer was merely a feeling—of longing and belonging. Of home. Did Dr. Elsass meet you, too?

Was the reaction amusement? Did they laugh? *Explain yourself.* I'd already seen them in their slumber deep under the water. The image rose again in my mind and with it an accessed memory: Dr. Elsass communing with this entity. Bargaining for wealth.

"And you, what could he give you in return?" I asked.

"My family needs souls." They spoke in a deep, guttural croaking cadence, measured and almost hypnotic. Utterly strange, yet familiar, somehow. "Souls willing to accept the life eternal Mother Hydra and Father Dagon offer. I am their prophet."

I shook my head to break the trance I felt descending on my consciousness. "Life eternal?" I laughed. "That sounds awful."

"Ah, you have suffered, child, I know that. I came to this prairie, so far from the sea, for one purpose: to ease suffering through the good news of Father Dagon and Mother Hydra."

"I...I...I don't see how they can help me."

"Our life eternal is joyful, free of painful memories. A life of companionship, discovery, and adventure, growing in strength and devotion to the gods. It is good, but lonely as things have transpired for me."

"How is this possible? Elsass is—was—a human."

"I have power. You've seen my control of water in all its forms." He gestured to the horizon, where lightning strikes of purple and silver illuminated the clouded sunset.

If I can get them to brag a bit more, I may understand the threat better. "Hmm, weather magic. I think my husband learned that from a spell book."

A glower passed across their face. "I have deeper powers. I communicate through the mind, as you know. And my will can possess the weak."

I thought as much. "So, it's been you in my head all along? And speaking through Berta?" I thought of my experience with Dr. Elsass's corpse. "And the body?"

"Mere tricks. Trivial. My real power is the transformation from the imperfect human form to my own, the sacred image of the almighty Dagon. I've studied and trialed my methods for years. The spell is almost—no, it *is* perfected. If I hadn't been interrupted at the most crucial point..."

They sounded too much like my late husband, convinced that magic was the only way to achieve his goals. A ruthless man, always looking for a shortcut. And thinking on Taylor, I thought of Sean Joye. Taylor's killer. And my defender. Once again, I'd left him behind. "And

Dr. Elsass agreed to undergo your magic?" I had my doubts about that.

"He would have. He was almost ready. And then… Allow me to show you."

In my mind's eye I saw Dr. Elsass slipping and sliding in the dark, running away from a shadowy figure who grabbed and pulled at him, shoving him to the ground. He fell, his head clunking against the pavers. The person tended the wound, then ran away.

"And you, what did you do to him then?"

"His life was seeping away. I put him into the water and began the ritual. I held his vital essence, a vibrant spark, his body ready to begin the transformation. A large portion of my essence spent—I'd no time to hunt a proper sacrifice. But then—"

"The attacker returned. With first aid supplies." I'd just found a roll of gauze among the leaves and forest debris. It all made sense.

He nodded, as if agreeing with my thoughts. "The most destructive force on earth. Love."

Yes, I had to agree with that. Love was the great slayer.

An accident, as Carrie had long maintained. A hasty, emotional outburst followed by a miscalculation of the cook's health and fortitude. At least, that was what I chose to think.

I had to notify someone.

While I absorbed their testimony, the creature wound its upper appendage around me, hugging my neck and shoulders. I rested in their arms, ready to cry. Comfortable and safe, I reluctantly freed myself from the pliant, muscular grasp. "Not now," I whispered. "Someday soon, I'll come to you."

Violet

CHAPTER THIRTY-FIVE

> *Grotesque beyond the imagination of a Poe or a Bulwer, they*
> *were damnably human in general outline despite webbed hands*
> *and feet, shockingly wide and flabby lips, glassy, bulging eyes, and*
> *other features less pleasant to recall.*

> ~From "Dagon" by H.P. Lovecraft,
> *The Vagrant Magazine,* November 1919.

"Now." Their grip on me tightened. "This is a lonely place. Few people of the air understand. You must stay with me." Their tone was desperate, frightened, even. "This can be your place, your heritage. I appreciate your help and have gifts for you."

I pulled away, struggling against their enormous strength, a few flakes of luminous scales clinging to my hands. For as easy an escape as the water seemed to me earlier, my life, its possibilities and responsibilities, now unfurled before me. Yes, many of my loved ones were dead and gone: my baby, my husband, my parents—but my niece remained, her mother a murderess on her way to the gallows if the court system offered any justice at all.

And Kyffin, my oldest friend, as close as a brother, barely recovered from a near-deadly attack. And I had some responsibility in that. "I don't understand. How have I helped you? Who are you?" There was something about the shape of its eyes, the square of its jaw—

All glamour dropped in their eagerness to overpower me. I could see my ally-adversary clearly, even though the evening gloom gathered along with smoke rolling across the ground. The smoke mixed with the mist rising off the water.

The eyes were large, dark orbs, set in an iridescent, scaly face. Sharp, white incisors shone behind a thin-lipped, wide-mouthed grin. The figure was as tall as me, perhaps even taller if not hunched over so. Their neck was thick, with rough gills along either side. Powerful shoulders jutted forward, and a prominent dorsal ridge extended from its head down its spine and ended in a long tail.

I tried to escape but fell on the ice.

"No, don't go." I heard their words in my head as I crawled away.

"I...I...must. People need me."

"People," they scoffed, this time speaking aloud. "People limited to the air. My progeny is as blind as the rest of the poor, air-sucking fools."

They helped me to my feet. Their touch was clammy, and my blood ran ice cold. *What did they mean by 'progeny?'* "You have children?"

"I'm Jürgen Osteen; the patriarch of this family. The gods sent me to establish an outpost here, a mission you might say, not so long ago. I had—I continue to have—a vision of a great city. We are the pioneers."

"Jürgen" sounded familiar. "You are...Finn's grandfather?"

He looked irritated, even angry. "And yours, although the connection is long forgotten. But that is how I could so easily bid you help me."

"What?" Grandfather Antoine's stories, that I remembered anyway, revolved around his Osage family members exiled by the government to the Oklahoma territory reservation. "I've never heard of...anyone like... you. And I still don't understand how I've been of any help."

"Nevertheless, it's true. You removed the wards set by that redheaded witch whenever I asked. Because we are family. And I care for my family."

My hands, so often dirty with nails broken. I found a misty memory of me digging with them in the Grove. And holding an incised stone. I glared at him and noticed his eyes were moist. Was this creature about to cry? "Your son, I could take you to him," he said. "The child abides with the old one of the deep earth."

Rage flashed through me. "Don't lie to me. We buried my Tony over a year ago. We were talking about Finn. Your...grandson?"

"Finley, son of my son Noble, has rejected our ways. Perhaps the metamorphosis will still bless him, then he'll have no choice. But to you I speak of the spirit, the essence of our life." He blinked. "You, too, are my child. I know magics that will allow you to visit me for a time under the water. The bond will not harm you, but, when you wish, it will change you completely. You will live forever."

My mind reeled. His proposal was absurd, but how long had he been here alone, existing in this aquafer? Preying on, or perhaps seducing, the unwitting inhabitants? Had Finn's father disappointed him? Was his suicide an avoidance of a dark and watery life eternal?

I had to get away, but knew I couldn't outrun Jürgen, not with those powerful leaping hind legs. And I had to stop him. Stop him from hurting us "air people" any further.

"You're right. You can't outrun me," I heard in my mind. "I can chase you as far as you care to run. You've removed the wards that confined me to this well."

I couldn't outrun or overpower him. I had no gun or club. As thunder rumbled overhead, a ray of the setting sun blinded me.

The winter solstice, shortest day of the year. I thought on the Earth whirling about the sun and spinning on its axis, and all of space beyond it. Benign stars, just there. Their power always available but never forced upon us.

I wasn't without protection, even if I'd neglected to use my resources of late. My teachers had trained me on the magic of the natural world, plants and animals, animated all by the warm energies of the sun and cool radiance of the moon.

"Your hedge magic is nothing against the power of water and earth that I command," Jürgen said.

"Maybe." If I kept him talking aloud, would that also keep him out of my head? "But…" I peered at him more closely in the gathering twilight. "Tell me more. Who are you to me?"

"I've lived here since 1834, me and my kin."

"Finn told me the Osteen family farmed here for many years." I probed, I hoped subtly, filling my conscious mind with images of Finn, the family burial plot, the huge vegetable garden, and anything that spoke of the property before Dr. Elsass moved his asylum into the mansion house. Deeper, more instinctively, I reached out to the energies of the stars as the sun set into the solstice.

His eyes snapped. "My firstborn, Winnie," he choked on the name, as if it hurt to speak. "That was your great-great-grandmother. Ran off with a city man in 1852."

"Who—or what, did this to you? Made you…" I'd been inching away, and my back now brushed against a juniper bush. I reached behind me to snap off a small branch.

"A monster? You mean gifted me with strength, intelligence, and eternal life? Taught me the deep magic of earth and water energies?" In one huge leap, he bound up and over the artesian well and stood on the rock path around the bubbling spring. "The blessing of Father Dagon and Mother Hydra on our people—your people—going back through all of time."

I had to keep him distracted while I wound the charm. I had the beeswax candle stub from the cabin, a bit of floss, and the five-pointed stone I'd dug up earlier. A rock that was apparently a warding stone placed by Comfrey. My teachers had mentioned such items, precious, rare, and so very dangerous.

I held the wax close to my heart, infusing it with my body heat and intent. And guilt. Because here I was, again, working magic on the unsuspecting without their permission.

"And what became of Dr. Elsass the other night?" a voice said.

Sean Joye. Where had he come from? Thankful for the distraction Sean provided, yet wary of what Jürgen might do to him, I pushed and pulled at the wax. I willed it to greater pliancy mixing in Jürgen's shed scales.

"Ah, you, sir. At last, we meet in the flesh," Jürgen said. "Welcome in. As for Elsass, a dross and mundane creature of little heart and less spirit. Perhaps all he really wanted of me was treasure."

"How so?" Sean asked. "You don't seem all that wealthy. These Institute folks got your house. Although you've got some interesting books, I'll grant you that."

My fingers worked furiously, the wax at last soft enough to form a head, a tail, and hind quarters. *It doesn't have to be perfect.* My gathered intentions and a link to his essence were the only requirements. My hands buried in my pocket, I wrapped the effigy, the warding stone, and the juniper with the floss in a clockwise motion. One wrap. Bind this entity to my will. Two wraps. Hold it to this place. Three wraps. Be silent.

Jürgen shrugged. "The Elsass man did hector and plague my son, Noble." Then he growled, "Drove my boy to self-destruction."

Protecting this property, these people, from Jürgen Osteen was my current problem. I'd deal with whatever happened to Dr. Elsass in due course. The time for my magic was now or never.

I ran to the well and dipped the juniper sprig in the water, just as Jürgen released a spell of his own, summoning a plume of water to rise out of the well and strike me with a glancing blow. I staggered, almost dropping the hex. What a fool I was. I hadn't even thought to put up a defense but realized Sean had tackled him at a critical moment, blunting the impact of Jürgen's spell.

My magical reflexes kicked in faster than my feeble thoughts and memories. I reached down deep to ground myself, rooting into the earth energies, the primal forces of the prairie, as a shield. But also, I cast my mind and heart up and out as I tethered my essence to the brilliant stars.

Jürgen staggered as he tried to regroup for another magical assault. I felt him tugging at my shield. "Good," I heard in my head, "I can turn your magics into my own," just as Sean punched him in the jaw.

At that moment the whispering trees chimed in. "𝔅𝔯𝔦𝔫𝔤 𝔲𝔰 𝔶𝔬𝔲𝔯 𝔢𝔫𝔢𝔯𝔤𝔶," they urged me. "𝔚𝔢'𝔩𝔩 𝔰𝔱𝔯𝔢𝔫𝔤𝔱𝔥𝔢𝔫 𝔞𝔫𝔡 𝔡𝔢𝔣𝔢𝔫𝔡 𝔶𝔬𝔲."

I ignored the trees and thought again of my little niece and what I owed her. And my obligations to the idiot apparently set on a boxing match on my behalf with a powerful supernatural entity.

And what I owed myself. I'd lived a life, if not in service of others, then in thrall of their expectations. It was time to make a stand.

"I abjure you to this well from this day forth." I brandished the totem. "Trouble the water if you must but leave the people of the air in peace. Leave Finn and his people in peace. Do not reach out in words or dreams, through your own voice or that of any minion beings. You are bound here for— "

I knew the form of the conjuring. I had to define the terms exactly, including an end. And I knew my power, or more accurately, lack thereof. That I was even able to do this much after two years of ignoring the Lady and Lord was a testament to their benevolence rather than my skills as a witch. "A year and a day." That would buy me some time to study and seek help.

Jürgen swatted Sean away, my friend crumpling into a pile of snow and ice, then our attacker crouched to leap at me. "King Holly, lend your aid," I shouted, gesturing at the foliage all around us.

Jürgen paused, perhaps surprised, then shouted words in a language old and harsh. The waters roiled and bubbled, bursting the confines of the well and swamping Sean and me. And I saw Jürgen, really saw him, in his hideousness and uncanniness. I felt my mind slipping into that dark place I'd inhabited for so long. *No, no, no.*

The nearby creek rose, a deluge crashing in on us as he pounced, and I fell into the rapidly freezing water next to Sean's unconscious form. I struggled to lift my head above the flood as debris smacked me in the face and pulled me under. Snarling, Jürgen raised his right claw to strike me. I braced for the blow, all the while fighting to stay afloat. Instead of a blow, I felt him release me.

I scrambled to my feet to see him entangled in vines, which pulled him toward the well. Sean stood up out of the receding flood, blinking and unsteady, but at least he was alive. I thanked the gods with all my heart and commenced the binding circle clockwise round the well. Drenched and shaking from the sudden, bitter cold, I had to do this. And do it now.

I stopped at the point from which I'd watched the winter sun set. "Guardian of the East, bind Jürgen Osteen to this place." My teeth chattered as I proceeded to the south, while Jürgen snarled and snapped at me. The waters continued to recede without his attention to his spell.

"Watcher of the South, keep Jürgen safely home at this place." I hurried on to the point where the last purple hues faded from the western horizon and the storm clouds dispersed.

"Spirits of the West, turn back any intruder into this sacred circle."

Jürgen made one last assault, his voice in my head threatening, "I'll drown you. At your own hand. And keep you alone in the dark. You'll see no one in the afterlife. Child, mother, father—never."

I banished his voice from my head. Perhaps he was right. But I had to do this for the people in my charge now. "Sentinels of the North, hold Jürgen Osteen apart in this place."

I moved on to the eastern gate and gave a moment of thanks. Only then, in the quiet, did I take in the full import of my thoughts. Duty to the people who the Lord and Lady had given me now. I heard a splash behind me. Turning, I saw Jürgen Osteen disappear into the artesian well. Sean staggered over to me and with clumsy, frozen hands helped fix the totem to the well's stone pavers under a cairn of rocks, charging each with its role to protect the land. For a year and a day.

Violet

CHAPTER THIRTY-SIX

I can't shake the feeling of being watched. I've often felt it when out and about on the grounds. I tell myself it is just Cook, feeding tramps again, but after what I thought I saw…no, I did see it! Someone is out there, and they are up to no good.

~From personal journal, Carrie Bartowski,
December 21, 1924.

We hurried to the mansion, wet and shivering, to find the staff dousing the last embers of a house fire, the wide wrap-around front porch a charred ruin and shattered glass from the windows glittering in the light.

Following a gaggle of patients and nurses, we soon found ourselves at Finn's farmhouse. Carrie greeted us with blankets then moved through the house, directing her nurses.

"I'm going to make myself useful," Sean murmured in my ear.

I nodded and gave his hand a little squeeze. "You were helpful back there."

He shrugged. "Truly, you had the bloke well in hand." Then he vanished into the kitchen.

Tomás was serving hot drinks to everyone. The staff had organized the patients by their room assignments, and someone had had the presence of mind to grab the admission ledger in the hubbub of evacuating the building.

Carrie began checking off each person against the list as she took a moment to squeeze their hand or hug them. When people asked what happened, she merely said, "We're looking into it," but her expression hurled daggers at Percy. *What has he done now?*

I saved my news about the murders and let her do her work. But my heart went out to Teddy, obviously itching to help, but confined to a rocking chair in the corner. "Don't think you're going to slip away in all this, young man," Percy said. He got right in the boy's face. "I know you understand me."

Sean appeared from the kitchen, hair still frozen, with a steaming mug of coffee, which he pressed it into my hand. "You got it all worked out?"

"I think so."

His quizzical expression gave way to a grin. "Then spill the beans." I realized there was no better time to put an end to it.

I strode to the center of the room, which buzzed with chatting, coughs, and nervous laughter. "Can I have your attention?"

A few people, dozing in their chairs from the unaccustomed physical activity and overexcitement startled, looked at me in shock, as if the farm dog had suddenly started talking. Most, though, intent on their conversation, didn't even hear.

"Listen to me." A few more glanced my way, then at Carrie. *Nurse, come get your unruly patient.*

"Quiet," a male voice boomed from the kitchen doorway. That got their attention. "Quit your yapping," continued Tomás. "Lady's got something to say." He turned to me. "Sorry, Mrs. Humphrey. Go ahead."

By chance the room was arranged into a little theater. I moved to the stage—an open area at the hearth.

"Are you going to tell us what started the fire?" said Dr. Lieberman.

"I don't know anything about that. But we've been through a lot since Friday." My voice was a hoarse whisper from inhaling ether and shouting magical incantations, and it hurt to speak. "We've been afraid and blaming someone, anyone, to make ourselves feel safe and innocent. But the deaths here aren't your responsibility. You didn't make a bad decision or fail to see an obvious warning. Not your fault..." I looked around the room at the faces, now staring at me in rapt attention, "except for one of you."

Berta stood closest to me, staring into the flames in the hearth. On a loveseat sat Blanche, her eyes red-rimmed. Carrie was next to her; her arm draped across her patient's shoulders. Dr. Cole looked distinctly uneasy in an easy chair, while Mrs. Elsass sat in its matching piece, looking even more uneasy. Percy hovered over Teddy, his prisoner. Board members filled several kitchen chairs pulled into the room. Sean lounged in the threshold leading out into the hall and beyond it the front door, while Tomás more obviously guarded the exit to the kitchen. Except for the patients with their attendants scattered throughout the house, I had everyone's attention.

"If you think you know what happened to Dr. Elsass," said Dr. Abel, "Please explain. I'm sure the sheriff will be here soon."

"And don't forget Mrs. Holmes, the cook. She has died of her injuries," I said.

"We've got our man, right here, Abel. All wrapped up for the sheriff," Percy said, clamping his hand on Teddy's shoulder. "The evidence is as clear as glass."

Tomás protested and crossed the room in a few strides to glower at Percy, his fists balled. Sean scooted away from his station to separate the two.

"You have no real evidence. And Teddy is not 'your man'." I shifted my gaze to Tomás. "Please, all of you. Hear me out. Have a little patience."

With that, Percy shrugged, raised his hands in mock surrender, and stepped away. "Then deduce away, police lady. We're all ears."

"Come on, son," Tomás said to Teddy, hugging him as he walked him into the kitchen.

"Don't go far," Percy called after them. "My money is still on the kid," he said to the rest of us.

A log clunked as it shifted on the andiron, and wind rattled the windows. I took a deep breath and began again.

"Dr. Elsass posed a threat to several of you, but we didn't know that last Friday. His death appeared to be an accidental fall, unlikely, but understandable given the weather conditions. Dr. Cole concluded the head injury was consistent with a fall. Is that correct, Doctor?"

"Yes, although he had water in his lungs. Consistent with drowning. And injuries to the body, as if he'd been held under the water."

I held up a hand to stop him. "Exactly but we need to take it slowly." And I needed to pause: I couldn't avoid my memory of the man encircled by mist and crumpled on the path of the artesian well. I blinked to clear the image and looked again at the faces staring at me.

"While some maintain this was an accidental death," I turned to Carrie, "others are determined to see murder." I gestured to Percy.

He glared at me. "Someone lured him out there. With a note."

"Yes, the note. Anyone could write a note," I said. "In fact, this story is full of notes, the waterlogged invitation being only one. We have medical progress notes, financial records, a deed, institutional bylaws, and a notebook to consider, too."

"Alright, get on with it," Percy said, lighting a cigarette. "Who did it?"

"The attack on the cook leads me to agree with you, Mr. Emerson. Dr. Elsass was murdered. Mrs. Holmes saw or heard something that would incriminate the killer—whether the director's death was accidental or deliberate, the killer feared being found out."

"Then they are guilty of a second murder," Dr. Abel said.

"Yes, although I suspect they didn't mean for the cook to die, just to be out of the way for a while, long enough for the killer to make an escape. They didn't count on the roads being impassable all weekend or the cook's frailty."

Dr. Bertinelli spoke up. "Isn't this place full of inmates who could take it into their head to shove someone down the stairs into a coal cellar and lock its door?"

"Shame on you," Dr. Cole said, rising. "As a board member, you represent this facility and should know better. Mentally troubled persons are no more likely to be violent than you or I. If one did lash out, unlikely, but— they wouldn't have the presence of mind to lock up. They'd be sobbing in a corner somewhere, frightened."

"We're wandering off topic," I raised my voice, and the room quieted. "Given the attack on the cook, we can assume, for the moment at least, that someone needed to silence her on the subject of Dr. Elsass's death. Thus, something is suspicious about his death. Mr. Joye or I have talked to most of you privately," my eyes caught Sean's, and he gave me a thumbs up, "but let's review. Who saw Dr. Elsass last, before I found the body around seven PM on Friday?"

"Most of us were together," said Dr. Abel. "We had cocktails before dinner, then the director left us, shortly before six, I think."

"Yes, the clock chimed six, and he was in the room," said Carrie. "I remember thinking I needed to go check on the musicale in the parlor."

"You all agree on that?" I looked around the room. Most nodded. "And who was there, at six?"

"I was," said Carrie. "The board members. Servers. Blanche."

"He wasn't," Percy pointed at Dr. Cole. "Not a sign of him all afternoon."

"As I've shared with Mrs. Humphrey—not that it's any of your concern," the young doctor said, voice icy, "I was traveling from Chicago. I arrived here around 6:30."

"And I believe you left the cocktail party shortly after Dr. Elsass," I said to Percy. "Isn't that so?"

"I just went to speak to Elsass, privately. Then I returned to the party."

"Don't remember that," said Dr. Bertinelli, his brow furrowed.

"You were asleep, you old coot," said Dr. Abel.

"So, we know Dr. Elsass left the cocktail party a bit before six, and Lottie saw him leave through the kitchen not long after six. He had his coat on. And Violet found him just before seven," Sean said.

"And that makes her the most likely suspect," said Percy.

"You say everyone, except for you, is the most likely suspect," Dr. Cole snapped. "And Mrs. Humphrey was under observation when the cook was attacked."

"It was obviously an accident," Carrie murmured. "Both incidents."

No one paid her much attention.

"In a way, I'm grateful for your suspicion," I said. "Putting me under observation immediately meant that I was in the clear for the attack on the cook, who must have witnessed something from her vantage in the kitchen. The question is, what did she see that her helper didn't?"

"It could be what she knew." Blanche spoke for the first time.

"Did you say something, dear?" Percy said.

"Not what she saw, but what she knew." Blanche spoke a little louder. "Or, what the person who attacked Elsass thought she knew." She rubbed her knees. "Whoever it was must have been very frightened. Or ashamed."

"Very true. Now, picture the scene. We have people coming and going in the parlor, awaiting the meal, having drinks, mingling," I said. "Dr. Elsass has left, for reasons unknown, to go outside, dressed for the weather—"

"What's the relevance of how he was dressed?" Carrie asked.

"Not just stepping out for a moment," Sean said. "And he ended up a quarter of a mile away."

"Yes," I said, "tell us about the note, Dr. Cole."

"As you know, it was waterlogged. The ink had run, obscuring some of the letters, but "Meet at the well," is a reasonable hypothesis for the message."

"Or "Need to talk," I said. "You and I saw evidence— footprints in the snow— that someone went to the cabin that night."

"The meeting, wherever it was, and the attack on the cook both indicate some deliberate action," Dr. Bertinelli said, "as opposed to an accident."

I shrugged, "I suspect a bit of both. Hear me out." I turned to Dr. Cole. "Could you describe, again, your thoughts on the injury and the body's position?"

"Certainly. As I've said, he slipped on the ice, his feet went flying up in the air, and he landed in a supine position, hitting the back of the head."

"But you found him later, in the water," Percy said.

"Correct," said Dr. Cole. "With his head wound bandaged with a pressure dressing made from his necktie and handkerchief."

"He could have done that himself," Carrie said.

Dr. Cole shook his head. "That would be awkward, even if he weren't dazed from the fall."

"And he ultimately drowned. What I don't understand is why someone would give first aid for the head injury, then drown him." Some aspects of this tale weren't consistent, but I wondered if my audience would be sharp enough to notice. I certainly couldn't talk to this group about Jürgen.

"He may have recovered enough to be able, even in his confused state, to bandage himself and move a bit, but unfortunately, into the pool of water rather than away from it," Dr. Cole mused. "Yet, don't forget the bruises around his neck and shoulders."

Percy stood, walked over to the fireplace, and poked at the logs. "He went to meet a note writer at the well, maybe argued, then walked, ran, whatever, away, and he falls, or they hit him with a rock—"

"A fall seems more likely—"

"OK, lady detective, he falls into the pool thing—"

"Artesian well," Finn intoned from the kitchen doorway.

Everyone turned to him. "You're back," Carrie gasped.

"Yes. Sheriff had quite a lot going on. But likely on his way by now."

"Finn," I said. "You know every inch of this place."

He snorted. "I expect so. Grew up here."

"I imagine it was a blow that your father sold the property."

The big man shrugged. "At the time—my father didn't consult me. I hadn't talked to him in years."

"When did you learn—"

He glared at me, defiant. I'd falsely accused him once. I'm sure he felt I was doing it again. "That the old sod had sold it all? When he killed himself. Not a word to me about his troubles." He sat heavily in a chair and buried his face in his hands. "This…legacy preyed on his mind, demanding a lot. It craves blood." He looked up, "He fed it his own."

"And the sacrifices didn't stop there, though," I said.

Finn laughed. "It always wants more." He glanced back at his family, huddled in the kitchen. "But…Tomás loves it here. It doesn't seem to touch him. I thought—"

"You could get your homestead back?" Sean said. "But Dr. Elsass wouldn't sell."

I'd just met Finn's legacy. Jürgen promised rest and everlasting life, but he was a murderous intelligence knitted to this land. I'd always felt the menace and heard his whispers. How could Tomás so easily ignore it?

"I see where you're going." Finn crouched at the hearth, tending the fire. "Elsass wouldn't even discuss selling, much less work out a payment plan. In fact, he'd found some paragraph in the sales contract about me owing him rent. But I didn't kill him."

"Yet you were alone, working on the coal stoker between six and seven PM," I said.

"Gall durn, you all heard me, banging and clattering in the basement."

"The clatter was on and off," Carrie said. "Not really verification of anything."

"Hell, it got fixed, didn't it? Heat came on. And Teddy was with me, most of the time."

"Miss—pardon me, Mrs. Humphrey, please come to the point," Dr. Lieberman said, gesturing at me with his ear trumpet. "If you've proof that one of us, or someone else here on the property, did away with Dr. Elsass, just present it."

"It was the kid," Percy said. "Motive, means, and opportunity. "Elsass owed him money—it's right here, in his notebook." He waved a small pad of paper around. "He's a big, strong boy and constantly writing notes to people. Elsass wouldn't think that odd at all. And he weren't with the rest of us from six to seven."

Chapter Thirty-Six

"He was with me," Finn fumed. "Working on the furnace."

"You're his father's...friend. What else are you going to say?" Percy was unnaturally calm. "Perhaps you two degenerates are in it together."

Finn glowered at Percy as the room fell dead silent.

I needed to change the subject and quickly. "As a number of people have reported and he himself admitted, Mr. Emerson wasn't with the group the entire time, either."

He sputtered but said nothing.

"My point is almost everyone here had a motive to wish Dr. Elsass was out of the picture. From jealousy—" I looked at Mrs. Elsass and Percy, "to fear of blackmail—" I continued to hold Percy's gaze, "to pure frustration at his stubbornness—" I turned to Dr. Cole, Carrie, and then Finn. "He was cheating the staff out of wages and cooking the books, all without the board's awareness."

The room erupted in a clamor of protests.

A sharp whistle from Sean punctuated the noise. "You'll be calming down now. Let the lady speak."

I sighed. "But sadly, none of these motives come into play. The motive for this crime was love." That got their attention. "And these deaths were accidents." In a way, at least. Clear thinking and a little foresight would have prevented both.

"This is what happened," I said. "Someone had an urgent need to speak with Dr. Elsass and set up a meeting during the time everyone would be milling about at the cocktail party.

"What was so private, so secret, it couldn't be discussed indoors? The house was fine for the director harassing me over my bill, Teddy talking to him about wages, and Percy sharing a concern."

Dr. Cole's mind seemed to be miles away. But suddenly he blurted, "The rabbit."

"Yes," I said. "We found, and Dr. Cole confirms, that one of his experimental animals was used for a pregnancy test, quite recently."

"And if someone wanted to discuss that with Dr. Elsass?"

"They'd want to be alone with the director. Where no one could possibly overhear. Far from the house, and at a time when everyone was too busy to roam the grounds."

"That's immaterial," Carrie sputtered. "Truly jumping to conclusions." She squeezed Blanche's shoulder.

"Of course," I agreed. "A pregnancy could be a coincidence. Although the only women here are patients and unmarried staff. It's not a stretch to assume Dr. Elsass would be informed immediately. By you, Nurse Carrie."

"Me?"

"Wouldn't that be the normal chain of command? And there's the question of who performed this test. Who would know how? Dr. Cole says he didn't; and why would he lie?"

Carrie blinked and clung to Blanche as Dr. Cole made a little disgruntled noise. "I most certainly would not."

"You don't know everything that goes on here, Violet. Strong feelings...swirl about...good people can be overwhelmed." Carrie glanced at Blanche and took her hand. The young woman stared straight ahead.

"Just what are you implying, Nurse?" Percy said.

"But people," Dr. Cole intoned, "are not slaves to their passions. They make choices."

I'd hope to lay out the facts, clear and precise, but my speech had been seriously derailed. "Let's focus on Friday night, shall we?" I said. "Dr. Elsass is outside, far from the mansion. There's snow and sleet. Maybe someone struck him from behind, or maybe he fell as he hurried. When I found him, he was curled on his side. A bandage fashioned from his tie and handkerchief was applied to the wound on his head. And I found this roll of gauze this afternoon—" I held it up, "—under some dead leaves and snow near the place I first saw the body."

"Why, I bet that's from the kitchen first aid kit," piped up Lottie, the only servant in the room, charged with watching over Berta. "I just noticed it was gone this morning. Mr. Sean asked me yesterday if anything was out of the ordinary, and it being such a topsy turvy mess, it was hard to say at the time—everything has been out of the ordinary."

"What time did you return from Chicago on Friday, Dr. Cole?" I asked.

"About 6:30."

"And what did you see from the rear parking lot?"

"As I said before, I thought I saw someone go into the kitchen, then out again by the time I'd gathered my things and started toward the house."

"Could you identify that person?"

He hesitated. "With certainty, no. But…"

Carrie laughed. "Ah, now I remember. I did step out. To fetch some…sage—from the garden. For Cook."

Dr. Cole exhaled sharply, and his shoulders relaxed. Don't get too comfy, I thought. We're not out of the woods yet.

"What would she be wanting sage for, then?" Lottie said. "We weren't having no sort of poultry. A nice rib roast, it was. All Christmas-like."

"But I didn't see Dr. Cole arrive," Carrie said. "We only have his word on that. And no explanation for why he was so frightfully late getting back from Chicago." She looked across the room at him. "If he was, indeed, late."

"As you know, Nurse Carrie," Cole's voice was ice. "At sundown, wherever I am, whatever I'm doing, and whatever the weather, I stop for prayer and thanks to Allah."

Carrie sniffed, then relaxed into the settee, as if vindicated.

"Cole being without an alibi is an excellent point," Percy said. "Will he be made director? As I've maintained all along, that's a motive. Ambitious young negro. Foreigner."

"And as I said before," I interrupted. "This murder is a love story. A baby on the way. An argument becomes physical. And dangerous. Dr. Elsass is injured. Someone cares for him, gives first aid. And sends for help? That would be the automatic response, wouldn't it, Nurse Carrie?"

All eyes turned to the head nurse. Blanche pulled away, stumbling to her feet and toward Dr. Cole, who leapt from his chair and guided her to sit down.

Carrie stood, glaring at me in silence.

"But what sort of help? A doctor? Dr. Cole goes to mosque in Chicago every Friday, and you knew that. Could he have returned yet, especially with the storm? Or one of the physicians on the board? That would lead to embarrassing questions."

Carrie made a dash for the exit, but Sean was there before her. She whirled around, her face tear-streaked and chest heaving.

"No, you'd have to care for him yourself. First: get him out of the cold and damp. You'd need someone strong. Trustworthy." In the kitchen, I could see Teddy taking muffins out of the oven.

Carrie's face grew pale, and she grabbed Sean's arm. "I'm going to be sick."

He stepped aside as she ran past him, then followed.

"Go on, what happened next?" demanded Evie, perched on the edge of her seat.

In the distance, a siren wailed across the prairie.

"Between six and seven, Teddy was helping Finn with the furnace repair, on and off. And at 6:30, Lottie was fetching out all the serving pieces." I said. "I think Carrie stabilized Dr. Elsass, then popped into the kitchen and told the cook to send Teddy out to her. She grabbed the first aid kit from the mudroom and went back to Dr. Elsass. We must have passed each other in the dark. Carrie returned to find the body moved and the man drowned in the few minutes she was gone."

Teddy brought us muffins from the kitchen, and Percy grabbed a newspaper from a side table and scribbled something on it, then handed it to the boy. He stared at it, then said, "No. I didn't see Cook all evening. No one told me to go out to help Nurse Carrie." He handed the basket to Lottie. "I would've said something before now."

"Of course you would." I turned back to the group. "Cook was a forgetful person, from all accounts of her. And busy with an important dinner. She remembered the errand later, unfortunately, right about the time Carrie realized she'd created a witness."

Evie had been quiet, but suddenly said, "And then the cook went to find Teddy in the basement—"

"If we were done with the stoker, she'd have been alone down there," Finn said. "You're saying Nurse Carrie followed her and pushed her into the coal cellar?" He shook his head. "Hard to believe."

"Unfortunately, it appears that way."

As if summoned, a disheveled Carrie appeared on the parlor's threshold, Sean's arm wrapped around her waist. "She's got something to say." He gave her an encouraging squeeze and walked her a few steps into the room.

"You, all of you, are like family to me. With your help, we built something fine here, Dr. Elsass and I. We understood each other in a special way—shared the same goals, opinions, and dreams of the future. I was more than happy to spend my energies building up his career."

Carrie looked at each of us, one by one, finally settling on Evie. "I'm so sorry," she said. "His death was a terrible accident. We'd hit a little snag in our relationship—"

Evie's brow furrowed for a moment before she gasped, silently mouthing, "No."

Carrie merely turned to me and plunged on. "And what should have brought us together even more closely was tearing things apart. But I know he would have calmed down and welcomed…" Her voice quavered. "Yes, I was out there. We argued, and he fell. I cared for him as best I could and ran for help. But when I returned, I saw…I thought I saw…" Her eyes glazed over, and she tilted her head as if listening to something. Or someone.

The sirens were louder.

"A…shape. A person. Pressing him down, into the water. I didn't kill him."

Dr. Bertinelli stirred. "I'd advise you to say nothing further. Can we call an attorney? Unless you'd like Mr. Joye to represent you."

Violet

CHAPTER THIRTY-SEVEN

Name: Mrs. Violet Arwald Humphrey

Date of Discharge: December 22, 1924

Facility: The Elsass Institute, Normal, Illinois

Clinical Course:

>   *Catatonia. No episodes x 4 weeks*
>
>   *Compulsive Behavior: No episodes observed x 1 week*
>
>   *Hallucinations: None observed x 2 weeks*

Condition: Greatly improved

Instructions: No restrictions. Regular meals, sleep, and physical activity. Follow-up with private physician.

Disposition: Care of family and friends, as desired. Patient given referral to Templed Trees Community.

~From Discharge orders, 12/22/24,
Violet Arwald Humphrey.

On Monday morning, I sat in the back hall of Finn and Tomás's house, hunched on a rickety wooden chair and staring at a closed door. I was dressed in bib overalls and a flannel shirt belonging to Tomás. And was most grateful for the clean socks. I allowed myself a rare cigarette while I waited to see whoever it was that required my presence. I felt like I'd been up all night but had actually caught a few hours rest. It just wasn't enough.

Between the fire in the mansion and Carrie being whisked away to the sheriff's office for questioning, the staff were taxed to the limit. Finn and Tomás had taken in the frailest patients, bedding them down on quilt bedrolls all over their parlor. The more independent men moved into the orderlies' quarters, and the sheriff's deputies found nearby farm families to take in the ladies, betwixt and between rural law enforcement's favorite activity: stomping around in the woods.

Given Carrie's eyewitness account of a figure standing over Elsass and the signs of a squatter in the log cabin, the sheriff had put two and two together and come up with five. They were looking for a non-existent tramp to arrest for Elsass's murder. The cook's death would likely be swept under the rug as an unfortunate accident related to the winter storm.

The door before me opened, and a middle-aged couple came out. "That's it then," the man was saying. "State Hospital in St. Louis?" He didn't sound happy.

"I think it for the best, at least temporarily." Dr. Bertinelli followed them out. "Several of our other patients are going there. So, she'll have friends, right? For the time being. Just temporary."

"But you will reopen?" the woman said. "Dr. Elsass and Nurse Carrie had made such progress with mother."

Dr. Bertinelli smiled a professional smile. It looked genuine, like he actually cared. I supposed an asylum board of directors was a nice job for a retired medical man. But I bet he never expected this particular task.

"I'm glad to hear it," he said. "But first things first. We must assess the building for safety, estimate the costs of repairs, and all the rest."

My, what have you gotten yourself into, doctor?

He noticed me, and I felt a bit guilty over my snappish thoughts. "Ah, and here's my next appointment." He gently prodded the couple down the hall. "We'll be in touch." He shook their hands and beckoned me in.

His makeshift office was tiny. It appeared to be a storage room; random items of farm life were shoved out of the way against the wall. A card table and a few folding chairs took up most of the space. He gestured to one, and I sat.

"Mrs. Arwald? I'm Doctor Bertinelli. I don't think we've ever been properly introduced."

"Humphrey."

He raised his eyes from the stack of forms on the table. "What?"

"I'm Violet Humphrey. Arwald was my father's name. I was married. Until recently."

"I'm so sorry. I knew that. It's been—"

Ashamed of myself for badgering a ninety-year-old man simply discharging a task he'd never signed up for, I interjected, "a long night. I know. My name doesn't matter."

"Oh, it does, it does. I'm writing out a legal document right here. In my defense, I spoke with your family's attorney on the phone, and he used the Arwald name."

My ears perked up at the words: legal document. "What legal things are you doing?"

"As you can imagine, with Dr. Elsass deceased, the Board is responsible for ensuring the safety of all the Institute's patients. And the fire—"

"Yes. That. What caused it? The faulty furnace?"

He stroked his magnificent muttonchops thoughtfully. "That's likely to be the public line. Although not fair to Mr. Osteen—"

"Finn?"

"Yes, the caretaker. Anyway, it likely will have to go down as negligent maintenance, but—we'll take care of him."

"So, what really happened?"

"I guess you, of all people, would understand the need for delicacy in these matters." He leaned over the table to whisper. "Emerson. He flew into one of his rages, knocked over that damn birdcage, and started burning his wife's paintings—everything, really, sketch pads and supplies, too, in the parlor fireplace. No screen. She fought him, well, tried to fight him."

"So, sparks flew."

"Yes, metaphorically and actually. By the time anyone noticed, the Christmas tree, curtains, and rug were ablaze."

"What an ass. What happened to the parrot?" I realized I hadn't seen it at Finn's house.

"Flew out the open door. Someone told me that they'd seen it in that grove of trees." Dr. Bertinelli cleared his throat and regarded the document in front of him. "Be that as it may, we must find safe placements for everyone immediately."

"You're not going to allow him to take Blanche, are you?"

He shrugged. "We took emergency measures last night, but…"

"She's his wife." I took a deep breath to calm myself. *This, I couldn't let stand.* But I was a committed person myself. "So, the family attorney, who couldn't remember my name, says…"

"Ah, yes." The doctor glanced at the papers. "You have two options. And in reading Dr. Cole's progress notes, I think either would be entirely reasonable."

I had started to like Dr. Bertinelli—the audacity of the whiskers alone was admirable. But what was he doing reading my medical record? Didn't sound like a board member's prerogative. I slammed both palms against the table and half stood, leaning over it. "And you're a psychiatrist, also?"

A warm pink flushed the thin skin of his cheeks. "Not specifically." He reached over to pat my hand. "Please relax. You have every right to question an intrusion into your privacy. But to safely discharge the Institute's obligations—"

"Dr. Cole knows all about me." That wasn't true, but he knew enough, certainly more than Dr. Bertinelli could have gleaned from skimming a few progress notes.

"And I have consulted Dr. Cole." Dr. Muttonchops steepling his fingers over a slight paunch. "Although his status here is somewhat…unusual." He sat up straight and rifled through the forms. "Be that as it may, I'm tasked with legally discharging all fifty-seven residents of this

Institute to safe and appropriate placements by the end of business today. You, Mrs. Humphrey, are, as of an hour ago, here under voluntary admission. Dr. Cole states you are no longer a danger to self or others, and your family representative concurs."

I let that soak in. I knew they were merely trying to expedite my removal from this place. I didn't believe, really, that anyone felt I was safe. More like, they were done caring. But Dr. Cole—maybe he did think so. That bit of faith, if it were true, meant…something.

"So, I can just leave?"

"You can just leave. Sign yourself out." Muttonchops produced a form. "I believe there is a young man here with a car ready to drive you wherever you want to go."

The room swayed as I felt hot, then cold. The doctor's face registered concern, and he stood. "Are you alright?"

I held up one hand to stop him. "No, it's fine. As much as I've wanted to be…anywhere else—"

"It's a surprise?" He chuckled. "After that performance yesterday, you shouldn't be. You'd put any prosecuting attorney in the city to shame. No, no, girl. Nothing wrong with your mind, in my opinion."

"Your opinion. And what is your medical specialty, sir?"

"I'm retired these twenty-five years. Just an old country doctor. Thrasher accidents, measles and mumps, delivering babies—human and bovine." He laughed at his resume. "And now I'm prescribing you a cup of tea." He shuffled out of the tiny room.

Dr. Bertinelli was a good egg, I decided. Maybe I could stay with him. And Mrs. Bertinelli. Perhaps they needed someone to do the heavy cleaning. I imagined a life on his small farm: Washing windows. Beating rugs. Cooking the noon meal. Because, as far as I knew, I had nowhere to go. Our old house in the city was gone. Grandfather's house was hopelessly tied up in a maze of legal actions, or perhaps my sister had sold it by now. I had no fantasy that my late husband's family in England would take me in; they probably blamed me for his death.

As I waited for the tea, I considered his praise. I *had* done well, hadn't I? Not only reasoning out the killer's identity, but also insight into myself. I'd worked to face my reality and forgive myself and others so that I could move forward. And so, I had.

Binding Jürgen Osteen, or, more properly, what Jürgen Osteen had become, was integral. For the house, the land, and the family, of course, but also for me. Finding my power again. Finding my voice.

I'd come to see any magic as a temptation to do harm in the name of good, to put my own needs ahead of anyone else. But perhaps it was possible...I mused. It had felt good. Maybe the key was magic in service—

"Here you go, my dear. Hot and black is my prescription. You don't need any milk or sugar clogging up your mucus passages after all that smoke last night."

I accepted the cup and realized how thirsty I was.

He checked a pocket watch, then handed me a letter. "I was just given this. Tomás thought it looked important."

It was a business-sized envelope, embossed with "Washington University" as a return address. It had been forwarded from my home address; a house recently auctioned to pay my dead father's debts. A faint whisp of memory unfurled in the back of my brain. *After all this time?*

"Now, you have another option. A facility further downstate, quite remote, has offered you a bed. I don't know a great deal about the place. Apparently, more of a rest home than a modern treatment institute such as this. A nondenominational religious community, if I understand it correctly."

"I'm not really religious," I said, sipping the hot liquid and fiddling with my envelope.

"And you don't have to be." He handed me a sheet of paper. "They care for distressed people as part of their vocation—the opinion and practices of their 'guests,' as they say, are immaterial. So, as you're free to go anywhere, you could go to this community."

"I don't have any money."

"Again, their mission is to help, not charge fees." He waved a hand. "I imagine they'd encourage you to do some chores or something. That's therapeutic, you know. I always got the farm hands right back to work after an amputation, as soon as possible."

Paralysis was coming on—decision paralysis. I gulped tea.

Dr. Bertinelli checked his watch. "I have ten more people to see in the next two hours." He offered a pen and a form, "Voluntary Discharge" emblazoned under the Elsass Institute letterhead. "Just sign yourself out on the top copy and keep the other. I'll give you this invitation from the Templed Trees Community also. Then you can take all the time you want to decide. Well, as much time as Mr. Osteen allows you to stay in his house."

I hesitated to pick up the pen, just staring at the form before me. I felt his hand on my shoulder. "Mrs. Humphrey?" I looked up into his white whiskers and pink face.

"You don't have to go home, but you can't stay here. Do you understand?"

I nodded and signed the form.

Violet

CHAPTER THIRTY-EIGHT

Tucked away among the slopes of the beautiful Shawnee Hills, the Community of the Templed Trees' mission is to defend our suffering world through spiritual intention and holy works. Always hospitable, we provide a haven of rest for beleaguered souls.

~ From "Is the Community of the Templed Trees Right for You?" tract. 1920, God's Garden Press, Harrisburg, Illinois.

I walked out of Finn's house clutching my paperwork and the letter from Washington University. I headed in the direction of Sean's waiting car where he'd already stowed my suitcase. He stood at the passenger door, smoking. His overcoat was unbuttoned, and he soaked up the winter sunshine. "Can you believe this weather, now?"

I'd hardly registered my surroundings since watching the sheriff drive off with Carrie the previous night. It wasn't clear if he intended to arrest her or not—the sheriff had seized on her story of seeing a figure over the body, along with the signs of someone using the log cabin for shelter. "Some tramp, squatting out there. Likely took off into the woods." He'd mentioned bringing in dogs but didn't seem to hold much hope for a successful search, given the time that had passed and the intervening snow accumulation.

The thrill of the past few days—finding murder clues, solving the puzzle, and summoning enough magic to bind a lonely creature had quickly faded. I was in danger of folding in on myself and knew it. Blinking slowly in the sunlight, I took in the bright white snow piled high and the lane wet with melt, a shining layer of mud. Beyond the fire-damaged mansion, the trees of the Grove swayed in a southern breeze. They whispered not a word. *Likely glad to be rid of the lot of us.* "Bye, trees," I murmured.

Sean ground out the cigarette on his heel and opened the passenger door. "Where to?"

I held out the two sets of documents: Discharge orders to "home," the other an invitation to the Templed Trees Community. My eyes began to sting and lips tremble.

"Oh, no. No crying. Not you. It must be bad." He crossed the wet ground and took me by the elbow. "What'd they say to you?"

I blinked away the tears and cleared my throat. *No tears!* I squared my shoulders, shaking him off, then marched to the car and slid into the passenger seat. "I'm to choose where to go next."

"What does that mean?"

"I could go home—but I don't have a home. Father's creditors have seized the house."

"Sure and—"

"Or I can go to this other rest home. A place I've never heard of. Even further out in the country than the Elsass Institute."

Sean shut my door, walked around the car to the driver's side, and climbed in. All around us, cars and even a couple of ambulances clogged the lane. Patients, most leaning on a nurse or orderly, filed out of Finn's cottage to catch their rides to the next stop on their journey.

He turned to me. "Come home. You can find a little room somewhere. I'd bet Kyffin would let you stay at his place for a while—it's sitting empty."

I thought of my best friend's roomy apartment overlooking the park; it was a lovely thought. For a moment. "But what would I do?" Although I knew exactly: Someone needed to rescue Blanche, somehow. An overwhelming task. "I...I...I'm not well." The car was hot in the brilliant sunlight, and I pulled off my gloves.

Sean took my hand, his thumb tracing lazy circles across my palm. "Sure, look what you did here. You sniffed out a murderer. And saved a good kid from a bad day in court. You're a natural at this stuff."

"What stuff? Murder investigations? Shall I become a policeman?" I sniffed. My palm began to itch.

"Naw. You're too honest. I was thinking something more like you cajoled me into. Detecting. I've kept it up, you know. With a few improvements."

I'd never once asked about the details of his life. "Which is what, exactly?"

"Well, I've done more than just try a spell on Kyffin. I've been teaching myself magic."

I'd suspected as much but could hardly believe it. Sean was the most observant Roman Catholic I'd ever met. "With Taylor's grimoire?" My husband was the most likely source of Sean's newly acquired magical information.

His face reddened. I'd swear a blush, but maybe he was just cold. He grimaced. "Bless me, Father, for I have sinned. I nicked your husband's journals back in all that hurly-burly last October."

I shook my head. "That's unbelievably dangerous."

He grimaced. "Yeah, and I've made a right bollocks of it, too. But you promised to help me. You know stuff."

"Hello there, Miss Violet. What have you decided to do?" I shaded my eyes in the sunshine's glare off the snow to see Comfrey standing just a few feet away. I wondered how much she'd heard.

I fluttered the two sets of discharge orders and the still-unopened letter in the air. "I guess word gets around, eh? Did they give all the patients a choice?"

"Not that I've heard about." She nodded at an ambulance, sliding into the muddy lot. Beyond it, a line of cars navigated the rapidly melting but still snow-packed road. "Most of these folks have family packing them up and into other institutions. You're lucky to have options."

I snorted. "I guess."

"Mrs. Humphrey's got a good friend with an apartment he's not using," Sean said to her. "Likely be happy to help her out. There'd even be plenty of room for the two of them, if Kyffin ever had a mind to move in." His eyes met mine with a sad, pleading expression. "You'd be a big help to him, I think." He got out of the car and walked around to Comfrey. "This friend was in a bad accident, end of September," he told her. "'Twas touch and go there for a while."

In all my concern for myself, I hadn't even thought about Kyffin, a victim of my sister's random lashing out, until Sean had shown up. *Now, be fair to yourself.* I had a nervous breakdown, and my memories were returning in fits and starts. Of course, Sean had kept up with my old friend; they'd apparently fallen in love or lust or something. Kyffin had told me as much in strict confidence. "But he's getting better?" I asked.

A darkness crossed Sean's face, and he looked all the world as if he wanted to hit something. "He walks with just a cane and speaks without much of a stutter anymore. But his memories aren't all there. Some are…flawed."

"Your friend will be in my prayers," Comfrey said to us both, then lowered her voice and leaned through the window to speak to me. "I bet you don't want to live alone in the city. Or take care of a sick man." I found her concern unusual, considering our superficial acquaintance.

"I might," I said. I didn't really like the idea of living by myself. Odd, since I've always been quite good at being alone. I guess I'd gotten used to being part of a family. Now that I didn't have one. Taking care of Kyffin, that could be rewarding. And perhaps I could do something for Blanche.

Comfrey was still talking. "Say, what do you think about going to the—"

But Sean tapped her on the shoulder. "Excuse me, but yesterday you started to tell me about something dangerous here. That situation, it's all sorted then?"

Comfrey turned to him and frowned. "Yes and no. What Miss Violet did yesterday—it did quite a lot to solve the problem."

It sounded like they were talking about Jürgen, and I was tired of unspoken agendas and hidden feelings. Suddenly stifling as the car warmed in the sunshine, I got out. Some issue, some matter of weighty importance hung in the air between Comfrey and me. "You've been a friend to me here. I appreciate it, and thank you. I think we should speak plainly to each other."

She sighed. "Certainly. I don't want to mess this up, so I'm pussyfooting around. I'm not aiming to trick you, it's just…I didn't want to sound crazy, especially to outsiders." She glanced over at Sean, intent on the cars sliding around in the muddy snow.

But he *was* listening. "I saw the fae steal my baby sister when I was two. I've spoken with saints, an angel, and too many ghosts. Chased down the Underwater Spirit—Osage call her, Panther." He looked her in the face. "I doubt you have much to say that will sound daft to me."

"I saw the Underwater Panther, too," I said. "I'm a practicing, if terribly out of practice, witch. And, of course, yesterday…" What *had* happened yesterday, I wondered.

"I hope I've protected this place for a little while. I did what I thought was best. But I didn't want to hurt Jürgen Osteen."

Comfrey nodded. "I thank you. That does set my mind at ease; to know you're no longer doing his bidding."

"Those stones?"

"Yes, I was aiming to ward off that old one, to keep him away from the house and the people. You, most particularly. But then you were digging up the amulets and charms, sometimes as quick as I could get them planted."

"I didn't mean to. I don't even remember it clearly."

Comfrey embraced me, comforting and protectively. "I'm from a community, a spiritual group. We take all seekers, of any faith or no faith at all. We've gathered to care for this material plane and guard it from outside attack. Our sister community in St. Louis has been watching over you, Miss Violet. Caring for you. Figuring out if you had the potential and the will to join our cause."

"Wait a minute," Sean said. "Sister community? That would be Mother Mary Gabriel's crew, wouldn't it?"

"Why, yes. Mount St. Michael Convent. Our community is called The Templed Trees. That's our invitation letter you got there. We have a place downstate, up in the hills. You can rest, relax, and get your bearings there. Learn more about us and decide your future."

"She has decided her future. She's going to open a detective agency with me."

"That's hasty," Comfrey said. "She needs to heal first."

"Honest work is the best way to get through hard times."

I felt my face flush. *Where did this man I hardly knew get the temerity…*

"Oh, that's served you plenty good," Comfrey retorted before I could say a word.

Sean reeled as if she'd hit him. Wordless, he walked over to a Rolls Phantom stuck in the snow. "Hey, need a hand, buddy?" he said to its chauffeur, then pushed the car as its rear wheels spun in slush.

Comfrey and I faced each other. I didn't know what to say. I'd churned up a head of steam over Sean's high-handedness, but realized Comfrey was being just as controlling, only more diplomatic about it.

"Sorry," she said. "I think I insulted your friend."

I waved a hand in dismissal. "I haven't known him long. We've just been through some difficult times together." A small voice in my head reproached me. I didn't think it was the trees—or Jürgen Osteen—this time. "Yet he's been better to me than anyone else I know."

"That doesn't mean you gotta do what he wants."

"I know." I turned away. "And I don't have to take your advice, either."

"No, you don't."

I felt her tap my shoulder. I turned, and she was offering me a small card.

"If you change your mind, here is our mailing address. We don't have a phone. But write, and we can find you a ride."

Chapter Thirty-Eight

I took it and nodded.

"Or just write. I'd love to hear from you. And answer any questions."

I got back in the car, still unsure where to go. I re-read the invitation from Templed Trees. In language couched in conventional, rest-cure terms, it explained a program of relaxation and recuperation for the convalescent. Simple food and clean country air. But, now knowing the hidden agenda, I could see deeper import in the words.

I sighed, reminiscing over my sweet, innocent pre-war days of studying magic in the English countryside. Rambling the hills, foraging for herbs of power, and raising energy skyclad under the full moon.

I heard someone walking up to the car and then crank it to start. The person climbed into the car via the driver's side. The scent of wet wool, pipe tobacco, and male sweat filled the car.

"Ain't I a prize eejit, now?" Sean said. We regarded each other in the rearview mirror. "Where to, ma'am?"

I took one last look at the letter from Templed Trees, then considered the now dog-eared envelope from the University, which Dr. Bertinelli had handed me back in his makeshift office. "I guess I have to decide, don't I?" But, maybe, the decision had been made for me a year ago by a ridiculously ambitious past-me. Such a crazy idea; the program would never accept me. The application had been a lark—a dare from my husband as we laughed over cocktails.

Sean shifted the car into gear and nudged it forward. "It'll take an hour to get out to the main road, anyway. You got that long." He pointed to a pile of cardboard scraps on the back seat beside me, scrawled with some strange symbols—interlocking circles and boxes with a dot in the center. "And I'm going to make a few stops; put up some warning signs for any unfortunate tramps that might happen this way."

"Oh, I'd almost forgotten. The ridiculous manhunt for the imaginary murder hobo."

I took a deep breath and tore the envelope open, then smoothed the letter on my lap. The sky darkened as a thin cloud covered the sun. "Dear Mrs. Humphrey," the letter said. "We are pleased to inform you of your admission to the inaugural class of our new program of study in Relativistic Astrophysics and Cosmology. Orientation will begin on Thursday, January 22, 1925, including a conference with our department head, Dr. Author H. Compton, who will also serve as your academic advisor. Classes commence promptly at 10 AM, Monday, January 26."

The wide universe beckoned. Another kind of magic. Or all part of the same.

AFTERWORD

Thank you for spending a few of your precious hours assisting Sean and Violet with their investigation of the strange events at the Elsass Institute. If you enjoyed your time together and are so inclined, they'd appreciate your brief review on Amazon or Goodreads.

This book is a work of alternative historical fantasy fiction, rooted in real history, yet entirely fabricated. It takes place in a reality very different from our own. Historical details may vary from the "real world" for narratively interesting reasons.

ACKNOWLEDGEMENTS

Thank you to everyone who held my head above water during this story's creation: my family, friends, and the Word Sisters writing group. A sensitivity reader was of great help regarding the portrayal of the Deaf, deaf, and hard-of-hearing characters, but, of course, any errors in facts and judgment are my own.

As an author exploring eldritch horror, I must tip my hat to the community of writers going back well over a hundred years who continue to inspire storytellers today.

ABOUT THE AUTHOR

Speculative Fiction with a Historical Twist!
Kathy L. Brown lives and writes in St. Louis, Missouri, USA. Her hometown and its history inspire much of her fiction. When she's not thinking about how haunted everything is, she enjoys blogging about tabletop roleplaying games. Additional Sean Joye investigations include the first series novel, *The Big Cinch*; a novella, *The Resurrectionist*; and a novelette, *Water of Life*; as well as several short stories. Learn more at kathylbrown.com.